TUSCAN BLOOD
ALI FALCO SERIES BOOK 2

JEFF CARSON

CROSS ATLANTIC PUBLISHING

ALSO BY JEFF CARSON

THE DAVID WOLF SERIES

Gut Decision (A David Wolf Short Story)– Sign up for the new release newsletter at http://www.jeffcarson.co/p/newsletter.html and receive a complimentary copy of the David Wolf story.

**NEW! Echoes Fade (David Wolf Book 17)

THE ALI FALCO SERIES

The Como Falcon (Ali Falco Book 1)

Tuscan Blood (Ali Falco Book 2)

1

The volcanic soil latched onto Ali Falco's shoes like wet cement, and she almost fell as she tried to step away from the vehicle. Her feet slid a few centimeters to either side, but she caught herself on the door handle before landing in a puddle.

Inspector Basso met her on the rocky, compacted road at the front of the vehicle and looked down. "*Cazzo*. My pants."

Ali stomped her feet, dislodging a brick of muck from each shoe, then zipped her jacket. When she lifted her head, movement to their left caught her eye. Two men were walking toward them along a narrow driveway, which curled down from a house standing sentinel at the apex of the hill.

"There they are," Basso said, nodding at the approaching inspectors. "What are they doing up there?"

Ali shrugged. "Maybe talking to the neighbors."

Basso rocked back on his heels, twisting to take in the opposite view.

She followed his gaze to their immediate right, where a farmhouse and a converted barn sat among rows of yellowing vines. The rolling terrain of the Tuscan country-side unfurled to the south, decorated with patchworks of freshly plowed fields and striped vineyards, and a tendril of fog snaked through the valley, set aglow by morning sunrays.

The peaceful setting was spoiled by a swarm of emergency vehicles—including one forensic van, one ambulance, and two police cruisers spewing scratchy radio communication—and a group of crime scene workers milling outside the farmhouse.

"I could live here," Basso said for the fourth time in twenty minutes, ignoring the nearby chaos. "Not so many trees. See how the land opens up and gives you a view?"

"There are plenty of views in Siena."

"Not like this," Basso said. "My soul can stretch out down here."

Ali made a non-committal noise. The surrounding landscape was beautiful, but as for choosing somewhere to live, she preferred the walled city an hour north. It had more dining options, and everything was within walking distance.

"Brunello di Montalcino," he mused. "The best wine in the world. If I lived here, I would sit on my porch and watch the sangiovese grow."

"You'd probably have some more chores besides sitting on your ass."

The wistful look in her partner's eyes evaporated, and his expression hardened to business as the other inspectors arrived. Turning in their direction, Basso asked, "What were you doing up there?"

Lieutenant Costa flicked his smoldering cigarette into a puddle as he walked past them, leading the way down to their destination. "Neighbors."

"Are they home?" Ali asked.

"*Sì*. And they had some interesting information."

Inspector Gatti followed a few paces behind the lieutenant. He nodded at Basso, but didn't bother greeting Ali.

"What took you two so long?" Costa asked.

"Traffic," Basso said, stepping in front of Gatti. "We had to take a detour."

Ali and Gatti followed their superiors through the open iron gate and into the parking area choked with emergency vehicles. One man stood apart from the crowd, leaning against the front of a van and smoking a cigarette. He looked to be in his fifties, thin, with weathered skin, wearing mud-streaked jeans and leather work boots.

"Giuseppe Sala," Costa said, keeping his voice low. "He's an employee of the vineyard. He says he was coming to aerate the grape juice while Salvatore and Martina Conti were away when he discovered the body."

They stopped a few paces from the farmhouse, prompted by Dr. Longo. The Siena provincial coroner was a squat, sturdy man who made Basso look tall. His white forensic suit was rolled at the ankles and wrists, and bright-yellow-framed glasses blazed circles around his eyes.

"Gloves," Longo said, pointing at a pair of boxes on the ground. "Booties."

They obeyed, knowing that if they crossed Longo, those intelligent eyes of his would go mean. A month ago, at the scene of a ninety-year-old man's death, clearly a natural-causes situation, Ali had stepped where Longo had not approved, provoking the coroner's wrath. Her main goal for the next few minutes was to not repeat that episode.

She donned latex gloves, wiped her feet on the brush mat

Longo had put down for mud removal, then slipped the booties over her shoes and straightened, surveying the farmhouse.

Up close, it looked humbler than from afar, the stucco cracking, the salmon-colored paint flaking off in patches. A portico supported by stacked-stone columns protected the entrance from the elements, and yellow numbered evidence tents had been placed on the patio beneath it, marking muddy streaks on the clay tile.

Against the wall sat a single wood chair and a circular wood table, a pack of cigarettes and a lighter waiting atop. Just beyond the cover of the porch, another evidence tent sat beside a mop, which lay in the mud as if it had been thrown carelessly to the ground.

"Follow me," Longo said, heading inside the farmhouse.

They entered a space that was part dining room and part kitchen. Immediately, Ali was hit with the stench of death. Sunlight lanced through the windows, reflecting off copper pots, illuminating a figure on the ground.

Unbidden, the memory of Colombo's body falling at her feet, Marco landing atop him, flashed in her mind. Nausea turned her stomach, making her mouth water. She blinked away the horror of the past, only to be slapped in the face by that of the present.

Basso looked at her, his expression asking if she was okay.

Ali pretended not to notice, hating how he watched her like a hawk now, and eyed the painting on the wall next to her, a depiction of the surrounding hills put to canvas by a master. The iron chains strung from the ceiling, suspending a bar and hooks. The hanging pots and pans. The hand-crafted chair that had been flung to the ground during the incident.

When she had stalled long enough, Ali dragged her gaze back to the body. A shiver coursed through her frame.

The man lay on his back, almost naked. He wore no shirt, and his pants had been pulled down to his ankles. There was a hole between his hairy pectorals, a starred split mark indicative of an exit wound from a high-caliber bullet.

Ali jolted with shock at the realization that he had been shot point-blank in the crotch, too, leaving his genitals ripped open and caked in dried blood.

"Any prints on that?" she asked, pointing at a wine bottle on the counter near the sink.

"Sì," Longo said. "We have a few sets we've lifted. As for the two wineglasses in the sink, they've been washed."

She nodded, then snuck a glance at Gatti. His normally tan complexion was blanched. She assumed hers looked the same.

Basso stepped forward, leaning down to study the dead man's crotch. "What's with the mop outside?"

"Can I talk?" Longo asked.

Basso straightened. "Of course. Sorry."

"Davide Conti," Longo said. "Age thirty-one. Shot once in the back, once in the genitals. Judging by the angle of entry and the blood spatter, he was standing when he was shot in the back. Perhaps running away, because he fell forward, hitting the chair here, knocking it over, pushing the table back. You can see his face took a beating as he went down."

The man's bottom lip was torn open, blood coating his mouth and jaw in a wide oval, like grotesque clown makeup.

"It appears he was then turned over and shot in the

crotch. You can see the perpetrator stood at his feet when he fired. Right there." Longo pointed at two muddy smears on the tile.

"Once in the crotch?" Basso asked. "Two shots total?"

"*Sì*. Two shots total. We pulled a bullet from the wood shelf above the kitchen sink, and there is no exit wound from the second shot, so we'll get that bullet during autopsy. And we just found a shell casing on the floor there." Longo pointed at a row of trash and recycle bins lined up beneath a countertop. "It's a .308 Winchester. Must have been ejected between shots, and then rolled behind the bins.

"Honestly, I'm surprised our assailant didn't find it and take it with him, because it appears he did some cleaning. He used the mop you saw outside to attempt to wipe up his shoe prints. You can see how they are smeared. He . . . or she"— Longo looked at Ali, raising his eyebrows as if she might take offense at his assumption of the killer's gender—"left a bunch of shoe prints and must have believed they were going to implicate him or her."

Ali nodded. "Prints on the mop?"

"It's been outside all night. It rained heavily during that time. Three centimeters. We found none."

"And the rifle shell casing?" Costa asked.

"*Sì*. We found some on it."

Costa's eyes narrowed. "He wipes his shoe prints, but he doesn't take the extra few minutes to find the shell casing with his fingerprint on it?"

"Maybe he didn't notice," Gatti said. "He had just let loose two gunshots. One tends to be in a hurry after something like that."

They stood in silence.

"What about the victim's phone?" Basso asked after a minute.

"We haven't found one," Costa said.

"He has to have a cell phone."

"One would assume," Longo said.

Ali imagined the molecules of viscera coating her throat and lungs as she breathed. It made her want to spit. Instead, she maintained the passive expression on her face and shifted her attention to the warped glass of the window, the dust motes floating in the sunlight, the white ceiling.

"I'd rather all four of you didn't traipse through the house looking for it," Longo said.

Costa nodded. "Let's go outside. I can't stand the smell."

Longo walked out first, then Gatti, then Costa. When Basso gestured for Ali to go before him, she didn't argue, keeping close on Costa's heels as they emerged onto the covered patio.

The outside air was like a splash of cool water on her face, scented with life. A few long inhales of burn pile smoke, emergency vehicle exhaust, and the salty sea breeze drifting inland from the Mediterranean scrubbed her nostrils clean. She slipped off her booties and gloves.

"You can see where they mopped out here." Longo pointed at the evidence tents.

"What did the neighbors say?" Basso asked.

Gatti opened his Armani jacket and removed a tiny notebook from his breast pocket. "They told us their two dogs went crazy last night at 10:15 p.m."

Somewhere far up the hill, the dogs in question were currently going crazy again, barking like they were in a death match.

"They looked outside to see what had alerted the dogs." Gatti flipped the page, taking a bit too long for Ali's patience. At twenty-seven years old—four years younger than her—he was extremely handsome and loved being the center of attention. "They, and I quote, 'Saw a dark vehicle leaving the property in the rain.'"

"How certain are they on the time?" Basso asked.

"I pressed them on that," Costa said. "The man of the house was watching *Calcio Tonight* on Rai 1. He swears it was during the commercials at ten fifteen. Says he checked the time when the dogs started barking."

Ali tilted her head in thought. "They said the vehicle was dark. Does that mean the lights were off? Or was it darkly colored?"

"Good question," Basso said, looking at Gatti.

Gatti tapped his notebook. "They said it was black or dark blue, sleek like a luxury vehicle. It pulled out of the gate, and then Davide Conti, our deceased, closed the gate."

"The gate was closed," Basso repeated slowly, seeming pensive.

"*Sì*. And there were actually two times the dogs went berserk," Gatti said. "The first at ten fifteen, and the second about fifteen minutes later. Around ten thirty, when they heard gunshots."

"They heard the shots?" Ali asked.

Gatti nodded. "Both of them. Spaced apart by a minute or so."

"They didn't call the police?"

"No. The man said his dogs were acting the same way they always do when there's a boar outside, so he assumed the Contis were shooting at one."

"And he's also certain about that second time?"

Gatti's turquoise eyes sparked with annoyance. "He heard the shots when *Calcio Tonight* was ending. The show starts at nine thirty. Ends at ten thirty."

For a moment, the group processed the new information. Then Basso folded his arms and gestured with his chin. "That's the winery in there?"

Ali swiveled to face the modernized outbuilding. It appeared to be the guts of the farm's winemaking operation.

"*Sì*," Costa said. "We checked inside. Nothing out of the ordinary. Vats of grape juice becoming Brunello di Montalcino."

Basso eyed the vineyard employee, who was speaking with a pair of uniformed officers near the emergency vehicles. "What's the man's name again?"

"Giuseppe Sala," Gatti said.

"Sala."

"That's correct."

Basso looked at Costa quizzically, and Costa nodded, taking the lead as they all walked toward the man.

"*Grazie*, officers," Costa said in dismissal.

The two uniforms walked away, leaving Giuseppe Sala alone with the four inspectors making a semicircle in front of him.

"*Ciao*. My name is Inspector Basso. This is Inspector Falco, my partner. I take it you've already met Lieutenant Costa and Inspector Gatti."

Giuseppe's pale-blue eyes bulged from their sockets, the skin beneath them sunken, as if he had lost a lot of weight in a short amount of time.

"You work these vines?" Basso asked.

"That's right," Giuseppe said. His accent was deeply Tuscan.

"I know you've already explained what happened many times today, but my colleague and I would like you to explain once more. We heard you were aerating the wine."

"That's right."

"What time did you arrive?" Basso asked.

"Just at sunrise."

"And was the gate open when you came in?"

"No." Giuseppe's gaze fell to the ground. The man seemed uncomfortable, probably more at home in the vines than among people.

"The gate has a lock on it, correct?" Costa asked.

"That's right," Giuseppe confirmed. "A combination lock. Just like any other day, I put the combination in, took off the chain, and pushed open the gate."

Basso nodded. "Nothing seemed out of place, then?"

"No. Everything was normal. So I got back in my car and drove over there." Giuseppe gestured toward a cream-colored Fiat Panda parked near the outbuilding.

The vehicle was covered in dents and scratches, and Ali pegged it at over a decade old. Quite the opposite of dark, sleek, and luxurious.

"I went straight to work cycling the wine. After I got the first and second tanks going, I stepped out for a cigarette." Giuseppe glanced at the farmhouse, then closed his eyes. "That's when I saw the door to the house was cracked open."

"It was open?" Basso asked.

"Just a little. I was . . . curious. I didn't know if Davide was up or not. He's usually not up this early, and so I was interested. I thought maybe he was making coffee. I walked over to greet him, and that's when I started to see strange things."

"Like what?" Ali prompted.

"I saw the mop on the ground. I almost picked it up, but something stopped me. I guess I figured it was so out of place that it must have been put there for a reason. Then I went to the door, and I saw the lights were on inside. I called Davide's name and knocked. He did not answer, so I walked inside." Giuseppe's closed eyes pinched tighter. A tear slid down his cheek, dropping off his jaw and onto his sweater. "Then I saw him."

"What did you do?" Basso asked.

"I called the *polizia*." Giuseppe shook his head. "I didn't want to call Salvatore. I dreaded it. But . . . then I called Salvatore, and I gave him the news."

Basso's face became a mask of sympathy. "I'm sorry, *Signor* Sala."

Giuseppe said nothing, but he opened his eyes to acknowledge Basso's words, letting tears fall without trying to wipe them away.

Ali watched the man, her heart aching.

"Salvatore," Basso said. "That's the deceased's father?"

Giuseppe's eyes flashed. "Davide. That's his name."

"Of course. I'm sorry."

"*Sì*, Salvatore is Davide's father."

"And where is Salvatore now?"

"He's on his way home."

Costa looked at Ali and Basso. "Salvatore was up at a wine distribution conference in Turin. With his daughter. What is her name again?"

"Martina," Giuseppe said. "Davide's sister."

"*Grazie, Signor* Sala," Basso said. "Now, I'm sure Lieutenant Costa has already asked you a question similar to this, but do you know of anybody who would want to kill Davide?"

Giuseppe shook his head vehemently, as if the question were absurd.

"No reason whatsoever for somebody to be mad at him?"

"No."

Basso straightened. "How about a woman?"

"What woman?"

"Was he seeing one?"

Giuseppe stared at the horizon for a moment, thinking, then shrugged. "He saw a lot of women. The boy was gifted with looks and charisma. Ladies liked him."

"Was there a certain somebody he was seeing now?"

Giuseppe shrugged again. "I'm not one to have these types of conversations with young folks."

Basso shot Costa a glance.

"*Signor* Sala," Costa said. "I know you've been through a lot this morning, but we will need to get an official statement from you in writing."

"Of course."

"*Grazie.* We will leave you in peace for now." Costa produced a card from his pocket and handed it over. "If you think of anything else, please do not hesitate to use this number. Any time. For any reason. Okay?"

Giuseppe nodded, wiping his tears with the sleeve of his sweater.

Costa strode away, Ali, Gatti, and Basso trailing close behind. Once they were out of earshot, he asked, "What do we think?"

Ali wanted to speak up, but her mind had gone blank. She was still reeling from the fact that her first case was truly happening. Four months ago, she'd solved the murders of her father, mother, and one of her mother's patients, but that had been a personal situation she'd found herself caught up in, like a boat carried downriver by raging rapids. This was different. This was the beginning of her career.

She felt a surge of power—and a surge of dread. Salvatore and Martina Conti were driving down from Turin right now, the road in front of them undoubtedly blurred by tears. She knew all too well what that kind of grief felt like.

Basso spoke first. "I think this is a crime that has to do with sex. Love. Jealousy."

Costa nodded. "Because of the shot to his genitals."

"I agree," Ali said, examining the property, searching for answers.

"One moment, please." Costa pulled out his phone and checked the screen. "It's Ferrari. Basso, come with me." He walked off, answering the Siena police chief's call. "*Sì?*"

"You two, don't get in any trouble," Basso warned, giving Ali and Gatti pointed looks before hurrying after Costa.

An awkward silence descended on the rookie inspectors, just as it did every time they were left alone with each other. Gatti eyed her, and his expression grew cold. She'd never had any siblings, but she assumed this was how it felt to be treated as an annoying little sister.

"What?" she asked, spitting the words in his face.

He turned around and marched toward the outbuilding.

Ali pursed her lips in frustration. She had tried to connect with the man multiple times in the past, but she'd since given up. Clearly, Gatti was all about the job, and for some unknown reason, he viewed her as a threat. If only he recognized how weak that made him appear.

Gatti stopped at the entrance to the outbuilding, peering inside at the shiny silver vats holding precious Brunello di Montalcino in the making. Ali was tempted to get a closer look at the winemaking operation as well, but she set out in her own direction.

Sloughing off all negative thoughts about the ultra-competitive, over-dressed, pretty-boy inspector, she stared at the rolling hills below, trying to piece together the details of their investigation in her mind.

The neighbors had reported Davide Conti closing the gate last night at 10:15 p.m. Presumably locking it in the process, because Giuseppe Sala had reported unlocking it this morning at sunrise. If the killer had come and gone between those hours, unlocking the gate upon arrival, then locking it upon departure, wouldn't the dogs have heard and barked like mad? Certainly, the neighbors would have seen any vehicle coming in or out of the gate, or pulling up to it along the road.

Ali shook her head. The murderer had approached some other way, unseen by canine eyes. On foot, most likely.

A low rock wall lined the property, meandering down the hillside toward a copse of dense forest at the bottom. The wall stopped at the trees, which seemed to take over as the property boundary.

Ali stepped forward, feet squishing in the water-logged lawn, and squinted into the distance. She made out a road on the far side of the wall, not the one she and Basso had driven in on. A vehicle was coasting down it now, traversing one edge of the vineyard. It reached the trees and disappeared from view.

Somebody could have parked in those woods and walked up the hill, she realized. Kept out of view among the rows of yellowed grapevines. It would have been dark, simple to remain hidden all the way to the farmhouse.

Intrigued by the idea, she walked to the edge of the lawn, searching the ground for shoe prints that led into or out of the vines. Finding none, she raised her gaze and stopped dead in her tracks. Amid the yellow, orange, and red fall foliage of the trees below, something dark stood out, like a tiny black void.

"What are you looking at?" Gatti asked from behind her.

She ignored him, intent on watching the black spot. It moved, pulling back into the forest and vanishing. "Did you see that?"

"See what?" Gatti stopped at her side. "The grapevines? They've been here the whole time."

"You're an idiot."

"They're done with the call." He snapped his fingers. "Let's move it."

Ali frowned at his tone and opened her mouth to retort, but Gatti was already sauntering toward Costa and Basso, who were busy lighting cigarettes. She swallowed the words she wanted to say, then glanced at the trees one more time. The dark spot was there again. This time, clear as day, she could tell it was a person. A pinprick of light reflected off an object near the person's head, spiking her adrenaline.

Back in training, the instructors had drilled it into her that culprits often liked to return to the scenes of their crimes for various psychological reasons. So, maybe that was the killer down there, observing through binoculars. Or just a reporter pointing a telephoto lens.

Either way, she was going to find out.

"Falco!"

She pretended not to hear Basso's shrill cry. Since she was already ducking among the vines, trotting at a full clip toward the trees, it wasn't too hard of an act to pull off.

2

Ali's feet slipped out from under her again, but this time, she went down. Hard.

She landed in the mud with a splat, limbs squishing deep into the saturated volcanic soil, and wetness seeped through her pants, all the way up to her waist. Still, she kept her eyes on the man in the trees, paying no mind to her ruined outfit.

As she climbed to her feet, the man swiveled his binoculars toward her, then melted backward into the foliage.

Cazzo. Despite flailing downhill like somebody on ice without skates, her approach had gone undetected until her fall. The man had been too preoccupied with watching the farmhouse to notice her and she had stopped twice to get a good look at him. Unfortunately for her, the hood cinched tight around his head and the binoculars pressed against his eyes had hidden all distinguishing features except a bit of facial hair. And now he was gone.

Ali straightened to her full height and peeked over the vines, not bothering to hide anymore.

"Falco!" Gatti called from above.

She waved a muddied hand, signaling for him to shut up, then held her breath, trying to see through the overlapping branches and bright leaves. She had spooked the man, and now he was getting away. She pictured him scurrying through the dense forest, aiming for a hidden vehicle.

"Falco, what the hell are you doing?!"

The foliage below erupted in sound. Feet trampled dead leaves, twigs cracked, and bushes rustled, their skyward-pointing branches swaying. The man's movements were urgent and frantic. He hadn't been escaping after all, only hiding.

Ali was just forty meters from the woods. If she moved fast, she could catch him. But it was a steep section of land here at the end of the vines, so she had to choose her path carefully. She assessed the ground ahead and then went for it, skiing more than running, picking up speed quick.

"*Cazzo*," she breathed, realizing the slope was even steeper than she'd anticipated. She dug her heels into the mud to slow her descent, but they slid about as if coated in olive oil.

Ali fell once more, and her momentum sent her tumbling, careening toward the forest. All she could do was ride it out, bringing her legs up in front of her for protection as she hit the wall of growth. Branches scraped up her legs as her shoes pushed through, and her backside slammed painfully into a thick root, wrenching her to a halt. Icy water cascaded off the overhead leaves, showering onto her.

Motionless, stunned, she groaned. Then the fading sound of frenzied footfalls spurred her to life.

"Stop!" she yelled.

The footfalls continued.

She got to her feet by rolling to her stomach and pushing up. "Hey you!"

An answer came in the form of a car door opening and closing, an engine revving, and tires squealing.

Ali lunged through the bushes. Branches snapped back and hit her in the face, streaming more water over her head and down her shirt. Shivering, she emerged into an open space covered by a canopy of leaves.

She spotted the road and sprinted toward it. To her right, the tarmac disappeared behind the trees, heading up to Conti Vineyards. To her left, it twisted in a hairpin turn, down and out of sight behind more trees and another hill. The sound of the engine came from that direction.

Clumps of mud flipped off Ali's shoes as she ran for the turn. Once there, however, she discovered the road soon twisted out of sight again. The vehicle was long gone.

Putting her hands on her knees, she breathed heavily through bared teeth. Pain punched her right shoulder with each pump of her heart, hurting worse where she had been shot months ago.

She collected herself, then walked back up the road, slowing as she heard an incoming vehicle. The engine sounded different, and yet she spun to face the newcomer. Maybe they had passed the vehicle she'd been chasing. Maybe they could give a description of it to her.

A small Fiat rounded the hairpin turn, engine whining as it struggled to climb the rise.

Ali raised her hands. "Hey! *Scusa!*"

The vehicle braked to an idle beside her, and she bent to look through the front passenger window. An elderly woman was leaning over, trying to reach the hand crank that would roll down the window. She glanced at Ali and lurched up, mouth opening in a startled cry. She put both hands on the wheel and floored the gas.

The engine moaned as the vehicle crept forward, ejecting black smoke into Ali's face. She coughed, waving away the exhaust.

"Falco!" Gatti called out.

"Coming!" She returned to the trees, following a thin trail, possibly formed by wildlife, to the other side of the woods.

Gatti was a few meters uphill, having just cleared the vines, still navigating a cautious descent. He stopped to give her a double-take. Then he laughed, quickly becoming breathless with glee. "*Cazzo*! What happened to you?"

She studied the hillside between them, refusing to respond. A fresh groove was carved into the mud from her tumble, but to the side of it, just below Gatti, there were other marks.

"Look at those prints in front of you," she said.

He barely heard her over his fit of laughter. "What?"

"I said, look at those prints."

He looked, frowning. "Animals?"

She shook her head, even though she couldn't be sure from this distance. Besides, if the prints had once been readable, they were now blurred by the three centimeters of rain that had fallen the night before. "They seem too big and spaced apart to be from a deer or a boar."

"What happened to you?"

"I fell. Now can we drop it?"

He snorted. "What are you doing down here, anyway?"

"I saw somebody."

"Who?"

"A man. He was watching us with binoculars."

Theatrically, Gatti held up his hands and looked side to side.

Ali glared at him. "He left. He ran away, got in his car, and drove off before I could get to him."

Gatti's expression finally sobered. "What did he look like?"

"He had a hood on, cinched around his head."

"Did you see his face?"

She sighed. "No. He had the binoculars to his eyes. I did notice some facial hair, though."

"And the car?"

"I didn't see it."

He smiled. "Great job."

Biting her tongue, she tracked the prints to a spot just meters away. "There are some by me, too. Here at the bush line. Now, are you going to come over here? Or am I going to do all the work for the both of us?"

Gatti's smile evaporated, and he resumed his journey to the bottom of the slope.

Ali went to view the nearby prints, and as she looked down, her attention was drawn to the mud-soaked slacks stuck to her legs. She trembled, the cold and wet seeping into her core as her adrenaline wore off.

Gatti covered the final few meters with athletic grace and paused beside Ali. Peering at her face closely, he said, "You're bleeding."

"I am?"

"A lot." Gatti pulled a handkerchief from the breast

pocket of his jacket and handed it over. "Under your right eye."

She reached for the tiny piece of stark-white cloth, then hesitated.

"Take it," he said, irritation in his voice.

"Thanks." She tapped the handkerchief to her cheek, and it came away with a coin of bright red.

"I don't know," Gatti said, gaze on the ground as he moved into the bushes. "They look bigger than animal hooves."

Ali joined him in the forest, taking a slightly different route. It seemed like a second wildlife trail. After a minute of searching, she froze. "I have a perfect shoe print right here! It's been sheltered by the leaves, so I can see a full shoe tread!"

"There's another one over here," Gatti said. "A few of them, actually. Large. Male, for sure. They look fresh."

"I see a clear trail. I think it's heading your way, so stay put." She followed the shoe prints until she encountered Gatti. "Same tread on all of them."

"So, these could be from that guy you just saw."

"Looks to me like they start blurry out there on the hill, smudged by last night's rain, and they're clear inside here, sheltered by the foliage."

Gatti considered her words. "Maybe."

"Which would mean they're the killer's shoe prints," she said.

"Or they're just this guy who was snooping on us. Could have been a reporter traipsing all around here this morning, watching us with his telephoto."

"Since when do reporters run away from the action?" she asked.

Gatti narrowed his eyes. "You're saying that was the killer you just saw?"

She shrugged. "Criminals return to the scene of the crime all the time, right?"

A vehicle drove by, flitting in and out of view. Ali and Gatti rushed between trees and bushes, ducking and swerving, reaching the edge of the road in time to see a delivery truck vanish around the hairpin turn.

Gatti's eyes became steely. "This could be where the killer parked and entered the property."

"That's what I'm saying," she said. "It would make sense to enter from here. Undetected."

He pulled out his phone and dialed a number. "*Signore,* there was somebody watching the crime scene . . . He's gone now . . . That's right. And I found some shoe prints in the mud. Could be our killer's . . . *Sì, signore.*" He ended the call and pocketed his phone.

Ali stared at him.

"What?"

"*You* found some shoe prints? *You* did?"

Gatti ignored her, walking back into the trees.

"You're a real piece of work, you know that, Gatti?"

Stopping to give her another once-over, he burst out laughing again. "You're one to talk, Falco."

3

"Their Bolognese tastes like dirty feet."

"How can you say that?"

"Ask my wife. She'll tell you the same. And the prices are astronomical . . ."

Ali tuned out the argument between Basso and Gatti and gazed beyond the third-floor window of the Siena police headquarters building. For six years, she had been on the floor below. Up here, the view was completely different, unobstructed. She could see clear across Siena. To the south and west, clay rooftops jutted at all angles, abruptly stopping as the city's walls gave way to rolling hills.

". . . and the wine was corked," Basso continued. "I tell you, if you want good, authentic, and cheap? Garibaldi's food takes the prize."

"I don't worry about price as much as you do, old man."

"I have kids. Mouths to feed." He scoffed. "Cherish the days you have without children."

"Aw," she said. "That's so sweet."

"Bah." Basso backhanded the air.

"How about you give this conversation a rest, eh?" Costa sat at his desk, working his teeth with a toothpick. "I'm about to burst from lunch, and all you people can talk about is pasta."

The door to Costa's office opened, and Longo walked inside. He paused, looking Ali up and down. "You . . . changed."

Ali felt her face flush. Thanks to Clarissa, who frequently brought an exercise bag to work, she now wore a sweat suit emblazoned with the provincial crest on the pants and top. As for her muddied outfit, it was wadded up in a plastic bag underneath her desk. She was still debating whether she would take it to the local dry cleaner or spare herself further humiliation by dropping it in a trash bin.

"Sit, everyone," Costa said.

Longo took the seat next to Basso in front of the desk, relegating Ali and Gatti to the pair of chairs along the wall. Gatti rubbed his wet pant leg, mumbling to himself about trying to scrub the mud off again when he got home.

"Okay," Costa said. "We confirmed Davide Conti had a cell phone. But where is it?"

"Vodafone was his carrier," Basso offered, clearing his throat. "We've submitted all the paperwork."

"And their lead time?"

Basso upturned his hands.

Costa cursed under his breath. "So what are we saying? That the killer took the cell phone?"

"Maybe," Basso said. "Or Davide could have, I don't know, lost the phone at some point before he was killed."

"Not likely. Let's go down the route of the killer taking it: He kills Davide. He takes the cell phone. He cleans up."

"But he leaves the shell casing with his fingerprint on it?" Basso scratched his head. "Longo, what have you got for us on that?"

Longo shrugged. "We could only pull a partial. One that's not hitting in the database, nor matching anything else we've pulled. Yet. We've only begun our lab work."

"*Cacchio*," Costa said. "Other prints? On the wineglasses? The bottle? Anywhere else?"

"We got hits on three sets." Longo ticked off his fingers. "Our deceased, his father, Salvatore, and his sister, Martina. Of course, they all three live there, so that's not too surprising."

"What about the shoe prints found down by the road?" Costa asked. "Have you examined the casts we took? Can you tell if they were left last night?"

"They were left last night," Longo said. "I'm certain of it. You can tell by the depth and sharpness of the details. And given that they led directly uphill, I'm confident we've discovered our killer's mode of entrance onto the property."

"And we found no fresh shoe prints near the spot Ali allegedly saw our crime scene spy?" Gatti asked. "Nothing to indicate somebody was hiding in the forest today?"

"I saw a man," she said coolly. "There's nothing 'alleged' about it."

"No, we did not find any," Longo confirmed, glossing over the tense exchange. "Too much ground cover in that area."

"Either way, Falco did a good job this morning." Basso twisted to face Ali. "I might add you look radiant after your mud bath."

They all chuckled, Gatti a little too hard, and Ali smiled despite herself.

When the room quieted, Basso continued, "We can match the shoe prints against known brands."

"We're on top of that," Longo said. "We'll look."

"So he tried to mask his shoe prints, to no avail." Costa swiveled in his chair, making a sucking noise with his tongue through his teeth. "The bullets?"

"We'll send them to ballistics in Florence and see what we can find," Basso said.

"I'll put my thumb on them." Costa fired hard looks at his inspectors. "The jackals of the press out there are hungry for a hot scoop. I don't want anybody talking to them. No comments other than from me. Or my shoe will be firmly lodged in your ass. Got that?"

"*Sì, signore*," they said in unison.

"When's the autopsy?" Costa asked.

"Fontana's preparing for it now."

"Then don't let me hold you any longer. Keep us posted on your progress."

"Of course." Longo left the room.

Costa got up and looked out the window, leaning forward with increased interest.

"What is it?" Basso asked.

"I think that's them."

Their small group gathered by the window and peered down. From high above, they watched an old, dented Volvo wagon, dark paint fading on the hood, slow and park. There would have been nothing exceptional about the scenario had the press not swarmed the vehicle. Clearly, somebody of interest was inside.

The doors opened, and a man climbed out from behind the wheel, a woman from the passenger side. Camera lights flashed, shutters clicked, and shouted questions floated up to the open window.

"Salvatore and Martina Conti," Costa said.

A trio of uniformed men greeted the father and daughter, parting the sea of reporters to escort them inside.

"They're to be brought to Interrogation Room A, like you requested," Basso said.

"Good." Costa tipped his chin toward Gatti. "Everything you have on them."

Gatti already had his notebook out. Ali pulled hers, too. After changing clothes, she had researched the Conti family.

"Salvatore is the owner and chief operator of Conti Vineyards," Gatti said, "a boutique Brunello di Montalcino winery that was passed down by his father two decades ago. Salvatore is sixty-two years old. His daughter, Martina, is twenty-four. She went to school in Bologna, obtaining a degree in viticulture and enology. Taking a look at Conti Vineyards' website and social media, she's the forward-facing person of the operation. Her brother, Davide, was also working at the vineyard, although it's unclear how involved he was."

"And the mother?" Costa asked. "Where is she?"

Ali chimed in before Gatti could. "She died ten years ago. Lost a battle with breast cancer."

"They named their flagship wine label after her." Gatti tapped his notebook. "Maria-Maria."

"And what else about Davide?" Costa asked.

"He has a record," Ali said. "Drunk driving just after his mother died, in that same year."

"He ran his vehicle off the road," Gatti added. "Crashed into a barn."

She nodded. "He's been in trouble with drugs before, too. Cocaine possession. First offense, so he got off with a four-month driving ban. Davide's social media—"

"—is non-existent," Gatti said over her.

Scowling, she clarified, "The last time he posted was over a year ago."

Costa raised an eyebrow. "It's like watching Wimbledon. What else?"

Ali shook her head, relinquishing the floor to Gatti.

"Not much else," he said. "They seem to be a small winery."

Costa blew out a long breath. "We need those cell records."

"That we do, *signore*," Basso agreed.

"I'll give Vodafone a call myself. Gatti, Basso, make sure Salvatore and Martina Conti are comfortable in the interrogation room. Coffees, waters—get them what they need. Basso and I will talk with them in a few minutes. Go."

Ali began to follow them out.

"Falco, wait here, please."

She stilled, watching the door shut behind the others.

"How is your hand?" Costa asked.

"My hand?"

"Is it healing?"

"*Sì, signore.* It is." She closed her right hand into a fist, rubbing her thumb over the backs of her fingers, feeling only half of them.

With the casualness of somebody stirring sugar into a

cup of coffee, Costa took out his Beretta, removed the magazine and chambered bullet, and threw it to Ali.

The gun twisted in the air, lobbing toward her half-healed arm.

She reached up and caught it with no problem.

"Aim at me."

She raised an eyebrow but did as she'd been told.

Striding to her, Costa lashed out and snatched the gun from her hand. With a deft, nimble move, he twirled the weapon and aimed it at Ali in less time than it took her to blink.

"Once more," he said, stepping away and pitching the gun at her again.

This time, she fumbled the catch. The gun bounced off the chair beside her and clattered across the floor. It was clear to her, and to Costa, that she would have caught the weapon if her pinkie and ring fingers hadn't struggled to open all the way.

Costa left the gun on the ground and grabbed her hand, turning it like he was examining a fossil he'd unearthed at the beach.

She watched, face blooming with heat as she waited for him to comment on the obvious bend in her two rightmost fingers. The bend that remained no matter how hard she tried to straighten them.

"Can you feel this?" He pinched her pinkie between his thumb and forefinger.

"*Sì.*"

Costa's eyes flashed. "You can?"

"*Sì, signore.*"

Still holding her hand, he shook his head in disappointment. "Now, I want you to look at that picture on the wall and tell me what you see."

She looked. It was an old black-and-white photo of the Siena police headquarters building, taken sometime in the late 1800s.

"I don't understand," she said. But as she turned back, she did understand, because he had jabbed a toothpick into her finger, hard enough to draw a bead of blood, and she hadn't felt a thing.

Costa smiled, but his eyes were cold. Letting her hand go, he picked up his gun and returned to his desk. The air grew thick with tension as he reloaded the weapon and put it in his holster. When he finally met her gaze again, his expression was dead serious. "I spoke with Dr. Stefani today."

Her breath caught.

"He says you haven't been to see him in four weeks. That the last time you were there, you weren't progressing at the level he would have liked to see."

"I didn't know that was legal—doctors talking to people about their patients like that."

"It is when the patient is an inspector licensed by the province of Siena to carry a firearm and the person requesting information is the inspector's boss."

"*Sì, signore,*" she said with a nod.

"I made you an appointment for Monday morning. Seven thirty. I want you there."

"*Sì, signore.*"

"And you will take another firearm proficiency test next Thursday at 4 p.m. We need to prove you are still fit for field duty."

Ali swallowed. She hadn't tried shooting since the profi-

ciency test a month and a half ago, after Dr. Stefani had
deemed her healed enough from her shoulder repair surgery
to get back to work. At the time, she had been able to feel all
her fingers, so she'd scored perfectly. Her recovery had
progressed quicker than anybody could have imagined.

However, a week or two after being hired on to the
inspector squad, things had abruptly gone south. The scar
tissue in her shoulder had impinged a nerve, turning half her
hand into a brick. Since that diagnosis, she had avoided
follow-up visits to Dr. Stefani's office.

She needed to get into the shooting range for practice.
Fast.

"Did you hear me, Falco?"

She nodded. "*Sì, signore.*"

"Let's go."

4

Ali stepped into Observation Room A, joining Gatti by the one-way glass to watch Basso talk with Salvatore and Martina Conti on the other side. Costa continued past her, into the interrogation room. The father and daughter turned to face the door as he entered, their clay-brown eyes identically puffy and red-rimmed from crying.

Salvatore was tall and skinny, dressed in a pair of jeans and a sweater. Martina was also thin, though much shorter than her father, and she wore a pair of jeans and a sweater, too. Her hair was dark and curly, cut just shy of her shoulders. She would have been classically pretty if not for the scar that slashed across her face, starting above her left eye and ending below her bottom lip. The tight line slightly skewed her facial expressions.

"*Signor* Conti," Costa said, voice solemn, "I'm so sorry for your loss. And for yours, Martina. I'm Lieutenant Carlo Costa. I'm head inspector of the Questura di Siena. We've been working all morning to investigate this heinous injustice to your family, and I want you to know we will not stop until we find who is responsible."

"*Grazie*, Lieutenant Costa, we appreciate your dedication," Salvatore said. "Before we begin, however, could I please get some coffee? I declined Inspector Basso's earlier offer, but I have since changed my mind."

"Of course." Costa returned to the door, leaning out into the observation room. "Falco, Gatti, some coffees, please."

"I'll get them." Gatti left the room.

"*Grazie*." Costa gestured to the interrogation table. "Please, let's have a seat."

The group settled at the table—Costa and Basso on one side, the Contis on the other.

Ali watched Martina through the one-way glass for a few moments, noting the dead expression on the woman's face. It must have been an impossibly long day for her and Salvatore so far, driving five or six hours down from Turin and then dealing with the media and police upon arrival in Siena.

Gatti returned with a tray of small plastic cups. He delivered four to the interrogation room, then retreated, taking up position next to Ali, sipping a coffee of his own.

She glanced at the tray, seeing it was empty.

"I'm sorry, did you want one?" he asked.

"No."

She focused her attention on Costa, who was talking.

". . . and we will be recording this conversation, just in case you tell us something that might aid us in finding Davide's killer."

"What did Costa want with you?" Gatti asked, keeping his eyes on the window.

"Nothing."

". . . we were up at the Italian Wine Exposition in Turin," Salvatore said. "It's an important event every fall season, where we meet with our distributors from around the world to talk about the year's harvest and our upcoming releases. We sign orders, and we hopefully get new ones." He shrugged.

"That makes perfect sense," Costa said.

"How come Davide wasn't there with you?" Basso asked.

"Martina and I take care of the business side of things more than Davide does—did. He never liked schmoozing, and so he was happy to stay home and tend the harvest. Every day, the grape juice needs to be pumped out of the tanks, aerated in open tubs, then pumped back in until fermentation has fully set. And there are other chores that need tending to, as well."

Costa nodded. "And Giuseppe Sala? He does what for you?"

"He works full time at the winery. Giuseppe has been with us for over twenty years. His son also helps out, but not as much."

"His son?" Basso asked.

"*Sì*. His name is Luigi. Luigi Sala."

"And how old is Luigi?"

Salvatore frowned. "Twenty-three?"

Martina blinked out of a distant stare. "He's twenty-five."

"And where does he live?" Costa asked.

"With his father, just a few kilometers from us," she said. "Toward Montalcino."

"*Grazie*, Martina."

Ali pulled out her notebook and wrote down the new information.

Gatti eyed her, making no move to abandon the coffee hovering at his lips, but she could tell he was seconds from pulling out his own notebook.

"Do either of you have any idea who might have done this to Davide?" Costa asked.

Salvatore and Martina shook their heads.

Basso raised an eyebrow. "Not a single person that he's upset in the recent past?"

"No," Salvatore said. "Davide had no enemies. People liked him. He was a pain in the ass sometimes, but that was only with me. Not other people. He was such a good boy. He was funny." Tears streamed down Salvatore's cheeks. "He was smart. A hard worker."

Basso handed Salvatore a tissue, allowing the grief-stricken father a moment to expel his emotion. When Salvatore had composed himself, Basso continued, "I'm sorry to bring this up, but we know Davide was arrested ten years ago for possession of cocaine."

Salvatore sighed. "He was a kid. He had just graduated university and gotten a job in finance. He had a lot of money for the first time in his life and ran with a bad crowd. He was not a drug addict, if that's what you're asking."

"Of course not," Basso said, raising his hands. "But other people, his friends, perhaps . . . Do you know any that still use drugs?"

"His friends from that era are now spread far and wide across the country. He didn't see them anymore. Or, if he did, I don't know about it."

"And where was this finance job?"

"Bologna."

Ali wrote some more notes. *Bologna. Finance. Cocaine.*

"Okay," Costa said. "*Grazie*. And what about women? Who was he seeing? Do you know?"

"I don't know." Salvatore did not expound.

"I don't know, either," Martina said.

"He didn't talk about his love life?"

The Contis shook their heads again.

"Who was the last person he dated?" Basso asked.

"I'm not sure," Salvatore said.

The inspectors looked at Martina. She shrugged.

"A woman? A man?" Basso chuckled. "What are we talking about here?"

"The last woman he was serious about was up in Florence," Martina said.

"Florence?" Costa asked. "When did he live there?"

Salvatore cleared his throat. "After his mother died, we went through a rough time as a family."

"That was ten years ago, correct?" Costa asked.

"*Sì*. He moved up to Florence. Stayed there for five or so years. Then he came back."

Costa nodded. "And he didn't work at the vineyard at all during that time?"

"No. He worked at a small investment firm. It wasn't going well. He came home, asking me for money. When I told him no, in the end, he decided to stay and work at the winery with us."

"What is the name of this investment firm in Florence?" Basso asked.

"I have no idea."

"Florence Wealth," Martina said.

"Oh, *sì*," Salvatore said. "That was it."

"And he dated somebody up there in Florence?" Costa

asked.

"She worked at a pizzeria," Martina said.

"Her name?"

She stared at the ceiling in thought. "Bella."

"Last name?"

"All I know is her first name. Sorry."

Gatti peered down at Ali. "You got all that?"

She ignored him and kept scribbling down the details, feeling slightly mortified by her messy penmanship. Writing had been difficult lately, but it was even worse with him hanging over her.

"What about rival wineries?" Costa asked. "Are there any of those?"

"All other wineries are rivals," Salvatore said. "Anybody else producing Brunello di Montalcino is our competitor. But I would say we are on good terms with all of them. My father used to say that it's bad business to have enemies. It's a mantra we follow. Of course, I'll make an exception for whomever killed my son."

"Of course," Basso said. "I can't imagine, *signore*."

After a brief pause, Costa continued, "The neighbors reported spotting a vehicle around the time your son was killed. It was a dark-colored sedan. More of a luxury model, they told us. Do you have any idea who that could be?"

"No," Salvatore and Martina said, glancing at one another.

The room fell silent.

Basso sat back, folding his hands on his lap in conclusion. "Is there anything else we should know that we haven't asked about?"

"I can't think of anything," Salvatore said.

Martina shook her head.

Costa slid two contact cards across the table. "Please, in the coming days, when you return home, if you see anything out of place, if anything comes to you that you forgot to tell us today, or if you just need somebody to talk to, do not hesitate to use my number. That is my cell. I will answer."

"*Grazie*," Salvatore said, scraping up the cards and putting them in his pants pocket. "Where do we go? We can't go home, can we?"

"No, you cannot. For now, your property is still a crime scene. However, I give you my word that we will clear it as fast as possible."

"When will that be?"

Costa scratched his chin. "It's difficult to say. I want to make sure we've gathered every piece of evidence from the scene possible. But I promise I will contact you the second it is cleared."

"I'm not even so sure I want to go home." Salvatore began crying again, harder this time. Martina reached up to touch her father's shoulder, and he clenched her hand, leaning into the comfort she offered. Wiping his face, he said, "The media. They are everywhere outside."

"We will get another group of officers to escort you to your car," Costa said. "We will keep the media at bay for you."

"*Grazie.*"

The Contis rose from their chairs and exited the interrogation room behind Basso and Costa.

Ali followed, stepping out into the humid air of the second-floor squad room. Faint evening light slanted through the windows, casting the space in a soft orange

glow, and the smell of food backdropped the more immediate, recognizable stench of sweat and coffee. The sun had
almost set on a tiresome day, and her mouth watered at the
prospect of eating something.

Costa escorted the Contis past her, recruiting Rossi,
Taglia, and Patucci to take the grieving father and daughter
outside. Once they had disappeared down the marble stairs,
Ali scanned the squad room, seeing her old desk was still
empty. Fabiano sat at his near the window, observing them.
She caught his eye, and he glared at her.

Months ago, Ferrari had chosen Ali over Fabiano to be
promoted to inspector. Fabiano's father was a city official
and businessman with vast wealth, clout, and connections,
so by means unknown to her, he had tried hard to overrule
the decision. It hadn't worked. In fact, it had even backfired a
little, since Ferrari had told Ali he would rid the building of
the Fabianos afterward.

And yet, both were still hanging around. The younger
Fabiano with his job intact, the elder with his influence.

She returned Fabiano's hateful glare, and her father's
words echoed in her mind: *You did nothing wrong, Ali. Do you
believe it?*

When it came to Fabiano, she believed it. If he wanted to
hold a grudge, then that was his problem.

Turning away, she was surprised to see Gatti staring
daggers at Fabiano, too. Not only that, but when she looked
back, she realized Fabiano could have been glaring at him
instead of her.

"It would be nice to speak to Martina alone," Basso said,
pulling Ali from her confused thoughts. "There might be
something to that job in Florence. Or that woman he was

dating. Maybe they were still involved. Bella was her name. Gatti, you paying attention?"

"Huh? Sorry."

Basso's gaze flicked to Fabiano, who was now head down, completing some paperwork.

"Listen up," Costa said. "I'll repeat: talk to the press, and my foot goes in your ass."

"*Sì, signore,*" they said.

Costa rubbed his neck, then waved a hand. "Everyone go home. Eat some food. Get some rest." He looked at Ali. "Wash some clothing. We'll let Longo and his team do their work, we'll let the cell phone company trudge through their bureaucracy, and then we'll see where we are in the morning. Seven o'clock sharp in my office."

5

"That's not a bad grouping."

Ali startled upon hearing the man's voice through her sound-suppressing headphones. She hadn't realized she'd had an audience for her first go at the fifteen-meter target.

"*Grazie*," she said, voice muffled to her own ears.

The officer ambled away, sweeping the brass behind the line.

Relief flooded through Ali as she verified all her shots had landed squarely in the red or not too far from it. Considering she lacked feeling in the outer half of her right hand, the officer had been more correct than he'd known: the grouping was not bad.

Of course, during her upcoming firearm proficiency test, she would be in a high-stakes situation, shooting from behind obstacles, sometimes with her off-hand, and from various distances, all while the training officer watched her every move.

She put the Beretta on safe and pressed the button to

eject the magazine, readying the weapon before reeling in the target for a closer inspection of her grouping. But the magazine failed to drop.

What the hell? She pressed the button again, and nothing happened. Either it was jammed or . . . Using her off-hand thumb, she tried to eject the magazine once more. This time, it easily dropped out of the handle.

Her stomach sank. Shooting had felt entirely foreign without the full sensation of the gun kicking into her right hand—which had resulted in her clenching the weapon extra hard with her left hand to compensate—and now she couldn't apply enough pressure to eject the magazine with her right thumb. That wasn't going to look good during the test. Not at all.

"Everything okay?" the man asked. He was back, watching her.

"Fine." Ali finished clearing the gun and took off her headphones.

"I'm Orsi. Leonardo Orsi."

She put the weapon inside the case, closing it up.

Orsi presented her with the paper target. "Do you want this? Like I said, solid grouping. You have the proficiency test soon or something?"

"Huh? Oh. No. *Grazie.*"

She bent down to tuck her headphones in her bag. Maybe she could have the gun modified to loosen the release button. Or have it modified to make the release button larger, giving her a better grip on it. Who could do that? She would have to talk to the weapons office.

"Well, nice to meet you."

When she looked up, Orsi was already gone.

"Oh, nice to meet you," she mumbled to herself, decidedly not in the mood to speak to another human, anyway.

Ali spent the next two hours of her Friday evening returning to her apartment, changing into exercise clothing that fit, and jogging the streets of Siena. As always, her lungs started out rusty, battling to work through the years of cigarette tar she had accumulated, and eventually warmed up.

Veering between masses of autumn tourists, she ran to the Stadio Artemio Franchi and lapped the track twice, then took a few trips around the nearby Fortezza Medicea. Slick with sweat, she finally made her way home, threading along the narrow streets and through Piazza del Campo, where the Friday night crowd was already starting to grow.

Half a kilometer past the square, she reached her apartment. The four-story pink stucco structure stood near the city's defensive wall, which had been erected sometime in the eleventh century. She jogged in place outside the courtyard entrance as she inserted her key into the tall iron gate.

Ramping up the intensity of her workout to eleven out of ten, she climbed the building's stairwell two steps at a time, her lungs and legs protesting. She did not stop until she emerged onto the third floor. Hands on her hips, she breathed heavily through her teeth, leaning hard against the wall.

The door beside her opened, and an elderly woman poked her head out. "You have to calm down."

Ali pushed off the wall, wiping her forehead.

"You're going to die if you keep that up."

"Hi, Isabella."

"I'm ninety-two years old, and I never ran around like a crazy person until I almost keeled over and died."

"It's called exercise."

"And look at me. I'm almost a hundred. What are you trying to do?"

Striding across the hall to her apartment, Ali laughed. "It makes me feel good."

"That's feeling good?"

She pulled out her keys.

"When are you going to bring a man around? A man can make you feel good."

"Okay. Wow." She opened her door, pausing at the threshold. "Wasn't it improper for your generation to have a man over?"

Isabella's eyes glazed over. "I used to put on a trench coat and a hat, with my long, luxurious hair tucked under, and act like a man as I snuck past the building manager to spend the evening with Paulo."

Ali smiled. "I'm sure there will be no sneaking past you when I finally do have a man over."

"You're such a beautiful woman. Men must be falling all over themselves for your attention. Why aren't you letting any of them in?"

"Because none of them deserve to be let in."

"Somebody has to be good enough."

"Good night, Isabella," Ali said, ducking inside her apartment, shutting the door quickly.

Except for the modest bathroom, the whole place was one L-shaped room. She had a kitchenette with a table and a couple of chairs, a small couch she'd purchased from IKEA a few years ago, and a bed meant for two people, though most nights, it served only one.

Dropping her keys on the table, she went to the faucet and drank down a glass of water, then set the glass in the sink and gazed out the window at the night sky, the sliver of rolling hills visible to the south. Any better view, and she would have to pay out the nose. This apartment was already more than she could comfortably afford, but she liked it, and she was grateful to see a glimpse of the Tuscan countryside, no matter how small.

Turning around, she caught sight of her reflection in a wall mirror across the room. Her hair was sticking up on the sides and top, with one curly strand extending off her forehead like a lightning bolt. The small scrape from earlier that morning reddened one cheek, and her deep-brown eyes were wide open and alert.

Ali sighed. Even after the especially long run, she could tell sleep would be elusive tonight. Since the action up in Como, she had found it challenging to rest without exercising to the point of exhaustion first. Bone-deep fatigue was the only thing that could quiet her anxious mind, which was way too active as of late.

Her gaze drifted down to her right hand, and she winced at how deformed it looked compared to her left. The pinkie and ring fingers were curled in, as if superglued together. With a little effort—too much effort—she straightened the digits, studying the tiny scab where Costa had stabbed her with the toothpick.

She went to the closet and retrieved the exercise band from the doorknob. Staring at the loop of rubber dangling from her bad hand, she gritted her teeth, threaded her right foot through one end of it, then stepped down and lifted her arm straight in front of her.

Pain pierced the front of her shoulder, but she continued to raise and lower her arm slowly. Once. Twice. She had just counted her seventh repetition when a memory careened through her mind like a runaway train.

She stood in the kitchen of the Como villa again. Twin guns blasted simultaneously. Marco and Colombo landed in a heap at her feet, convulsing. Blood spread across the tile.

Ali flung the band across the room. "*Cazzo.*"

Rubbing the ache out of her shoulder, she walked back to the sink and stared at the unopened bottle of wine sitting on her counter. A sealed pack of Marlboro Blacks and a red Bic lighter lay next to it. With a small shake of her head, she abandoned the vices and went to the couch, collapsing into the cushions.

Her eyes locked on the framed photo she'd placed on an end table. Taken years ago, it showed her standing with her mother and father on a Ligurian beach. They were all rotisserie-baked from the August sun, mouths stretched wide with beautiful, joyful smiles.

After all these years, Ali finally had her parents back. They were both dead, but their memories were no longer wrapped in a cold blanket of shame. Now, when she studied the picture, she felt a warm presence, as if her mother and father stood behind her, watching over her in that moment.

One night not long ago, she had allowed herself to view a batch of online videos starring a famous American medium. She had lounged on the balcony, drinking the red and sucking down Marlboros between glasses, while the man had done some convincing readings, supposedly connecting people with their departed relatives.

At first, she had been more than skeptical. Borderline outraged at the man's brazen con. But the alcohol had pushed aside the rational part of her, and she had found herself dripping tears, sobbing uncontrollably as she'd watched clip after clip, feeling the same warm, loving presence she did now.

Maybe her parents were here. Maybe her mother was floating next to her, stroking the stray hairs away from her eyes like she used to do. Maybe her father was squeezing her shoulders, murmuring about how she was his *principessa*.

"I miss you," she whispered, voice cracking.

Her phone buzzed on the counter. She went to it and saw a text from Clarissa, plus two missed calls. A shock pulsed through her as she read the callers' names: Clarissa and Marco Vinci. There was also one voicemail. From Marco.

Wow. That was new.

She pressed the button to listen but saw from the transcript displayed onscreen that he hadn't said anything. Or nothing intelligible, at least.

With piqued curiosity, Ali put her phone on speaker. She heard soft breathing, followed by shuffling sounds, before the voicemail ended. Realizing how tight her grip had become, she relaxed her fingers and pressed Clarissa's name.

"*Ciao!*" Clarissa shouted over the noise of a crowded bar. At least somebody had a social life. "Where are you?"

"I'm home," she said, leaving the phone on her bed as she undressed.

"I called. What were you doing?"

"I was out on a run. And before that . . ." She decided to keep the shooting thing to herself. "At work."

"How's your face?"

"Fine. Listen, I'll get the sweat suit back to you Monday."

"Like I'm worried."

Ali put her sweaty clothes in the hamper. "What are you doing?"

"We're out at Buco Nero. You coming?"

"No. I have an early morning."

"Oh . . . the case. Whatever. Why don't you come for just a drink?"

She looked at herself in the mirror and grimaced.

"He-llo?" Clarissa asked.

"He called."

"Who? What?"

"Marco."

Clarissa went silent for a few moments. "What did he say?"

"Nothing. He left a voicemail that said nothing, and then he hung up."

"You're not going to call him back, are you?"

"No."

"Good. He had his chance. He didn't answer your calls, and now you're supposed to answer his? You left three messages pouring out your heart, and he never responded."

"*Sì. Grazie.* I remember clearly."

"Just making sure you do." The sound of Clarissa lighting a cigarette came through the speaker. She exhaled. "Why the hell is he calling now?"

Ali didn't respond.

"Come out. Have a glass. Talk with other humans. Get

ogled by men. Maybe take one home. Give him what he wants."

Ali brought her phone into the bathroom and set it on the counter. She took out her hair tie, unleashing chaotic curls, as she debated how to respond. Truth was, she had all the energy in the world to go out, and she wanted to. Almost desperately so.

"I have to rest," she said. "It's a big day tomorrow. It's my first case, and I'm not going to screw it up." She looked at her claw-like hand. "I *can't* screw it up."

"Ugh." Clarissa's grunt of disapproval echoed across the tile bathroom. "Fine."

"*Ciao.*" She ended the call and turned on the shower.

While the water warmed, Ali stared at the Instagram icon on her phone screen, trying and failing to resist its lure. She opened the app and searched Marco's name. Two pictures from years prior were still the only tumbleweeds rolling around in the man's ghost town of a profile.

Ali knew she should stop there. Put the phone down, get into the shower, and wash off the day. But curiosity nagged at her. She had to check.

She typed, *v-a-l-e-n-t*, and Marco's former fiancée's name auto-filled. *Valentina d'Elia.*

Ali hovered her finger over it. Then she pressed, watching the beautiful woman's life appear onscreen. According to her profile, Valentina spent her days eating at fancy restaurants, riding boats in Ibiza, and lying on the beach, showing off her perfect bikini body.

A dozen more photos had been added since the last time Ali had snooped. She scrolled past them all, freezing when she reached the familiar picture of Marco. Posted a month and a half ago, right around the third time Ali had called him and left one final heartfelt message, it once again told her everything she needed to know.

Marco and his fiancée had gotten back together. He and Ali did not have the connection she'd thought. And the kiss they'd shared during their harrowing adventure had been just that: a small, intimate moment brought on by extraordinary circumstances. He had just broken up with Valentina, and Ali's lips had comforted him. Nothing more.

To her, however, it had been an impossibly electrifying connection, something she hadn't experienced since leaving Matteo all those years ago.

Steam billowed from the shower. She closed the app, set her phone face down on the counter, and stepped beneath the hot spray.

6

Ali hurried down the final stretch of cobblestone road, legs straining after the prior evening's run.

At 6:55 a.m. on a Saturday morning, she had most of the streets to herself. The air was cool and damp, scented of pastries, coffee, and baked goods. Her mouth watered as she entered Oscar Bar and ordered at the counter.

"You're late." Basso stood near the register, sipping a coffee, leafing through the *Corriere della Sera* with stern concentration.

Ali checked the time and saw they only had a few minutes until they were due in Costa's office. She paid the attendant and glanced behind Basso, spotting three patrons holding tickets at the other end of the counter.

"Don't worry," Basso said absently, reading an article. "We're not meeting this morning."

"We're not?"

He peeled his eyes from the newspaper to look at her. "We're going straight down to Montalcino."

"Why?" She moved closer, sensing he was about to lower his voice.

"They matched the print on the bullet casing to Giuseppe Sala last night."

She frowned. "Giuseppe Sala?"

The barista took Ali's ticket and moved to the espresso machine.

Basso turned the page, revealing two megalithic columns separated by an AC Milan player sliding across turf, shirt off, a triumphant battle cry twisting his face.

"Giuseppe was the one who called it in," she said. "Why would he do that if he killed him?"

"We have warrants for search and arrest."

"Huh," she said, remembering the anguish on Giuseppe's face as he had told them about his discovery of Davide's corpse. The man had seemed genuinely shaken up. "But why would he shoot Davide in the crotch? We're clearly looking at a crime of passion, aren't we? Giuseppe's an old man."

The barista returned with her cappuccino, a packet of cane sugar, and a spoon.

"*Grazie*, Marta," Ali said.

"*Prego, signora.*"

When Marta was gone, Basso raised an eyebrow. "You're saying old men don't have passion?"

"No." Ali sipped her cappuccino. "It just seems odd to me."

"Murder is odd. He could have been trying to mislead us." Basso folded the newspaper and tucked it under his arm. "No brioche?"

"I ate oatmeal at home."

"Why?"

"I'm trying to be healthier."

"Why?"

She rolled her eyes, taking another sip.

Basso checked his watch.

"All right, all right." She downed the entire cup, wiped her mouth, and followed him out.

"I'll drive," Basso said, as if there were any question. The man always drove. It had been that way for as many years as she'd known him. Early on, she'd learned that offering to drive was an affront to the man's firm sense of control, like slapping him on the shoulder while he stood on the edge of a cliff.

They walked the short distance to the parking spots outside headquarters and climbed into Basso's Citroën. Ali buckled up, kicking a juice bottle lying on the floor.

"Give me that," Basso said.

She handed it over, and he threw it in the back before firing up the engine.

"How are the boys?" she asked.

"Hellions." He checked his mirrors and pulled out. "Absolute hellions."

Thirty minutes later, they turned onto Strada Provinciale del Brunello, a two-lane highway that thread like a vein through the hills near Montalcino. Vineyards striped the landscape, reminding the traveler they were in wine country.

The pavement was dry, no hint of a cloud in the azure sky. Autumn leaves tumbled across the road on a southerly wind that occasionally hit the car, rocking it side to side. Each time, Basso cursed under his breath and clutched the wheel a little tighter.

"It's too late for a GSR test on Giuseppe's hands," he said

eventually, breaking their comfortable quiet. "But there may be something usable on what he wore. We want all the dirty clothing he has in the house. The sheets off his bed, too. We're obviously searching for the rifle, cartridges, and shoes that left those prints. Longo identified them as boots."

Ali nodded. "Costa and Gatti?"

"Costa had an early meeting, and you know Gatti always drives him. We'll probably get there first. Some local units will join us for backup in case things go bad."

Her heart started beating faster at the prospect of things going bad.

"How's your hand?"

She eyed him. "Why?"

Basso shrugged. "I heard from Costa."

Ali turned away to hide her frustration. If Basso knew, who else did? "Who can I ask to modify my gun?"

"In what way?"

"Just . . . I want to have my gun modified. Do you know somebody?"

He looked at her, and the car swerved into the oncoming lane.

"Watch out!"

He corrected. "Are you having trouble shooting?"

"No. I just don't like the way the magazine release is set up."

"Why?"

"Forget it."

They rode in silence for a beat.

"Talk to Rossi. He has access to anything you need."

"*Grazie.*"

Basso pointed at the GPS readout on the dashboard

touch screen. "How much longer?"

She pinched and zoomed with her fingers. "We're taking a left in ten kilometers. Then it's a few minutes after that."

They continued tracking the blue line onscreen, weaving through the same hilly terrain as the day before. Montalcino was in full view to the west, a crust of buildings and walls perched atop a mound of cultivated land. However, their route would soon take them away from the picturesque town, down toward the low country.

"Next left," she instructed, pointing at a dirt road.

Two police cruisers were parked at the intersection of dirt and pavement, a pair of men in each. Basso slowed to take the turn, then pulled up beside the front vehicle and stopped, rolling down Ali's window. The noxious odor of animal dung hit her nose.

"Pew," she said.

"That's the smell of the country." Basso leaned forward to speak past her. Smiling wide and using the male ribbing tone that Ali wondered if she'd ever muster the courage to try, he said, "*Ciao.*"

"Basso?" The man behind the wheel frowned, like he was disappointed with God's choice. "*Mamma mia.*"

Basso made some comment about a *calcio* player, and the officer acted deeply offended before looking at Ali. "I'm Sergeant Rustica. This is Umberto."

The taciturn man beside Rustica nodded.

"Falco," Ali said.

Basso sucked in a deep breath through his nostrils. "Smells like *merda* out here."

"Pig farm," Rustica said.

"I thought it was you two."

Rustica rolled his eyes. "You have the warrant?"

"Glove compartment," Basso said to Ali.

She popped the latch and pulled out the papers, waving them in front of her open window.

Rustica nodded, apparently satisfied, so she gave them to Basso.

"You will make the arrest," Basso said. "Falco and I will start our search once you have him out of the house. He has a son named Luigi that lives there, too. We'd like him out of the way—detained, if necessary—while we do our thing."

Rustica chewed his lip in thought. "Are we waiting for Costa?"

"No. The six of us should be able to handle this."

"Okay," Rustica said. "Suit yourself. We'll follow you."

Ali rolled up her window as Basso stepped on the gas.

The dirt road ran along the top of a hill for a kilometer or so, then dropped into a valley. At the base of the depression, nestled amid yellow-leaved trees, sat a humble farmhouse with a run-down outbuilding. A rolling door was open on one side of the outbuilding, affording a view inside. It looked like a workshop.

Two small Fiat Pandas, both aged and battered, were parked in the driveway, along with a tractor and a rusted-out trailer. Other decayed junk was strewn about the property, machines that had been stripped of parts, their metal carcasses flung aside.

Basso cut the engine, and the two cruisers blew up dust as they stopped behind the Citroën.

Wind pushed hard at Ali's back as she got out. Slamming the door shut, she zipped her jacket to her chin and burrowed within the fabric, seeking relief from the cold.

Rustica and Umberto collected the two men from the other cruiser, then joined Ali and Basso. The unintroduced officers eyed the inspectors, and one of them flashed Ali a cheap smile.

"Let's move," Rustica said, snapping the group to attention.

Basso handed over the arrest warrant and stood beside Ali near the vehicles. They watched the officers approach the house with tense anticipation.

Ali caught movement in one of the upstairs windows.

"I see it," Basso said.

A young man, shirtless, opened the window and leaned out. "What's going on?"

"Luigi Sala?" Basso called up to him.

"*Sì*."

"Is your father here?"

Luigi turned his head, like he had heard a noise inside. He yelled something over his shoulder, then shut the window and disappeared.

Rustica knocked on the front door. "*Polizia*! We're here to talk to Giuseppe Sala!"

The four officers fanned out, resting their hands on their guns.

Ali kept her eyes glued to the window, but Luigi never reappeared.

Giuseppe answered the door. He was dressed in an identical outfit to the day prior, and she guessed they were the same clothes, only dirtier.

Rustica and Umberto wasted no time taking Giuseppe into custody, cuffing his hands behind his back and informing him of his rights.

"What is this?" Luigi burst out of the house, pulling a shirt over his skinny torso, trying to wedge himself between his father and the police. He was barefoot, and he cursed as he stepped off the tiny porch and onto a rock.

"Stay inside!" his father yelled.

Luigi shook his head, face red. "Why are you arresting him? What for? I demand to know."

Ali noted the stoic way Giuseppe gazed at his son. The man offered no resistance as he was led toward the cruisers.

"Is this about Davide?" Luigi asked. "It wasn't him! Are you seriously arresting him for killing Davide?"

"Be quiet, Luigi!"

"He was at the bar that night! There is no way he could have—"

"I wasn't at the bar!" Giuseppe screamed, halting, craning his neck to face his son. "I wasn't at the bar. Now shut up."

Luigi froze mid-protest, mouth hanging open. "What?"

"I lied to you about where I was last night. Now go inside."

Ali and Basso glanced at each other.

The fight seemed to leave Luigi's body. His shoulders slumped as he returned to the front door.

Rustica patted Giuseppe on the shoulder, and they resumed their march toward the vehicles. The man offered no resistance as he was deposited into the rear cruiser.

Ali and Basso stepped onto the porch.

"Luigi, my name is Inspector Basso. This is Inspector Falco." Basso pulled the search warrant from the breast pocket of his jacket and presented it. "I know your father told you to go inside, but we would like it if you stayed out here for a while. This is a warrant to search the property."

Luigi's eyes were wide open, staring at the floor. He looked up, and the desperate glare he latched onto Ali made her straighten. "There's no way he killed Davide. You have to believe me." He turned to Basso. "My father is not like that. My father did not kill Davide!"

They didn't respond, so Luigi implored Umberto, then the other officers, with a begging expression. Everyone avoided meeting his eyes.

"We're going to need you to step aside while we do our search," Basso said. "Why don't you get some shoes first?"

Luigi walked into the house. Basso kept close on his tail, holding up a hand to Ali and Umberto, who had lunged to follow. When the two men put their backs to the door, Ali moved closer.

"Leave the boots," Basso said. "You can take any of the other shoes, but you have to leave the boots."

Luigi sat on the floor, laced up some trainers, stood, and went outside.

Basso gestured to Umberto, who ushered the young man away from the house.

"I'll have Amigoni and De Luca take Giuseppe to Siena," Rustica said. "That's where you want him, right?"

"Sì," Basso confirmed. "*Grazie*. Chief Ferrari will be expecting them."

Rustica nodded. "Umberto and I will keep an eye on this kid while Costa gets here."

"You're a good man."

"I won't forget you told me I smelled earlier."

"And I won't forget what you said about Inter last time

we saw each other." Basso pulled gloves and booties from his pocket. Ali followed suit, donning both.

"What is it with you men and *calcio*?" she asked, walking into the house.

The small entryway was littered with footwear, all dirty, old, and well-worn.

"Boots," Basso said. "We'll take all those."

"Right."

Her hands were buzzing, Ali realized. She had anticipated violence instead of a relatively uneventful arrest, so her adrenaline had spiked during Giuseppe's outburst at his son.

"You okay?" Basso asked.

"I'm fine."

Bending down to study the soles of the boots, she saw immediately that the tread was all wrong on the first pair. The second appeared more like a match. She pulled out her phone and scrolled to the pictures she had taken of the boot prints in the trees.

"Well?" Basso asked.

She shook her head. "The patterns are all wrong."

"He might have gotten rid of the boots, just in case. Let's at least find a rifle and the cartridges that go with it."

They strode into the kitchen. An electric burner glowed red-hot, a moka pot vibrating on top. Ali shut off the stove and moved the coffee maker to a hot pad, sending the room into silence save the ticking burner.

On the counter lay a partially open pizza box, empty inside. A single bottle of wine, stoppered with a rubber cork, stood at the edge of a worn metal sink. She identified it as a three-euro bottle of Chianti from the supermarket, not quite a Conti Vineyards Brunello di Montalcino.

There was a narrow living room beyond the kitchen. Two small couches lined one wall, and a bookcase leaned against another, eating virtually all the available floor plan. A door off the kitchen stood open, revealing a cramped bathroom with a toilet and a sink.

After a few minutes of searching through kitchen cabinets and drawers, under furniture, and on shelves, it became clear that anything significant they might find would be upstairs, or perhaps in the workshop.

They headed to the second floor and discovered a small hallway with three doors, two of which led to Giuseppe's and Luigi's bedrooms, the third to a television room.

Basso entered the first bedroom. Ali followed, making a face at the smell but keeping the expletives pushed down, along with the vomit that wanted to come up.

"Luigi needs foot spray," Basso said.

"And deodorant."

Dirty clothes were strewn on the floor, and a bed sat unmade, Inter Milan sheets giving off a musty scent. Ali wagered they hadn't been washed since purchase.

She backed out and moved to Giuseppe's room, pleasantly surprised to encounter the gentle scent of cologne. The bed was made, and the window was open, letting in fresh air. She pulled aside an accordion door, revealing a neat row of hanging shirts and a few folded pairs of pants. A hamper contained muddy clothing.

"Got some dirty clothes here."

"I see," Basso said from behind her. "Still no gun?"

She checked the corners of the closet. "Nothing."

The sound of tires crackling over dirt and gravel came in through the window.

Ali looked out and saw two familiar vehicles. "Costa and Longo are here."

They reached the porch as the cars parked.

Gatti emerged from the driver's side of the front vehicle, an Audi hatchback, and Costa climbed from the passenger side. Longo and Fontana spilled out of the other vehicle, both carrying duffle bags.

Costa dropped a cigarette butt on the ground and smothered it with his shoe. "Rustica, Umberto, good to see you."

The officers responded with somber nods, and then Costa shifted his gaze to Luigi, who sat on the earth near Rustica's vehicle. The young man was picking rocks off the ground, flinging them into the distance.

"Luigi Sala," Costa said.

Luigi squinted up at him.

"My name is Lieutenant Costa. I'm the head inspector in Siena. I'm sorry to barge in on you like this, but we have found some evidence that led us here. Specifically, a shell casing with your father's fingerprint on it."

"At Davide's?"

Costa nodded.

Luigi shook his head. "That's impossible."

"Unfortunately, it is not." Costa eyed Ali and Basso. "Have you found the gun?"

"Not yet, *signore*," she said.

Costa looked back at Luigi. "Where's your father's gun?"

Luigi said nothing, only stared at Costa.

"The less cooperative you are, the more I'm concerned you're hiding something," Costa said.

Luigi scoffed, then gestured to the workshop. "It's hanging on the wall in there."

Gatti hurried off, Ali and Basso right behind him. They rounded the Fiats and entered the spacious outbuilding. Made of creaky wood, it seemed hundreds of years old. Tools of all kinds hung in neat rows on the walls. A long worktable stood off to one side, blackened from grease, dinged from heavy use.

Gatti made a show of inspecting each wall. Upturning his hands, he asked, "Where?"

"Here," Basso said.

Ali followed his gaze to a brown bolt-action hunting rifle with a leather strap hanging off two hooks above the sliding door.

With gloved hands, Basso plucked the gun from its storage spot, taking care to aim the weapon at the ground as he pulled back the bolt. A spent shell waited in the housing. "It's a .308 Winchester."

"The smoking gun," Gatti said.

"Looks that way." Basso slid the bolt forward and turned around.

Longo and Fontana were there, suited up to process the scene. Basso handed the gun to them.

Ali pointed at a shelf, where a box of rifle cartridges peeked out behind two cans of paint.

Gatti removed them from the shelf. "More .308 Winchesters."

For the next half hour, Ali, Gatti, and Basso helped gather potential evidence from the property, bagging clothes, boots, and trash that would be sifted through later. When their usefulness ended, they moved outside, letting Costa, Longo, and Fontana wrap up the morning's work.

Basso took a phone call and walked up the drive,

cigarette smoke billowing in his wake. Gatti stood by the workshop, tapping on his phone. Ali went to lean against the Citroën, wanting her own space.

She lifted a foot and held it behind her butt, stretching her tight quadricep.

"Did somebody use our gun to shoot Davide?" Luigi asked, still seated nearby. He gathered dirt from the ground, sifted it through his hands, and flicked the remaining rocks toward the metal scraps in the yard.

Ali opted to pull out her phone rather than come up with a response. She discovered no missed calls or messages, but she pretended like she had something to do.

Costa exited the house, Longo and Fontana in tow. The forensic experts brought their evidence bags to the vehicles, then Longo directed Fontana where to place each one while he took notes with a pen and a clipboard.

"Luigi." Costa motioned for the young man to rise.

Luigi stood, brushing dirt off his backside and legs.

"We would like to ask you a few questions," Costa said.

"Please do."

"Where were you Thursday night?"

"I was here."

"Doing what?"

"Watching television."

"All night?"

"*Sì.*"

Costa folded his arms. "Did you see your father that night?"

Luigi sighed. "No."

Basso materialized next to Ali, joining the interrogation. "Why did you say your father went to the bar?"

"I . . . I thought he did. He usually goes out on Thursday nights."

"What's the bar called?" Ali asked, poised to write his answer in her notebook.

Luigi stared into nothing, shaking his head.

"You don't know the name of it?" she pressed.

"No."

For the first time, Ali suspected he was lying.

"What time did he come home?" Costa asked.

"I'm not sure. But it was after eleven. Eleven thirty, maybe."

"But you said you didn't see him."

"I didn't. I heard him. I don't remember exactly what time."

Costa and Basso exchanged a glance.

"He didn't kill Davide Conti," Luigi ground out forcefully. "He's not a killer."

Basso stared at Luigi. "You said you stayed home all night?"

"That's right."

"What about the pizza? Was that from Thursday night or last night?"

"Oh." Luigi flushed. "Thursday night. I went and got a pizza, but after that, I stayed home."

Gatti joined the semicircle of inspectors in front of Luigi.

Eyes bouncing between them, the young man looked like a cornered animal. "When can I visit my father?"

"It will be a long day for your father," Costa said. "I would suspect you'll be able to speak to him tomorrow morning."

"Where?"

"We took him to headquarters. He'll likely be held at the penitentiary on remand."

"Where?"

"In Siena."

"Are we done here? Can I go inside now?"

Costa waited a beat, then nodded.

Luigi stomped toward the house, and Ali watched him, noticing his unique gait. Did his father walk the same, with his feet splayed out? She couldn't remember.

Phone in hand, she scrolled through the pictures of the boot prints again.

Basso peered over her shoulder, smelling of smoke. "What are you looking at?"

"I was just checking something."

"What?"

"Luigi walks with his toes pointed out."

"So?"

"So, the boot prints in that mud at the scene . . ." She gave him her phone. "See here? They were almost the opposite, with the toes pointed in. Did Giuseppe have the same walk? I didn't notice."

Basso shook his head. "I didn't, either."

"And the boots we found don't match," she added. "I don't need to be a forensic expert to see that."

"See what?" Costa asked.

Basso handed back her phone. "Falco here was telling me she doesn't think it was Giuseppe Sala."

"Oh?"

Ali shrugged. "The boots aren't going to match."

"Maybe not," Costa said. "But the gun is. Now, let's get out of here. I'm hungry."

7

"He's not talking."

Ali lifted her head and saw Basso standing at her desk. "Giuseppe Sala?"

"*Sì.*"

"I know. I watched you and Costa try to interrogate him."

Basso took a sip of coffee. By her count, it was his fourth cup since they had returned from the Sala property this afternoon. She would have slumped over from a heart attack.

"He's playing the quiet game. But why?"

"He's also not looking at you," she said.

"Never once," Basso confirmed. "No eye contact. Not even before, at his house. Did you catch that? The man is determined. As unyielding as a marble statue."

She nodded.

"But why?" he repeated.

She shrugged.

"Maybe Luigi was involved, and Giuseppe is trying to protect him." He tapped his chin. "Luigi said he was home alone with no one to corroborate, and he conveniently forgot to mention the pizza he went to pick up. What if he conveniently forgot to mention killing Davide, too? What if he was jealous of Davide for some reason? That might explain the shot in the crotch."

Ali waited for Basso to continue, knowing from experience that he wanted to talk at her right now, not with her.

"But . . . like you said, Luigi walks like a penguin. So does his father. I noticed it when Giuseppe was leaving the interrogation room. You were right to bring that up, Falco. You think those boot prints look like Giuseppe's? Knowing he's got the legs of an arctic bird?"

"Antarctic."

Basso frowned, meeting her eyes for the first time since he'd arrived at her desk.

"Antarctic. Get it right." She yawned, stretching her mouth wide. "I don't know. There were only a few usable boot prints. And besides, the killer would have been moving carefully—intentionally—across difficult terrain during a rainstorm. Not like how they'd walk in the halls of a police station."

"Then what about the boots? Why didn't we find a match?"

She shrugged again. "Maybe it's like you said earlier: Giuseppe ditched the footwear somewhere so we couldn't tie it back to him."

"And then he hung the murder weapon over the door of his workshop?" Basso grunted, tipping the cup to finish off his coffee. "Costa says we can go home and take tomorrow off."

"We can?"

"*Sì.*"

"Why didn't you tell me earlier?"

"I am. I just did. But he wants to see you in his office first."

"Now?"

"*Sì*. See you Monday." He shuffled over to Gatti's desk.

Ali stood up, wincing at the tightness in her legs. It was worse than ever now. She gathered her things and put them in her backpack, then turned off her desktop computer, slipped on her jacket, shouldered her bag, and walked to Costa's office.

The door was open a crack, and she saw him sitting inside, back to her, attention on his phone. He was staring at a picture of a young woman, no older than Ali, holding a baby. The woman was in the throes of laughter as she poked the baby's stomach. The baby was smiling, gripping the woman's finger.

Ali knocked twice on the door, noting the speed at which the phone dropped out of sight.

Costa swiveled his chair to face her.

"You wanted to see me, *signore*?"

He nodded. "Take a seat."

"*Sì, signore.*"

"I hear you were at the shooting range last night."

"*Sì, signore.*"

"How did that go?"

"It went well."

Costa squinted at her, as if reading the lie. "Good. And you're going to your doctor appointment Monday morning? Seven thirty?"

"*Sì.*"

"Good. You can take tomorrow off. Longo and Fontana

have a backlog of work, so we may as well give them time to do what they do without us breathing down their necks."

"Basso told me. *Grazie*. Is that all?"

"One more thing." Costa steepled his hands on his desk. "What is your gut telling you on this?"

Her brow furrowed in confusion. "*Signore*?"

"You saw inside that house, what we found. What do you think?"

She said nothing, fearing her thoughts might be too extreme.

"I don't want voiceless inspectors on my team, Falco."

"Okay," she said. "My gut's telling me it wasn't Giuseppe. The man seemed genuinely heartbroken yesterday when he talked about finding Davide's body. Also, the boots we found at his house don't match the prints. I deduced that from sight and then confirmed by comparing a couple pictures on my phone. If Giuseppe killed Davide, then he hid the boots. And if he hid the boots, why not hide the gun as well? And why leave the spent shell in the chamber like that? Same goes for Luigi."

Costa looked at her long. "It's what I'm thinking, too. But the evidence is pointing at Giuseppe, and so we have to follow it. I'm sure you understand."

"I'm not sure I do, *signore*."

"Then let me tell you." He leaned back in his chair and sighed. "People in power, with the constant pressure put upon them, want things like this solved quickly and cleanly. If it's slow and messy, it's not good for anybody involved. Right now, we have some clean evidence pointing at Giuseppe Sala."

"So we lock him up and throw away the key, ruining the

lives of two innocent people because of one fingerprint? You can live with something like that?"

A hint of amusement gleamed in Costa's eyes.

"What about the boot prints?" Ali asked. "We can't prove those were made by Giuseppe."

Costa tilted his head. "What if they were made by some-body other than the killer?"

"That's not likely."

"Prove it, Inspector Falco."

She raised her chin. "*Sì, signore.*"

"And do your shoulder exercises."

"*Sì, signore.*"

"And get into the shooting range again before your test."

"*Sì, signore.*"

"Which is at what time?"

"Four o'clock. Thursday afternoon." How could she forget?

"All right. Now go home."

"*Sì, signore.*" She paused at the door. "*Signore?*"

"What?"

"Who's the woman with the baby?"

The easy smile on Costa's face vanished. "I'll see you Monday."

8

Ali set a brisk pace as she walked down Via del Sole. A chilly breeze funneled through the walls of the medieval buildings, spreading aromas of a thousand different meals cooking across the city.

It had been weeks since she'd gone out on a Saturday night. Clarissa was likely heading to a bar right now. All it would take was one phone call to join in on the fun. But the thought of standing in a sweaty crowd, listening to people scream over the music to be heard . . . The pack of Marlboros and the bottle of red sitting on her counter sounded more her speed.

And that was downright depressing.

Her phone chimed in her pocket. She pulled it out and found a text message from Marco.

Hi. I tried calling last night. I would really like to talk to you. I have some big news to share.

Big news to share? What kind of news? Was he getting hitched to Valentina?

Maybe he wanted to invite her to the wedding.

She reread the text, considering a response, and decided he deserved the same silence he'd treated her to for so long.

Then again, she was curious. Maybe she would call him. Later, when she was home and comfortable.

Ali's route took her straight through Piazza del Campo, where a sea of chaos was already churning. She stuck to the edge of the square, passing a group of teenagers lounging on their 50cc motorcycles, and turned onto Via di Salicotto by Torre del Mangia, the iconic Siena clock tower that was visible for kilometers beyond the city's walls.

It was quieter within the narrow confines of the street, only a trickle of people passing by, and the noise of Siena's most famous square faded into the background.

Her phone rang, and with a tap of her finger, she ignored Clarissa's call. A few seconds later, a text message came in.

We're at Il Rosé if you want to join!

Rolling her eyes, she typed out a response.

Can't do it. Have fun!

Ali waited for a reply. None came. Maybe her friend had given up. It wouldn't be a surprise.

She rounded a corner and glimpsed a man walking a dozen or so paces behind her. At first, she didn't give his presence a second thought. But then he jerked his head down, as if he had been caught staring, and her adrenal glands fired.

Suddenly, she was back on the shores of Lake Como, being chased and attacked by the man with the Egyptian eye tattoo.

Ali forced the memory away and willed her racing heart to calm, reminding herself that she wasn't out in the middle of nowhere. She was in the middle of Siena during the busiest time of night.

Of course, at the moment, nobody was in her immediate vicinity. Nobody but the man.

She did a double take and saw he had pulled his hood up, dousing his face in shadow. There were no lights mounted on the walls here, but even so, she could tell he was thin and had sloping shoulders. Very different from her former attacker. That didn't comfort her any.

The man slowed, sensing she was onto him. Or maybe he was an innocent bystander, traveling the same direction as her, who had just realized he'd gotten a bit too close, freaking out the woman in front of him.

She wasn't taking any chances.

Up ahead, a couple strolled past on a perpendicular street. Ali knew if she took a right at the intersection, she would be only fifty meters from Piazza del Mercato. The place was always choked with people doing their shopping and socializing.

She started jogging, checking over her shoulder as she picked up speed.

The man lurched into a jog, too.

There was no doubt about it now. He was coming after her.

Something about the situation—the way the man's feet stumbled on a crack in the cobblestone, how his skinny arms pumped almost clumsily, or the fact that he was chasing her straight to a crowded area—stoked her anger, pushed away her fear.

Ali ran full steam around the corner and saw Piazza del Mercato blazing with light. However, instead of closing the short distance between her and the square, she skidded to a halt, pressing herself flat against the building.

Then she waited.

The sound of slapping feet reached her first, wheezing breaths next. A moment later, the man launched into view, right in front of her.

She used her right arm as a club, slamming it into his hooded face. Pain erupted from her bad shoulder, and she felt the crunch of a nose collapsing against her forearm.

The man cried out, twisting sideways as he fell. He landed on his back, hitting the ground hard, head knocking on the pavement.

Ali prepared to stomp him, but froze when she saw the terrified, anguished face of Luigi Sala looking up at her.

"Please! No!" He pulled down his hood and raised his hands. "It's me, Luigi! Ow! I just want to talk! Ah!" He gripped the back of his head, baring his teeth in pain. "I just want to talk!"

"What the hell are you doing running after me like that?"

"I was calling your name."

"When?"

"Just before. When you started running."

"Well, not loud enough!" She stood over him, fists balled, shaking her head.

Hurried footsteps approached, and she saw two young men running from the square.

"Are you okay?" one of them yelled.

"What's going on?" the other shouted.

"I'm sorry," Luigi said, shifting to a seated position. "I'm sorry. I just want to talk. I called your name."

"I could have killed you," she said.

"I'm sorry."

The men came to a stop, panting.

"Are you okay, *signora*?"

"Was he attacking you?"

"What's going on?"

"It's okay." She forced a smile. "He's drunk. He was just playing a stupid prank. He's my friend."

They frowned, looking between her and Luigi.

"It's okay. Really. *Grazie*. You two are brave. I appreciate your help."

The men shrugged and turned around, laughing as they made their way back to the square.

She eyed Luigi. "Well? What do you want?"

He got to his feet, grimacing as he checked his wounds. "I want to tell you my father did not do it. He did not kill Davide."

"You already told me that this morning. That's what you chased me down for?"

"No. I mean, I have proof."

"What kind of proof?"

"I told you he always goes to the bar on Thursday nights. Always. In fact, he's there most other nights, too. But on Thursday nights, especially. That's when he plays cards with a bunch of other old men."

"A bar you don't know the name of."

"I . . . I do know the name. I was lying."

She squinted. "Why?"

"I don't know. I . . . was confused by what my father told me. I didn't believe he wasn't there. I wanted to check for myself."

Ali folded her arms across her chest. "So you checked?"

"*Sì*. And he was lying. I went to the bar and talked to his friends, and they all said he was there from eight until just after eleven. The newspaper said the neighbors heard gunshots at ten thirty." Luigi's eyes went wide and earnest. "Don't you see? There's no way he could have done it."

"What's this bar called?"

"Mickey's Bar. Like the mouse."

"Where is it?"

"Just east of our house. A few minutes away."

She stared at him. "Why would your father lie, Luigi? Why would he tell you he wasn't there?"

Luigi chewed his lip. "I don't know."

"Okay, but why are you out here telling *me* this?" she asked. "Why aren't you at the station right now, making an official statement?"

"I went to the station. I was going to come in, but . . . then I saw you leaving, and I . . ."

"Followed me? Why?"

"I don't know. I'm sorry. I guess I was scared."

"Scared of what? Admitting you withheld information from the *polizia*?"

"Not just that." Luigi looked at her. "I think he thinks it was me."

"Who thinks it was you?"

"My father."

Ali blinked. "Why would he think you killed Davide?"

"I didn't."

"Okay, but why would he think that?"

Luigi stepped backward, shaking his head.

She remained still. "What exactly were you doing that night, Luigi?"

"See? This is exactly why I didn't want to go in there and talk to the *polizia*. I'd be sitting in jail right now with my father if it were up to you people."

"Did you do it?" she asked.

"No!" Luigi's voice echoed off the tall buildings.

"Then there's no reason to be scared to talk to us. If you tell the truth, then you can rectify the situation."

"Mickey's Bar," he said. "Like the mouse."

Before Ali could utter a word, Luigi turned and ran.

She took a few steps after him, but he veered down an alley and out of sight.

9

"You punched him to the ground?" Basso's voice blared out of Ali's phone.

"*Sì.*" She sat on the edge of her bed and rubbed her forehead. Her tongue was dry, tasting of the three glasses of wine and the equal number of cigarettes she'd ingested the night before.

"Well, the bastard had it coming. He followed you out of the station?"

"*Sì.*"

"I have a mind to go down there and beat his ass."

Ali regretted the details she had opted to share. "It wasn't that bad. He was scared and wanted to talk to me. He made a mistake."

"He was scared of what?"

"Going on the record."

"Why?" Basso's kids squealed in the background, and there was a loud thump. "Shut up! I'm on the phone!"

The chaos ceased.

"Luigi told me he was lying," she explained. "That he

knew the bar where his father went. It's a place called Mickey's Bar."

"He lied?"

"*Sì.*"

"Why would he do that?"

"I don't know. He told me he wanted to see for himself if his father was actually at the bar before he talked to us or something."

"Or something? Or he's a *pezzo di merda* that killed Davide himself, and he's letting his father take the blame."

She sighed. "Luigi thinks that his father thinks he did it. That Giuseppe said he wasn't at the bar to protect him. That's why he followed me instead of going into the station. Luigi was worried that once we learned about his father's alibi, and about him lying to us, we would take him into custody."

"Well, of course we would! It looks like he did it now! Think about it . . . He's closer to Davide's age. He works at the vineyard. Who knows what was really going on between the two of them? They could have been mortal enemies. They could have been after the same woman, and that's why Luigi shot him in the *cazzo.*"

"I think we need to check out the bar before we start theorizing," Ali said. "At least corroborate Luigi's statements that his father was there."

"It's our day off. We can go tomorrow. Besides, it's Sunday. The bar's probably closed."

"It's not. I checked the hours. It's open until two this afternoon."

Basso growled into the phone.

"Giuseppe Sala is sitting in jail right now," she said. "If he has a solid alibi, we need to know about it sooner than later."

"He's sitting there by choice," Basso argued.

"Maybe. Anyway, I just wanted you to know. I'm going to drive down to the bar to ask around."

"On your day off." He blew air from his lips. "*Cacchio*, Falco. You're not going alone. What time is it?"

"Eight fifteen," she said.

"Be ready in thirty minutes. In the parking lot behind your building."

"Okay."

Ali took a quick shower, dried her hair, got dressed, and went out to the parking lot to wait. When the clock struck nine, there was still no sign of Basso. His kids, or his wife, must have presented some stalling.

A white Volkswagen Golf pulled up in front of her. She stepped aside, giving the car some room to do whatever it was doing. The window rolled down, and a man shouted, "Falco!"

Walking over, she saw it was Gatti in the driver's seat.

"Get in," he said.

Ali scowled. "You're here?"

"Because of you."

"Where's Basso?"

"I don't know. Doing whatever he does on a Sunday. He called and told me to pick you up because you have a bug up your *culo* to go check on a clue down south."

"You know what? I can do it myself. You can go home."

"Just get in," Gatti said, voice softening. "Come on."

She opened the door and slid into the front passenger seat.

"Buckle up," he said.

Rolling her eyes, she fastened herself without protest, then reclined the seat to a more comfortable angle.

Gatti put his foot on the gas. The vehicle had some zip, and she wavered in her seat as he left the lot, took Via Roma to Porta Romana, exited the fourteenth-century gateway to the city, and went downhill toward Strada Regionale Two.

She had to admit his clutch work was smooth. He kept the bumps and jerks to a minimum, driving at a speed that implied time was valuable, but he regarded life. She couldn't say the same about Basso.

"You look terrible," he said.

"*Grazie.*"

"You go out last night?"

"No."

She eyed him. As always, he was dressed smartly, wearing a pair of designer jeans and a felt jacket with the collar up. His chestnut hair was styled with product, his sideburns shaved with laser-precision.

He eyed her back. "What?"

"Nothing."

"So where are we going?"

"A place called Mickey's Bar. Near Giuseppe Sala's house."

He pointed at the screen on the dashboard. "Enter that into the navigation."

"You always this demanding?"

He glared at her. "*Sì.*"

"Okay."

"What, you want me to be more polite? I can start opening doors for you, *signora.*"

"Forget I said anything."

It took a few minutes and most of the brain cells she had online to route the GPS. "There. Forty-eight minutes."

"You going to tell me what happened last night? Basso said you got a tip from Luigi Sala."

She recounted her run-in with Luigi, excluding the part about clotheslining him to the ground this time. Still, as she remembered the painful impact, her fingers drifted under the right sleeve of her sweater. A tender spot on her forearm made her flinch. Pushing up the fabric, she saw broken skin and an angry bruise.

"What happened there?"

"Nothing."

"So Luigi was lying to our faces."

She nodded. "He was scared. He wanted to see if his father had lied to him before he told us about the bar."

Gatti frowned at her, and they drove a few kilometers without speaking. Ali's mind wandered to the way he and Fabiano had been staring daggers at one another two days ago.

"What happened between you and Fabiano?" she asked.

Gatti's jaw clenched.

"None of my business?"

"I hate people like Dimitri Fabiano. He's gotten where he is by being his father's son. That's about all he has to offer this world."

"I guess I can't argue with that logic."

"Let's just hope you can hang on to your job." He chuckled. "If you screw up, his father's got him poised to take over for you. You'd better believe that. And then I'll be stuck riding in the car with that asshole."

She raised an eyebrow at him. "And if he takes your job?"

Gatti snorted, like that was the dumbest thing he'd heard all year.

"You know," she said, "I did have a few drinks last night, so I'm not feeling that well. Mind if I rest a bit?"

"Be my guest."

She lowered her seat all the way, closed her eyes, and tried not to think about changing gun magazines, or about Fabiano.

A tap on Ali's shoulder startled her awake. She was slumped sideways into the door. Sitting straight, she wiped her face and looked out the window. They were on a two-lane road traveling through the Montalcino countryside.

"We're almost there."

"*Cacchio.* How long was I asleep?"

"Forty minutes, give or take."

She pulled down the visor and checked the mirror. Bloodshot eyes stared back at her. Gatti's earlier comment about her appearance echoed in her head, somehow making her feel much worse than she looked.

"It must have been fun," he said.

"What?"

"Last night."

"Not really."

"Oh? Where'd you go?"

"My couch."

She saw him glance at her in her peripheral. She didn't care.

"Left here?" he asked.

She consulted the twisting GPS line. "*Sì*. We're about three minutes away."

Passing through farmland, they approached a small cluster of buildings. A red sign with white lettering hung off one of them, reading, *Mickey's Bar,* signaling their arrival loud and clear.

Gatti turned into a dirt parking lot next to the building, slotting his Volkswagen between a scooter and a Fiat 500. They got out, and Ali stretched her arms overhead.

High clouds blanketed the area in shadow, but the fields to the south were alight with mid-morning sun, putting the beauty of the landscape on full display. If she hadn't been hungover, she might have been awed.

Mickey's Bar was a stand-alone structure, rectangular and painted bright yellow, with big windows looking out over the parking lot. Inside, a couple of men sat at tables along the glass, watching Ali and Gatti with interest.

"You ever been here?" Gatti asked.

"No."

He opened the front door for her, and she went inside, vision adjusting to the dim light.

"*Buongiorno!*" the barista said, smiling. With a full head of gray hair, he seemed to be in his late fifties or early sixties. He wore a checked shirt, sleeves rolled to his forearms, and a pair of thick corduroy pants.

"*Buongiorno.*" Ali's stomach rumbled. Now that she thought about it, she was desperately hungry and thirsty.

Gatti stayed beside her as they approached the counter. "*Buongiorno.* We'd like to—"

"I'll take a cappuccino, please," she interrupted. "And an apple juice. And one of those Nutella cornetti."

"*Sì, signora.* And for you?"

Gatti appeared taken aback, but he recovered quickly. "*Caffè*, please."

The barista got busy, presenting Ali with her pastry on a plate, then making the drinks.

"Didn't know we were coming here for a meal," Gatti said under his breath.

"I'm hungry."

They settled in to wait, using the time to look around.

Mickey's had all the necessary fixings for a bar that served day and night. Next to the espresso machine, an impressive selection of grappa and whiskey bottles lined the counter. A single tap served Peroni, and a rack of wineglasses hung above a stack of beer mugs.

Peeking at the two patrons seated by the windows, Ali saw one had a glass of white wine. Out of reflex, she checked the time on a clock hanging above the cash register. Only 10 a.m. A bit early to drink alone, but she couldn't judge. It would be hypocritical.

"Are you traveling through?" the barista asked, setting a cappuccino and a juice in front of Ali and an espresso in front of Gatti. His wrist bore a watch with Mickey Mouse's iconic ears on the face. "Sugar?"

"*Sì*, please," she said.

"No, *grazie*." Gatti drained his cup in one gulp.

Ali bit into her cornetto, finding it stale yet delicious. "We live in Siena."

"Oh. What brings you down here?"

She exchanged a look with Gatti, then lifted the waist of her sweater, revealing the badge on her belt. Gatti did the same with his jacket.

The barista's eyes flicked between their badges, but he gave no indication he cared one way or the other.

"We have a few questions we would like to ask you, if it's not too much trouble," Ali said, mustering her most formal Italian. "I noticed your watch. Is this your place?"

"*Sì.*"

"We're investigating the murder up at Conti Vineyards. Do you know about it?"

"Of course."

Gatti nodded. "Are you familiar with a man named Giuseppe Sala?"

"Why?"

Ali sipped her cappuccino. "We'd like to know if he was here on Thursday night."

"I couldn't say." The barista backed away from the counter. "I work in the mornings. It's my brother-in-law that works the nights."

"Who are you asking about?"

Ali and Gatti turned around. The man who'd spoken held up his glass of white wine in greeting. The other man sat a few tables away, observing them. They were similarly dressed, each wearing a button-up shirt, tie, and jacket, all earth tones.

"We're asking about Giuseppe Sala," Gatti said.

"What about him?"

"We're wondering if he was here on Thursday night."

"He was. He's usually here on Thursdays." The man ticked off his fingers as he added, "Thursdays, Fridays, and sometimes Saturdays."

"At night, you mean," Ali clarified.

"*Sì.* We play Scopa." He shrugged. "Cards."

"Do you know what time he stayed until?" Gatti asked.

The man shook his head. "I normally don't last very long. They all stay and play, and I go home and sleep." He laughed and looked at the other man, who was too busy glowering at the inspectors to share the humor.

"And what time was that?" Ali asked. "What time did you go home?"

"Eight thirty or nine. I couldn't tell you the exact time."

"And you?" she asked the glowering man. "Were you here with Giuseppe Sala on Thursday night?"

"I'd like to know why you're asking first. I wouldn't want to implicate a friend."

"Who says you'll implicate him?" Gatti challenged. "Maybe you'll give him an alibi."

"You think Giuseppe killed Davide Conti?" the barista asked.

Ali suppressed a cringe, keeping her expression neutral. "That might be a possibility, so we're here to find the truth. You men like the truth, don't you?"

The glowering man deliberated for a few seconds. Then he admitted, "I don't drink. I have no use for this bar at night."

"*Grazie*," Ali said before finishing her cappuccino. She chugged the glass of apple juice.

The barista grabbed a pencil from a cup near the register and jotted something on a notepad. He ripped off the page, then slapped it on the counter. "You've come at the wrong time. Here. That's my brother-in-law."

Gatti held the paper between them to read. The name Pino Acquaviva was written in neat script, along with an address.

"He lives down the road a few kilometers. I'll call and let him know you're coming." The barista walked to a phone hanging on the wall.

"*Grazie,*" she said.

"*Prego.*" He picked up the handset and pointed at a bill. "Now, that will be twelve euro."

10

Gatti fired up the Volkswagen's engine as Ali punched Pino Acquaviva's address into the GPS.

"Thirteen kilometers," she said.

He studied the GPS readout.

"What?" she asked.

"We'll be going right past Conti Vineyards."

He was right. Ali tucked the information away for later analysis.

"Have they cleared the crime scene yet?" she asked.

"They did yesterday."

Ali nodded, then shut her eyes to rest some more. The memory of Davide Conti's body came unbidden. Close behind was an image of her father lying on a gurney in the Como morgue, his skin ashen and his face misshapen from the bullet that had torn through his head.

Sometimes, she woke up in a cold sweat with that sight burned in her mind.

"There it is," Gatti said.

She opened her eyes, welcoming the distraction. In the

distance, rows of sangiovese vines had come into view, along with the Conti farmhouse and outbuilding.

They passed a vehicle parked on the side of the road, glossy black and buffed clean to reflect the sky, but she barely registered it, thinking instead of Davide's body and the prospect that the wrong man was locked in jail. If they had arrested an innocent, then that meant the killer was out there, getting away with his crime.

Was it Luigi? Or somebody else?

The passenger side-view mirror caught the sun and sent a ray of brilliant light into Ali's eyes. She hissed, reaching out to block it, pausing when she noticed a dark reflection in the glass. "Wait. Who was that?"

"What?"

"That car back there."

"Where?"

"Stop."

Gatti checked his mirrors, then stopped the car and twisted to peer out the rear window. "That one?"

The black vehicle was over half a kilometer behind them now, and it was moving, driving the other way at speed. Its brake lights bloomed as it disappeared around the corner.

"It was an Audi sedan," she said. "A luxury sedan with dark paint. That's exactly what the neighbors said they saw."

"*Cazzo.*" He slapped the wheel. "Should I go after it?"

"I don't know. Maybe."

Gatti turned them around, having to reverse twice due to the ditch on the side of the road, and punched the gas, revving high to the corner where the vehicle had disappeared. Their view opened up, but there were no cars in sight. He slowed.

"Did you at least see the license plate?" Gatti asked. His tone was incredulous, like she'd let a goal through her legs in the final moments of a World Cup match.

"No."

He snorted.

"Did *you* see the license plate?" she countered.

"No. I was too busy driving."

Her face heated.

Gatti turned the car around once more, tense silence descending upon them. As they approached Conti Vineyards a second time, he maintained double the speed he had been doing before.

The gate was open, and two vehicles were parked in front of the house: the Volvo wagon she had seen Salvatore and Martina Conti step out of at headquarters, and a beat-up gray Fiat Panda.

"Whose Fiat is that?" Gatti asked.

She slid him a cold glare, then reverted her gaze to the window. There was no action outside the farmhouse, nobody working in the fields or in the outbuilding. They passed the property, reaching a stretch of road she had never seen.

Gatti downshifted and coasted into a low valley, then revved up and over a hill covered in olive trees. At last, they came upon a house in the middle of a plowed field.

"That it?" he asked.

She said nothing.

"Look, I'm sorry. I was upset."

So you blamed everything on me without hesitation, Ali thought, though she was pleasantly surprised by the apology. She hadn't known Gatti possessed the ability to feel remorse.

"Whatever," she said. "Let's get this over with and get back to Siena."

"Good plan."

The house was one story, long, rectangular, and made of blond stone. It had a well-kept lawn in front, a garden and patio off to one side.

Gatti parked under the shade of a canopy tree. He shut off the engine, and they got out.

A plump woman with long hair pulled up in a bun stepped from the side of the house, heading toward them. She wore an apron, and she wiped her hands on it. "You must be the inspectors!"

"*Sì, signora,*" Ali answered.

The woman waved them over. "Come."

Sunshine warmed her skin as she and Gatti moved out of the shade. They met the woman halfway to the house, holding their badges in the air.

"I'm Inspector Falco. This is Inspector Gatti."

The woman waved their badges away. "My name is Giulia. Come. Come and enjoy this beautiful morning."

Behind Giulia, Ali noticed a gray-haired man seated at a table on the patio. Four plates had been placed on the white tablecloth, and between the plates waited a decanter of red wine, a basket of bread, and a platter of cheese and meat. Ali glanced at her watch. It was only 11 a.m.

Smiling sheepishly, Giulia said, "I know it's early, but I don't let visitors go hungry. You'll eat with us while we talk."

"Oh, we couldn't," Ali said.

"Nonsense." Giulia spun on her heels, motioning for them to follow her along a pea gravel trail that wound between sculpted bushes.

The man rose from the table, holding out a hand. He seemed more suspicious than his wife.

"*Signor* Acquaviva?" Ali asked.

"That's me."

She and Gatti introduced themselves, flashing their badges again.

"You're investigating Davide Conti's murder," Pino said.

She nodded. "*Sì, signore*. We are."

Giulia indicated the table. "Please, sit."

"Wow," Ali said, surveying the selection. "We really didn't expect such hospitality."

"Sit." Pino rubbed his stomach. "I'm hungry."

Ali and Gatti took chairs next to each other, facing the couple on the other side of the table.

"Eat," Pino said, diving into the breadbasket.

Gatti wasted no time gathering a generous amount of salami and cheese. Ali took some, careful to leave plenty for their hosts, though she could have shoveled the whole table into her mouth for how hungry she still was after the cornetto at the bar.

"*Vino*?" Pino asked.

Ali shook her head. "No, *grazie*."

"*Sì*," Gatti said.

Pino clicked his tongue at her. "Follow your partner's lead."

"Oh, we're not partners," she and Gatti said in unison.

Pino looked at his wife, then poured some wine for everyone. "*Cin cin*."

"*Cin cin*," Ali echoed with Gatti and Giulia.

Everyone tapped their glasses, and then Pino downed half his wine in one gulp. Gatti took a healthy sip himself, so

Ali relented. The calming effect was so immediate that it bordered on disturbing, as if the alcohol had untied a knot inside her body.

"We hear that you work at Mickey's Bar with your brother-in-law," she said.

"*Sì*," Giulia confirmed. "We own three-quarters."

Pino lifted his fork. "Eat."

Gatti wolfed down his food like he was at his grand-mother's house.

Ali selected a piece of bread and took a bite. Once she had swallowed, she cleared her throat and continued, "We also hear that you work nights."

"Most of them, *sì*."

She smiled. "That's good, because we are hoping you can clear up a couple of questions we have about Giuseppe Sala."

"He was at your bar on Thursday night, correct?" Gatti asked around a mouthful of food.

Pino chewed for a beat, staring at Gatti. Finally, he nodded. "That's right. He was there. And when he didn't show up Friday or Saturday, they were all looking for him. Of course, now we know why."

"Who was looking for him?" Ali asked.

"His friends. There's a group of decrepit *anziani* like myself who frequent the bar together. Giuseppe's one of them. When he stopped showing up, they started talking about Davide Conti's death. Nobody mentioned Giuseppe was under suspicion, though. Of course, how would we have known? It was quite a shock to read in the papers this morning that you have him in custody. I thought he got along fine with the Contis. They're like family to him."

Gatti wiped his mouth. "So, you are saying that Giuseppe Sala was at the bar on Thursday night?"

Pino raised his eyebrows. "That's what I said."

"I'm just making sure. When did he show up and when did he leave? Do you remember?"

"They usually trickle in from seven to eight. He was there at the normal time. Otherwise, he would have lost his spot in cards. Nobody wants to have to sit out the first round."

"And he left at . . . ?" Ali prompted.

Pino peered up at the sky. "Must have been around eleven. That's when they usually wrap up. They're always ending about the same time, and nothing was different Thursday. I close the place at eleven thirty, so I'm always kicking them out at eleven."

"Sometimes twelve o'clock," Giulia said. "Or one. Or two."

"Sometimes twelve or one if it's a weekend." Pino wagged a finger at his wife. "Sometimes. Rarely. Never two."

Gatti met Pino's gaze. "*Signor* Acquaviva, we would greatly appreciate it if you could come up to Siena and give us an official statement regarding this matter. It's very important."

Pino nodded. "I was going to."

"You were?" Giulia asked. "When?"

"Today!" Pino exclaimed, face redder than the tomato on his fork. "Inspectors, I will come up and make a statement today."

"*Grazie*," Ali said. "This information is very important to the case, and to Giuseppe Sala. It will be a big help."

"*Sì*. Of course, of course."

"Okay, it's settled." Giulia pointed at the table. "Now don't let this food go to waste."

Gatti grabbed another serving and added it to his plate. The four of them proceeded to eat in comfortable silence, listening to the breeze on the bushes and the clanking of silverware.

"What do you think of the wine?" Giulia asked, smiling proudly. "It's Castello Monaco."

Ali realized she was holding her glass to her lips, and it was already half gone. "It's good."

Giulia sipped. "They have the best Brunello."

"But they're assholes," Pino said.

"*Pino.*"

"It's true! They think they're royalty."

"Why shouldn't they? Their wine is the best quality in the world."

"Eh." Pino waved a hand.

"My husband has a personal vendetta against the Monaco family."

Pino jabbed a finger at the table. "Anybody who has that kind of money—so much they live in a castle—is involved with the Mafia. When you inspectors are done with this case, you should look into the Monacos. You'll see."

"Paulino Acquaviva, we are not making accusations tying people to the Mafia." Giulia's lips quivered as she turned toward Ali and Gatti. "We are not saying that."

"Of course." Ali understood the fear in Giulia's eyes. It was dangerous business, spreading rumors about the Mafia. Especially to police, who could possibly be on the Mafia's payroll.

"And this is Quattro Luci Farm prosciutto," Giulia said,

moving on. "The best prosciutto in the world. Grown and produced right here in Montalcino."

"Apparently, we also have too much money," Pino grumbled. "Buying all these best-in-the-world products . . . Give me a cantina red any day. I don't need a fancy castle to tell me a wine is good or not." He pointed a piece of bread at Ali and Gatti, bouncing one eyebrow. "You two going steady?"

"Pino!" Giulia reared back and punched his arm.

"Ow, woman!"

"No," Gatti scoffed, shaking his head like the thought disgusted him. "We are certainly not."

Ali smiled, but her chest stung.

"Please excuse my husband," Giulia pleaded.

"*Grazie* for your hospitality, *Signor* and *Signora* Acquaviva." Ali put her napkin on her plate. "We hope to see you this afternoon, *signore*. You can go to the main reception desk at the station and tell them why you're there, and they'll lead you the rest of the way. It really shouldn't be more than a few minutes of trouble."

Pino nodded. "Plus the drive."

"They have him in jail!" Giulia punched Pino's arm again, then looked at the inspectors. "He will be there. I will see to it."

Ali and Gatti stood, shook hands with the couple, and allowed Giulia to escort them back to the Volkswagen. After one last goodbye, they drove away from the Acquavivas.

Gatti turned up the radio, filling the cabin with music, but it wasn't enough to keep his harsh rejection from replaying in Ali's mind over and over again. She opened her mouth to say something but thought better of it.

"What's up, Falco?"

"Nothing," she said, not wanting to let on how much his earlier words and tone had bothered her. Unfortunately, her willpower was only so strong, and before she could stop herself, she asked, "You have a girlfriend, Gatti?"

A smirk tilted his lips. With a shake of his head, he returned his focus to the road, pretending she hadn't spoken.

What was that reaction? "Is that a no?"

"No, I don't," he said, smiling to himself.

He thinks I'm into him, Ali realized.

Cold fury ignited inside her. The nerve on this guy. She was tempted to tell him off. Inform him that nothing about his shimmering tide-pool eyes impressed her, that his perfect grooming and expensive attire were just smoke and mirrors, scarcely covering the competitive asshole underneath.

"I'm gay."

Ali's mind went blank, and her jaw dropped open. Twisting to meet his gaze, she saw he was dead serious.

"Is that going to be a problem?"

"What?" Her cheeks heated. "No. I don't care about that in the least."

"Okay. Good."

"Good." She looked away, trying to wrap her head around this new insight into Gatti's identity. She had never heard a single word about his sexual orientation. Which was strange. Usually, one couldn't have an off-schedule bowel movement without everyone in the department knowing. "Who else have you told? At work, I mean."

"The people that matter. Let's put it that way."

Ali was touched. Honored. The complete opposite of her emotions from a minute ago. Now she *mattered* to him.

Afraid of ruining the moment, she shut her mouth and watched as they neared Conti Vineyards. This time, Gatti slowed, giving them more time to scan the property.

Martina Conti was out in the fields, standing motionless between the vines. Her hands were by her sides, her head tipped back, her face to the sky, as if she were trying to commune with her dead brother.

Ali lowered the volume on the radio, feeling the scene demanded respect.

At the sound of their approach, Martina looked down, and Ali felt a jolt of pain at the obvious sorrow in the young woman's expression.

Gatti accelerated.

"If it's not Giuseppe Sala, then it's somebody else," he said. "It's about time we pull our heads out of our asses and figure out who."

Ali leaned back and closed her eyes, seeing Davide's body haunt her one more time.

11

"Can you feel this?"

Ali glanced down and saw Dr. Stefani pressing a rubber reflex hammer into her right pinkie finger.

"No."

"Tell me when you feel something."

"Still no." The sun emerged from behind a cloud, shining into the office, pulling her gaze to the window. "Quite a view from here, Doc."

"Keep your concentration."

"I can't feel anything."

"Now?"

"No. I told you, nothing's changed."

"I beg to differ."

Ali glanced down again. The hammer was pressed into the center of her middle finger.

"What the hell? Let go." She shooed him away and massaged her hand. "What? Why? How?"

Stefani slid back on his wheeled chair. "The pinch is worsening. Are you doing your exercises?"

"*Sì*. I mean . . . no . . . not as much as I should."

He lifted his glasses to his forehead. "The exercises will help, but they can only take you so far now that the numbness is advancing. We're going to have to do another surgery to relax the constriction around the nerves. We'll go into your shoulder again, and possibly your palm."

"Can you do it today and have it fully healed by Thursday?"

Stefani gave her a compassionate smile. "I heard about your firearm proficiency test. Have you shot recently?"

"*Sì*."

"And how was that?"

"Fine."

Stefani rolled over to his computer and clicked the keyboard. "I have an opening next week. Tuesday morning. Is that okay?"

"For the surgery?"

"*Sì*."

"But I have the shooting test this Thursday. What's the point of taking the test if I have to do the surgery after? I'll just have to retake it later . . . if everything heals correctly."

Stefani watched her, raising his eyebrows ever so slightly.

In that moment, she realized there wouldn't be a firearm proficiency test on Thursday. Not after he relayed every detail of this appointment to Costa. Her days on field duty were numbered.

Stefani clicked more keys, then pulled out a card and wrote on it. "Here's your appointment reminder. Good luck."

"With what?"

"The investigation."

"Oh. *Grazie*."

Ali entered headquarters at 8:15 a.m., an hour and a half later than normal. She jogged up to the third floor, rubbing her hand as she took the marble stairs two at a time.

"*Buongiorno*," Clarissa said.

"*Ciao*," Ali replied, hurrying past her friend's desk. "I'm late. We'll talk later."

"Finally," Basso said by way of greeting. He was standing in the middle of the room, chatting with Longo and sipping an espresso.

"Sorry I'm late. Doctor's appointment."

"So I heard. How's the hand?"

"Fine. What's going on? Did I miss the meeting already?"

"We haven't had it yet."

She looked around. Gatti was sitting at his desk, and Costa's door was open, revealing an empty chair. Murmurs emanated from Ferrari's shuttered office, then the laughter of several men.

"What's going on in there?" she asked.

"Above my pay grade," Basso said.

Gatti averted his gaze.

Ali wiped the sweat beading on her forehead, dropped her backpack under her desk, and slipped off her jacket.

"Did you have a good Sunday?" she asked Basso, keeping one eye on Ferrari's office.

"*Sì*," he said. "Acquaviva came in yesterday afternoon

and made an official statement. Sounds like you and Gatti did well without me."

"*Grazie.*" She snuck another look at Gatti, who stared at the computer in front of him.

"Acquaviva brought in a man named Belfi," Basso continued. "He's a patron of the bar who was also playing cards that night. So, it appears Giuseppe has an alibi corroborated by two men now."

The door to Ferrari's office swung open, and he came out laughing, followed by Costa and two older men—Giulio Fabiano and the mayor, Enrico Tiraboschi. It had been a few weeks since Ali had seen the elder Fabiano. He and the mayor were dressed like royalty, wearing costumes of money and power found only at the most expensive tailors, jewelry shimmering on their wrists and fingers.

Dimitri Fabiano came into view last, wearing his patrol uniform and a backside-sniffing smile. His eyes latched onto hers, striking out a bolt of hate before he returned his attention to Ferrari. With a salute to the chief and a nod to his father, he sauntered away, past Clarissa's desk and down the stairs.

Again, Ali remembered the conversation she'd had with Ferrari at the end of the summer, remembered how he'd sworn off the Fabianos. But here he was, hosting father and son in his office, acting like old friends.

Giulio said something under his breath that caused the men beside him to briefly look her way. She wanted to crawl under her desk. Or throw something at them.

"Falco!" Costa waved her over.

Taking a deep breath, Ali plastered a smile on her face

and walked to the group. "*Ciao, Signor* Tiraboschi, *Signor* Fabiano."

"Nice to see you, Inspector Falco." Giulio accepted her offered hand, holding on too long, turning it like a specimen in his firm grip. He grinned knowingly. "How are you healing?"

She pulled back. "Fine."

"That's good." His beady eyes shone with a mixture of delight and disdain.

She let her expression cool. People might respect this man for various reasons, but she did not.

"Have you met the mayor before?" Costa asked.

"No." Ali smiled and shook Tiraboschi's hand.

His eyes flicked down, and she got the impression that her numb digits were the star of the show this morning.

"In my office, Falco," Costa said. "Basso, Gatti! Longo! My office."

Basso strode over, greeting Giulio and Tiraboschi like they were old friends. Ali broke from the group and headed into Costa's office, trying to clear her mind of whatever the hell had just happened as she took position near the side window.

Slowly, the others trickled in. Costa, Ferrari, and Basso claimed the chairs at Costa's desk, while Gatti and Longo found places to stand by the walls.

"We're all up to speed on *Signor* Pino Acquaviva, *sì*?" Costa nodded at Ali and Gatti. "Good work yesterday. The man said you were cordial and courteous with him and his wife. He said you persuaded him to come make an official report yesterday, which he did." He picked up a pile of papers and leafed through them. "He also brought in a man named

Belfi, who is a regular at the bar. Belfi corroborated everything."

Basso raised a finger.

"*Sì?*"

"Falco and I, along with four officers down in Montal-cino, heard Giuseppe clearly tell his son he was not at the bar that night."

Costa folded his hands on his desk, waiting for more.

Basso continued, "And now we have an owner and a patron telling us Giuseppe Sala was indeed at the bar. So, who are we to believe?" He splayed his hands like a lawyer during his closing argument. "If we are to believe the owner and the patron—and we have no reason not to—then I propose Luigi Sala as our next person of interest.

"Giuseppe told us that he was not at the bar, but he was. Why? Because he wanted to take the fall for his boy. Because he knows his boy is guilty. Also, Luigi lied to us when we asked about the bar. He pretended not to know the name. He lied because he knew we'd find out his father was there if we checked, which would lead us to suspect him." Basso wiped his hands together. Case solved.

The room remained quiet for a moment as his words sunk in.

"Where was Luigi the night of the murder?" Ferrari asked.

Ali shrugged. "He said he was home all night, but he did go out to get a pizza."

"Then he has no alibi," Ferrari mused. "Still, we have no evidence against him, so we can't arrest him. But I want Luigi Sala questioned again as soon as possible. I don't need to tell you all how important this is, but I will."

Ferrari pinned each one of them with his severe gaze. "The mayor came here today to discuss this case. The powers that be in this city are not liking the publicity. Threats have been made for us to solve Davide's murder expediently and efficiently, or else. So, releasing Giuseppe is not going to look good for us. We put the wrong man in jail!" He smacked his palm on Costa's desk. "We're back at square one with our hands empty."

Ferrari twisted in his chair and gestured toward Ali. "We've all heard about your encounter with Luigi the other night. Why don't you regale us with that tale firsthand?"

"I was walking in the city when he approached me—"

"Approached you?" Basso scoffed. "He all but attacked you. He followed you from the station. He was running after you when you clobbered him in the face, putting him on the ground."

"*Sì*, I put him on the ground. And *sì*, I feared he might be attacking. But now I don't think so. I think he was just scared and wanted to talk to me."

Basso flipped a hand.

"He was the one who told me about the bar."

"After lying about the bar," Basso countered.

"He admitted to lying, and he begged me to look into his father's whereabouts on Thursday night. He said we would see his father was innocent." She shrugged. "End of story."

Ferrari's eyes narrowed. "How long was he tailing you?"

"I don't know."

"That's the action of a dangerous man," Basso said.

Ali shook her head. "If he wanted to hurt me, he would have tried. He didn't."

"Because you floored him."

She shrugged again. She couldn't argue with Basso's logic.

"Then why chase you?" Longo asked. "Why not come in here?"

"He told me he was scared to come in. He had lied to us. He thought he'd be arrested. He was sure you would all think he did it."

"Which means he's probably on the run now," Basso said to Costa. "We have to find him and bring him in."

Ferrari shifted his attention to Longo. "What about gunshot residue? Did we find any?"

"None on the clothing taken from the Sala house," Longo said. "Neither Giuseppe's nor Luigi's. None on the bedding, either. And it's quite clear that Luigi has not washed his sheets in a very long time."

"He could have taken a thorough shower," Basso said. "Gotten rid of the clothing."

"What about Davide Conti's cell records?" Ferrari tried.

"Vodafone has been dragging their feet over the weekend," Costa said. "We'll get them today. Or I'll kill somebody myself."

"I will make another call this morning." Ferrari stood up, straightening his uniform jacket. "I don't want you bringing anybody else into this building until we see Davide's cell records. Especially not Luigi Sala. Talk to him elsewhere. Do not bring him past that hive of press outside. Understood?" He waited for everyone to nod, then exited the room, the door booming closed behind him.

Costa rubbed his temples. "Longo, how are the Salas' boots matching up with our prints from Conti Vineyards?"

Longo sighed. "Negative. None of them have the same tread marks as the prints."

"Okay," Costa said. "What else?"

"We have a receipt we found in the trash." Longo dangled a clear evidence bag containing a slip of paper. "It's for Thursday night."

Costa grabbed the bag and read the receipt through the plastic. "Pizza-Amore. The time stamp says 9:13 p.m."

"So Luigi went and got the pizza at 9:13 p.m.," Basso said. "He could have come home and eaten with plenty of time to get to Conti Vineyards and shoot Davide at 10:30 p.m."

Costa grunted, rising from his desk to pace. "We need to know more about Luigi."

"We can start by asking Salvatore and Martina about him," Basso said. "After all, he worked at the vineyard, too."

"Good." Costa crossed his arms. "What else?"

"The car," Ali said.

They all looked at her.

"The neighbors said they saw a dark sedan. Luxury model. Gatti and I might have seen it yesterday."

"You did?" Basso snapped. "Why didn't you tell us this earlier?"

"I'm sorry, *signore*." Gatti gave Ali a sidelong glance. "I forgot."

"We forgot," she said. "It was an Audi. An A8, I believe."

"Plates?"

She shook her head.

"We were preoccupied looking at Conti Vineyards," Gatti said. "It was parked along the road when we passed. We turned around and tried to pursue, but it was already driving away. We lost it."

Basso frowned. "Okay. Assuming this was the same vehicle the neighbors saw leaving the Conti place the night of the murder, that leaves us where? No closer to figuring out who this is."

"Okay, here's what we're going to do today," Costa said. "We're going to talk to Salvatore and Martina Conti. We're going to ask them about Luigi. And then we're going to find Luigi and talk to him, too. And when I say we, I mean Basso and Falco." He pointed at Gatti. "Gatti will stay here and put his foot on Vodafone's neck."

"And you, *signore*?" Basso asked. "What are you going to do?"

"I am also going to work on Vodafone. Then I have a press conference." He knocked on his desk. "But before any of that, we're all going to visit Giuseppe Sala in prison and ask him why the hell he's pretending he killed Davide."

12

It was easier to walk than drive, so they marched through the streets of Siena, Costa in front. They were giving the lieutenant space as he barked into his phone. He had already let out a couple of angry shouts, apparently making no headway with Davide Conti's cell phone records.

"Luigi's not answering," Basso said to no one in particular, pressing his own phone to his ear.

Ali stayed next to Gatti, happy to remain silent as she ran her thumb across her numb fingers inside her jacket pocket and ruminated about her future as an inspector.

The Ministero della Giustizia penitentiary was an ancient building attached to an old church inside a small square called Santo Spirito. The European and Italian flags hung limp over the entrance.

Costa pocketed his phone and led the way through reception. After their credentials were verified, a guard brought them to a visitation room. The space contained two long wood tables, a row of chairs on either side of each. A window covered with iron bars looked out on the street below, and a caged industrial clock ticked loudly on the wall. It read 10:22 a.m.

A short time later, Giuseppe Sala came out from behind a heavy door, wearing a black sweatshirt and black pants, escorted by another prison guard. With bloodshot eyes and bags underneath them, Giuseppe looked like he'd had a long couple of nights in his cell. He wore no hand or ankle restraints, but he shuffled toward them as if bound.

"*Ciao, Signor* Sala." Costa motioned for everyone to sit.

The room erupted in noise as they pulled out chairs, the four inspectors facing the man being held for murder.

Costa dug into his leather attaché case, took out a folder, and produced two sheets of paper. He placed both on the table, turning them for Giuseppe to read. "*Signor* Sala, Pino Acquaviva came into the station yesterday to confirm your alibi. He is an owner of Mickey's Bar, where you go to play cards with your friends every Thursday night. You know *Signor* Acquaviva well, do you not?"

Giuseppe leaned forward, squinting at the papers. "I don't have my glasses."

"You don't need glasses to answer the question."

"*Sì*. I know him."

Costa hovered his hand over one of the papers. "Since you don't have your glasses, I'll give you the gist of these reports. This one was filed by Pino Acquaviva under oath. It says you were at the bar all Thursday night, from just about 7:45 p.m. until 11 p.m., when he kicked you out, along with everyone else." He moved his hand to the other paper. "This report was filed by a man named Vittorio Belfi. It says the same thing, that you showed up at 7:45 p.m. Thursday night and left when he did, at 11 p.m."

Folding his arms on the table, Costa continued, "We know from Davide Conti's neighbors that there were two gunshots at 10:30 p.m. They remember this time because the shots occurred at the end of *Calcio Tonight*, the show on Rai 1. You know it, don't you?"

Giuseppe pressed his lips into a tight line.

"All of this means there is no way you could have killed Davide Conti. So, I'll ask you again, *Signor* Sala. Where were you the night of Thursday, November 15?"

Giuseppe shook his head.

"Are you trying to protect your son?"

Giuseppe blinked.

"*Signor* Sala," Ali said, clearing her throat, "Luigi was the one who told us about Mickey's Bar. He came to me and told me you were there. He checked for himself."

Giuseppe's gaze fell to the table.

"Why did you tell your son that you weren't at the bar?" Costa asked. "Why did you lie about that?"

Giuseppe shook his head again, keeping his eyes low.

"Fine, *Signor* Sala," Costa said. "You don't have to talk. However, I want you to know we will be looking at your son in the coming days. Very closely. As for you, we don't have anything, so you're going to be released this afternoon. But if we find that your son has done something—something you know about and are not telling us—well, then I'm afraid you'll be coming back here. And it won't be so easy to get out a second time."

Softening his voice, Costa added, "Of course, I understand what it's like, wanting to protect your children. I have a daughter myself. She lives in Rome. She just had a child of her own, which makes me a grandfather. Can you believe that? A young-looking man like me?"

Giuseppe's gaze lifted, but his expression remained stoic.

"Good luck to you, *Signor* Sala. Have a safe trip home, but please stay close. We might need to speak with you again." Costa rose to his feet and collected the papers. "*Andiamo.*"

The guard opened the door, letting them funnel out. When they reached the reception room, Costa's phone rang.

"*Sì?* No . . . Okay. We're on our way. Tell them an hour and a half." He hung up and returned the phone to his pocket.

"Who was that?" Basso asked.

"Ferrari." Costa paused his explanation while they exited the building. Once outside, he pulled out a cigarette and lit it. "Basso, Falco, change of plans today. We have an appointment down south in an hour and a half."

Basso's eyes narrowed. "Where?"

"Monaco Vineyards. Apparently, Enzo Monaco has something he wants to tell us."

Ali frowned, looking at Gatti. "That's the wine we had at Pino Acquaviva's house, right?"

Gatti made a face, like he didn't know what she was talking about.

"You were drinking while questioning *Signor* Acquaviva?" Basso asked.

"I . . ." She shook her head. "No . . . not really."

Basso smirked. "Relax, Falco. If somebody puts a Monaco Vineyards Brunello in front of you, you drink it. Now let's go. I'm driving."

13

"They age the wine for at least two years in the barrels. Not *up to* two years." Basso placed a hand over his heart to show his offense.

"Pay attention to the road. And okay, *at least* two years."

"We're going to talk to one of the biggest Brunello di Montalcino producers in the world. Get it right."

"Touché," she said.

"And I want you to know how connected this man is. If we rub him the wrong way, then we'll be looking for pizzeria jobs. Got it?"

"*Sì, signore.*"

Basso slowed, taking a right. This road was thinner, and it swept a long curve around a mountainside lined with tall cypress trees thrusting toward the sky. Costa's Audi was a half kilometer ahead, brake lights flashing as it rounded a bend and went out of sight.

Ali rubbed her thumb over her numb fingers again. "Do you know what was going on in that meeting today?"

"I told you, above my pay grade."

She rolled her eyes.

"It's the truth, Falco. I mean . . . obviously, something's going on. And it has to do with Fabiano."

"I need to have another surgery on my shoulder," she admitted.

"Why?"

"I just need to."

"The fingers?"

She nodded.

"If you need surgery, Costa's not going to hold it against you."

"Do you really believe that? Maybe the Fabianos were sitting in on a private meeting between him and Ferrari to discuss my future as an inspector."

"I'm sure the meeting was about something else."

They traveled in silence for a few minutes.

"We're here." He pointed out the windshield. "Castello Monaco."

Snapped from her thoughts, Ali saw the castle emerge into view at the mountain's peak. From their low vantage point, the regal structure was a silhouette against the darkening sky, with twin turrets extending high above tall battlements, one on either side of the gatehouse tower.

"*Madonna*," she said, whistling.

"You've never seen it?"

"I have, but not this close. Always much farther away."

"Well, get ready to go even closer."

Ali's blood hummed with the rush of adventure. She was grateful to have such a job. For the time being, at least.

Snaking up the mountain, they watched the storybook structure flit in and out of sight. Rows of vines draped the terraced slopes like a patterned apron, and state-of-the-art machinery moved between them. Hardworking men and women were bent over in the fields, preparing for winter dormancy. The massive operation made Conti Vineyards look like a household garden.

"Wow. This is heaven." Basso rolled down his window and lit a cigarette, as if the scenery had evoked a post-coital response. "You want one?"

"No."

He scoffed. "You think I don't know you're still smoking?"

"Not on the job. I've pretty much quit."

"Right."

The road leveled out, and they found themselves atop the mountain. The castle loomed large now, as did the gathering clouds behind it. Raindrops hit the windshield.

"*Cazzo*," Basso said. "Just one day without rain is all I ask."

Up ahead, a family with three children hurried from an opening in the castle, toward one of the vehicles parked in a dirt lot.

"Tourists," Basso explained. "The Monacos have a couple of shops and a visitor center in there. We're not going that way, though."

They tailed Costa past the parking lot and around the southwest edge of the castle. Rain pounded the windshield harder as they traveled north, into the blustering storm.

"You have an umbrella?" Ali asked.

"Of course. I have two."

A hulking gray wall, spiked on top, jutted out from the castle about halfway down the western side, blocking access to the back of the property. Costa stopped at the wrought iron gate leading through it.

A uniformed man came out of the nearby guardhouse, ducking to shield himself from the rain, tapping an electronic tablet with his finger. He spoke to Costa, then released the gate and waved them past.

The road continued through a stand of trees, deciduous and pine, all aglow in autumn colors. Leaves tumbled in the air on the storm outflow, drifting to an enormous sprawl of open land decorated in manicured grass and gardens. In the center of the lawn, a marble sculpture of Zeus spat a shower of water that slanted sideways on the wind.

A drawbridge yawned open before them, massive chains stretching at least three stories up. Without hesitation, Costa drove over the thick wood bridge and into the castle's innards, as if he were a regular. Basso followed, the wood making no sound under his vehicle, and they arrived in a courtyard.

Mesmerized, Ali leaned at every angle to take in her surroundings.

"Look at that car," she said, indicating a covered parking area on the other side of the courtyard. Three vehicles waited beneath the shelter: a Range Rover Sport, an Alfa Romeo sedan, and an Audi A8.

"They're nice."

"No, look at the Audi. That's the one Gatti and I saw."

Basso stared at her. "That one?"

"*Sì*. I'm almost sure of it."

Costa parked under the open sky, so Basso did the same.

Ali stepped from the vehicle and zipped up her jacket, examining the castle. Or, more exactly, this wing of the castle, which she assumed was the Monaco family's private residence. The high interior walls rose in an intricate pattern of glass and stone, and new tinted windows cut into the facade. Every detail was made to look ancient, but it was all subtly modern, even the drawbridge they had just driven over.

"*Buongiorno*, inspectors." A gray-haired man stood outside a heavy wood door. He was tall and muscular, wearing a tight-fitted suit with a black tie. If not for the blank expression on his face, he would have been good-looking. "My name is Girardo. Come with me, please. You can leave your umbrellas in this holder."

Girardo offered no hand in greeting to any of them, just pivoted and walked inside.

Costa and Basso went first. Head on a swivel, Ali trailed after them.

The relatively cramped entryway opened into a huge hall. Antique furniture sat on a polished marble floor, including a grand piano in one corner. A chandelier hung from an impossibly high ceiling, and its crystals shimmered in the natural light streaming through the tall bank of windows behind it.

Girardo stopped, motioning to an open door. "This way, please."

They entered another palatial room. It housed an endlessly long table with dozens of chairs lining the perimeter, and soft classical music played from everywhere and nowhere at once. A span of windows framed a breathtaking view of the vineyard outside and the rolling hills beyond.

"Enzo," Costa said, approaching the man seated at one end of the table.

"Ah, Carlo!" Enzo stood up, dropping a napkin over a half-eaten sandwich. "It's great to see you!"

The men hugged after shaking hands.

"It's good to see you, too," Costa said. "How is the family doing?"

"Ah." Enzo made a wishy-washy gesture. "And how is Gloria? She must be all grown up by now."

"She's doing well," Costa said with a smile. Then, remembering their audience, he added, "Inspectors, this is *Signor* Enzo Monaco. Enzo, this is Inspector Basso and Inspector Falco."

Enzo nodded at them each in turn. His salt-and-pepper hair was cut short, sculpted with product and razor. He wore a shiny shirt, which looked like it had taken somebody's hands months to make, and a pair of pressed slacks held in place by a sturdy leather belt with a buffed silver buckle. His sleeves were rolled up, revealing a Patek Philippe watch. Ali was pretty sure the timepiece had cost more than a few years of her salary.

"Come with me, please." Enzo led them out of the room, deeper into the castle's interior.

"The vineyard looks beautiful," Costa said.

"It does, doesn't it? I love it in late fall. That means harvest is over and we can relax for a bit."

They stopped at another door, where a man in a three-piece suit stood at attention, waiting to greet them. His face was hard, dark eyes framed by circular gold-rimmed glasses.

"*Buongiorno*, Lieutenant," the man said, putting out a hand to Costa.

Enzo smiled. "Carlo, I believe you know my lawyer, Emilio Torrero."

"*Sì*. Good to see you, Torrero." Costa shook hands.

"Likewise. I'm here to make sure this conversation goes appropriately."

"Of course."

"Please," Enzo said. "Come in."

The room they stepped into looked much the same as the last, except instead of a table and chairs, there was a pair of wide couches placed perpendicular to one another.

Two women sat close together on the far couch, both clearly upset. The younger one had blue eyes that were big as billiard balls and blond hair that stretched down her shoulders. She wore a pair of jeans and a button-up shirt. A simple outfit, but it might as well have been a ball gown for how beautiful she still looked. The older woman was draped in jewelry, wearing a sweater and slacks, and she resembled the younger woman, but much more stern.

"Take a seat," Enzo said, motioning to the empty couch as he joined the women.

Torrero stood behind the Monaco family, arms clasped at his back, and watched Ali, Basso, and Costa take their seats.

"Carlo, you've met Camille and Bianca."

"It's a pleasure to see you again, Camille," Costa said warmly.

The older woman nodded.

"And my goodness, Bianca. You have grown into a beautiful woman. It seems like yesterday you were up to my knee."

A hint of a smile played on Bianca's lips, and then sadness welled in her eyes.

Enzo patted his daughter's knee before meeting Costa's gaze. "*Grazie* for coming on such short notice."

"Of course," Costa said. "Camille, Bianca, these are Inspectors Basso and Falco. Now, what can we help your family with?"

"Go ahead, Bianca," Enzo encouraged.

A tear fell from the young woman's eye, and she swallowed hard. "I was with Davide Conti the night he was murdered."

Costa leaned forward a few degrees. "So it was your car at the property. The neighbors reported a dark sedan."

Bianca nodded, and her father shifted his gaze to the far wall, staring blankly.

"What time were you there?" Costa asked.

"I went over at six o'clock. We had dinner." She shrugged. "We stayed together until about 10:15 p.m."

"You're sure of that time?"

"Sì. I remember thinking I would be home by ten thirty when I got in my car. It takes about fifteen minutes to drive between here and his house."

"Was it raining at the time you left?"

"Sì." She looked down, shaking her head. "We were laughing about it. He was making fun of me because I was scared. It was a big storm."

"And then what?" Costa prompted.

"And then nothing. I got in my car and left."

"Was there anything out of the ordinary that happened right around the time you left? Do you remember, perhaps, passing a vehicle on the road? Anything that seemed suspicious?"

"Not then . . . but there was something later."

"And what was that?"

"Excuse me," Torrero interrupted. He bent down and spoke into Enzo's ear.

Enzo waved his lawyer away. "She has nothing to hide."

Bianca grabbed her phone from the couch cushion and tapped the screen. "I texted him when I got home. I told him that I got back okay. He wanted me to because I was making such a big deal about the storm."

She stretched forward and handed her phone to Ali. Ali passed it to Costa, who held it out for them to see.

I'm home. It was raining buckets! I wish I was back in bed with you. I am so happy. I am so happy for us.

Ali's eyes flicked to Bianca, and she saw the woman's face had turned bright red. She looked back at the phone, reading the reply from Davide.

I'm sorry, we can never see each other again. Goodbye.

Ali frowned. His tone was jarringly cold. She scanned the next three messages, all of which were from Bianca.

What? Are you joking? If so, it's not funny.

Davi? Are you there? What is going on?

Davi? What is going on? Call me. Call me!!

Costa pulled the messages to the side, revealing their time stamps. Davide had broken off his relationship with Bianca at 10:28 p.m. on Thursday.

Ali studied Bianca again. The young woman's cheeks were now wet with tears.

"I don't think he sent that to me. There's no way. Look." Bianca held up her left hand, flashing a ring on her finger. "We got engaged Thursday night. He literally asked me to marry me. And then he broke it off over a text message? No, that's not him. And he was killed . . . It wasn't him. It was . . ."

"You think it was the person who killed Davide?" Costa asked.

"*Sì.*" Bianca wiped her face. "It had to be. There's no way he would have said that. He loved me. We loved each other. We were just beginning the rest of our lives together."

"Davide Conti won the lottery when Bianca accepted his proposal," Enzo said. "It doesn't make sense that he would break up with her over a text message later that same night."

"Did you know he was going to propose to her?" Costa asked.

Enzo blew air from his nose. "No. They were seeing each other in secret, apparently. But I would have accepted him into the family. My daughter loved him, and I would have blessed the marriage."

Bianca lowered her gaze to the floor, and Camille did the same.

A prickle of intuition climbed Ali's neck. She glanced at Torrero and caught the lawyer watching her.

"Do you know who killed Davide, Bianca?" Costa asked.

Bianca shook her head.

"If it was the killer who texted you, it's odd that he did. Why not just let your message go unanswered? Is there somebody out there who would have been jealous of your relationship? A former boyfriend, perhaps?"

"No. My last boyfriend lives in Switzerland. I don't think he would be the type . . . Can I see my phone?"

Costa handed it over.

Bianca tapped the screen, then gave it back. "Here. This is my former boyfriend. He posts a lot on social media. Look. He was up in Lausanne on Thursday."

Again, Costa held the phone out for Ali and Basso to see.

There was a picture of a young man smiling, sticking his tongue out. He had his arm around a scantily clad young woman, and they were sitting in what looked like the back room of a bar. The photo was tagged with a location, the blue clickable text reading, *The Swan*.

Costa tapped the link, and a map swelled onscreen. A dot hovered over the center of Lausanne, a city nestled on the shores of Lake Geneva in Switzerland, far to the north. He pressed the back button and gestured at the man's name.

Ali took the hint, pulling out her notebook and writing, *Harold Beaumont. Old photo? Actually taken that night?*

Costa returned the phone to Bianca once more. "No one else comes to mind? No other former boyfriends?"

"No."

"What about Davide's demeanor lately? Has he looked concerned? Talked to anybody that made him upset?"

"I didn't notice anything. I mean . . . I saw that he was acting strange. That he was nervous. But after he proposed to me and I accepted, he confessed that he'd chickened out of proposing earlier in the week. I figured that's why he was acting strange. But . . . maybe not. Maybe he was worried about being in danger. I don't know. He never told me anything."

Bianca began sobbing uncontrollably, and Camille wrapped her daughter in a hug.

Costa looked at Enzo. "Obviously, you're deep in the wine business. Are there, I don't know, any rivals that you suspect the Contis may have? Opposing vineyards or angry distributors? Or any shady people they may be involved with?"

Torrero lunged forward, speaking in Enzo's ear again.

This time, Enzo nodded. "I'd have to think on an answer to that."

Costa glanced at Bianca, who was still sobbing in her mother's arms. "We would like access to her phone."

"We will cooperate by sending you any and all information you need," Torrero said. "I'll act as the intermediary."

"*Grazie*," Costa said.

Enzo stood. "I believe that is all we have to say, gentlemen. And lady, excuse me."

He escorted the inspectors from the room, leaving Torrero with his wife and daughter.

Girardo joined their procession in the great hall, guiding them to the entrance. When he opened the front door, the sound of howling wind and lashing rain rushed to greet them. Water was falling in sheets, streaming off the porch roof, sending mist wafting inside. Ali's face grew damp as she hurried to zip up her jacket.

"I'm sorry that was so short and sweet," Enzo said. "My daughter is very upset."

Costa sighed. "I'd like to get the data from her phone as soon as possible."

"I'll have Torrero send it over immediately."

Costa looked like he wanted to say something more, but he only nodded. "*Grazie*."

"Good luck staying dry. Girardo, help them out, please."

Girardo pulled a long umbrella from the bin, moving onto the covered porch to snap it open.

Basso signaled for Ali to go first, so she retrieved her own umbrella and strode out into the waterfall beside Girardo. The Citroën's lights flashed as it unlocked. She opened the front passenger door, closed her umbrella, and slid inside, remaining dry with the help of Girardo's umbrella, which loomed over her like a dragon wing as she shut the door.

Basso climbed in a minute later, grunting and swiping his shoes on the floor. He turned on the engine and cranked the heater. "*Cazzo*. It's freezing."

Ali watched Girardo disappear inside, then turned to Basso. Before she could talk, the vehicle's speakers erupted with the sound of an incoming call. Costa's name appeared on the dashboard touch screen.

"*Pronto*," Basso answered.

"Meet me in the tourist parking lot on the way out."

"*Sì, signore.*"

14

"Davide's phone is missing," Costa said. "So maybe the killer really did send that text. Or maybe he made Davide send it, and then he killed him and took his phone to hide the evidence."

"Or Davide simply changed his mind," Basso challenged. "But what the hell kind of psycho proposes, especially to that woman, and breaks it off fifteen minutes later? No, it couldn't have been that."

"In either case, the killer must have taken the phone," Ali said from the back seat of Costa's car. "There's no way Davide lost it in less than two minutes." She frowned. "I wish we could have talked to Bianca Monaco alone in there."

Basso nodded. "She and Davide were seeing each other in secret. Why? Because seeing each other out in the open would be unacceptable to her father?"

"Bianca is twenty-two years old," Costa said. "Davide Conti was thirty-one. That alone is slightly scandalous."

They went quiet. Costa sucked a drag from his cigarette

and blew it out the cracked window. The rain had let up, but it still pattered on the roof and windshield.

"How do you know Enzo Monaco?" Basso asked.

"We've been acquaintances for years. Since secondary school."

"That man went to the same secondary school as you?"

"*Sì.*"

Basso's jaw dropped, and he repeated, "That man—the one who lives in a castle—went to the same secondary school that you did?"

Costa lowered his cigarette. "*Sì.* Why?"

"Nothing."

After a brief stare-down, Costa said, "Enzo Monaco has the ability to buy and sell all of us, me included, and he wouldn't hesitate to do so. Let's not forget that moving forward. Because I can see the gears turning in your minds. You're thinking Enzo might have had motive to kill Davide Conti if he found out the young man was seeing his daughter. If he found out Davide was going to propose and didn't want to let the son of a competing vineyard become part of his bloodline. Is that right?"

Basso raised an eyebrow. "Sounds like the gears are turning in your head, *signore.*"

Costa waved off the accusation. "Bianca is a key witness here, but we can't do anything rash. No stepping on any Monaco toes, or you won't be doing any stepping again. Got it?" His eyes landed on Ali in the rearview mirror.

She put up her hands.

"Luigi Sala," Basso said. "He's young. He's closer to Bianca's age. He spends time at the Conti house. Maybe he saw the two of them together. Maybe he has a thing for her, and he was jealous of Davide."

Ali picked up the line of thought. "Martina and Salvatore Conti were out of town, so Luigi knew Davide would have Bianca over. He watched them. He got angry at what he saw. We all know what he saw."

"Careful," Costa said, glancing out his window as if Enzo Monaco were surveilling them.

Ali continued, "Luigi waited for Bianca to leave—"

"—and then he went inside to kill Davide," Basso finished. "Shooting him in the crotch. Making him pay for taking his girl."

Costa's phone rang.

"It's Ferrari." Costa flicked his cigarette out the window and answered. "*Sì*? Okay . . . *Sì*. We just concluded our meeting at Castello Monaco . . . It was very interesting." He gave a short summary of the visit. "Oh, really? . . . Okay, we're on our way there next. We were already going to pay them a visit." He said goodbye and hung up.

"What?" Basso asked.

"Salvatore Conti wants to speak to us. So go speak to him. Then I want you to go speak to Luigi Sala. But be careful this time."

Basso nodded. "And you?"

"I have a press conference, remember? I'm going back to Siena."

The rain was done, but a fog had rolled in, obscuring the view of Conti Vineyards until they were only a hundred meters away. As Basso coasted along the final bend, the farmhouse and outbuilding emerged from the mist. A mud-strewn Range Rover was parked inside the open iron gate.

"Whose car is that?" Ali asked, squinting.

"I have no clue."

Basso navigated into the driveway, parking next to the Range Rover. She met him at the back bumper, and they walked to the house, avoiding puddles as they traversed the coarse gravel.

Salvatore and Martina Conti stood on the patio talking with two men. One had a chiseled face laced with fine wrinkles, and the other was young, handsome in a rugged yet boyish kind of way.

The four of them appeared to be wrapping up a conversation, shaking hands and sharing somber words. Before Ali and Basso could interrupt, the men turned and stepped off the porch, nodding as they passed the inspectors.

Ali snuck a peek over her shoulder and saw the young man was looking back at her, too.

"*Signor* Conti," Basso said. "You may remember us. I am Inspector Basso, and this is Inspector Falco."

"*Sì. Ciao.*" Salvatore shook their hands, his grip large and leathery.

"*Ciao,*" Martina said.

Ali's gaze settled on a package of prosciutto sitting atop the small outdoor table. The label read, *Quattro Luci Farm*. She recognized it as one of Giulia Acquaviva's "best-in-the-world products." Beside it was a single rose. Perhaps gifts from the men.

"How are you two holding up?" Basso asked.

Salvatore looked down at his daughter, seeming unsure about something.

Martina lifted her chin, taking in a breath.

The Range Rover growled to life, then accelerated toward the road, mud flipping up off its wheels.

Ali glanced at the tile patio, noting the killer's smeared boot prints had been cleaned.

"Those were some friends of the family," Salvatore explained, still watching his daughter. "Of Martina's."

Martina blinked long, as if her father's attention bothered her. As if she were an embarrassed teenager. Perhaps she and the young man had a thing going.

Salvatore gestured to the house. "I would tell you to come inside, but we don't like spending much time in there now. We've been sticking to our bedrooms, mostly."

"We understand," Basso said. "Whatever you like. We can stay here. We heard you wanted to talk to us."

"Sì. I've been lying awake for the last three nights, agonizing over who could have done this to my son, and I keep coming up with something I need to tell you about. I know you have Giuseppe in custody, but if you want my honest opinion, I don't think he did it."

"No?" Basso asked.

"No. But as for his son? I can't say the same."

Martina closed her eyes, shaking her head.

"And why is that?"

"Please. Follow me." Salvatore's gaze dropped to their feet. "Sorry for your shoes."

They rounded the house, trudging through mud and grass. Ali's feet slipped this way and that, but she kept up. Martina lagged far behind.

"Back here." Salvatore stopped at a stand of bushes

growing against the rear of the house. He pointed at a window. "There. See in there?"

Ali peered inside. It was a bathroom with a shower, sink, and toilet.

"Eight months ago, Davide was walking by the barrel room." Salvatore pointed at the distant outbuilding. "He saw Luigi standing here, in this exact spot."

"He wasn't *standing* here," Martina said. "He was working here."

"Whatever he was doing, he was standing right here by this window. When Luigi saw Davide, he walked away, clearly startled. Davide came over to investigate what Luigi had been up to, and he saw Martina was inside this bathroom, right on the other side of this window, taking a shower."

"I see," Basso said. "And what happened then?"

"My son called Luigi back to him. And then he punched him in the mouth." Salvatore folded his arms. "That's what happened."

"I see," Basso said again. "That is definitely interesting."

Martina stood a few paces away, holding her head in her hands.

"Do you disagree?" Ali asked her. "Is that not how things played out?"

"I think it was all a misunderstanding," Martina said. "Everyone moved on, and everyone was fine. Eight months have gone by without drama. Davide and Luigi were friends, even immediately after the incident, because Luigi apologized with his hat in hand. And he wasn't snooping, he was working on the wires back here. I just happened to be taking a shower. If anything, it was my fault. I should have closed the shutters before I started bathing."

"I think it's something that needs to be investigated." Salvatore smacked a fist into the palm of his opposite hand. "We can't overlook the fact that the gun was Giuseppe's. And we still don't know what Luigi was doing that night." He eyed his daughter. "Martina, you and I were all the way up in Turin. Not here. You don't know, either."

Martina scoffed, then spun on her heels and stormed away, vanishing around the side of the house. Her squishy footsteps faded into the peaceful quiet of the countryside.

"*Grazie, Signor* Conti," Basso said, giving Ali a sidelong look. "We appreciate you letting us know about this."

"Is it true that Luigi apologized?" Ali asked. "And that everything seemed . . . cordial from that point on?"

Reluctantly, Salvatore nodded. "I do think it's strange that he would have waited eight months before deciding to retaliate. But it's all I can come up with. I just don't know who would have wanted to do this to him." His eyes brimmed with tears, and his lips quivered. In a whisper, he added, "I want to know. I need to know."

"We won't stop until we find out who did this, *Signor* Conti," Basso said. "And we will look into Luigi Sala. Rest assured with that knowledge."

"*Grazie.*"

"In fact," Ali said, glancing at Basso, "we were planning to come talk to you about Luigi, anyway."

"You were? You think he did it?"

She shook her head. "We're not prepared to make that claim, *Signor* Conti. I want to be clear about that. We just want to know more about him."

"You said Luigi works here part time, correct?" Basso asked.

"That's right," Salvatore said. "His hours have been cut down a lot now that harvest is over."

"And Giuseppe? Have his hours been cut down, too?"

"Not Giuseppe. He's the winery manager, so there is still plenty for him to do. There are things that break and need fixing. We will bring Luigi back in for bottling when it's time, but otherwise, he'll be done until next season."

"Is Luigi angry that you cut his hours?" Ali asked.

Salvatore considered the question. "I don't think so. He's not exactly a go-getter like his father. I think he is glad to be working less."

"*Signore*." Basso tilted his head. "Did you know that Davide was dating Bianca Monaco?"

"He wasn't dating Bianca Monaco," Salvatore said, laughing. He looked between Ali and Basso, expecting them to join in his humor. When they didn't, he frowned. "Wait, are you serious? Davide and Bianca?"

"*Sì*, we are serious," Basso confirmed.

"If he was seeing Bianca Monaco," Salvatore said, something akin to anger in his voice, "then this is the first I'm hearing about it."

"Does the news upset you?" Ali asked.

"No," he answered too quickly. "I mean . . . if we have one rival, it's Monaco Vineyards. Many of our clients have left us for Monaco. They have money signs in their eyes. You understand."

"I'm not sure I do," Basso said.

Salvatore shrugged, letting out a hard exhale. "Monaco is so big it can sell Brunello for less. Our smaller operation struggles to keep up, but we have loyal clients." His eyes snapped back to Basso's. "No, if he was dating Bianca Monaco, I had no clue."

Basso smiled without teeth. "*Grazie* again for the information you've given us."

"*Prego*."

They made their way to the front of the house, circling up on the gravel driveway.

"Is there anything else you want to tell us, *Signor* Conti?" Basso asked. "Perhaps something about Luigi or his father that we don't yet know?"

Salvatore gazed into the horizon. "I'll tell you what I've told my daughter a thousand times, Inspector."

"What's that?"

"There are two types of people in this world: those who can handle responsibility, and those who cannot. The Conti family can handle responsibility. We take the burden of caring for the land and the people who work on it. We provide the opportunity and the imagination. But the Salas? Giuseppe and Luigi? I love them. We count on their help, and we are very grateful for it. But if it were up to them, if the fate of this winery were up to the intellect and drive of this father and son, then we would be in trouble."

Salvatore slid his hands into his pockets. "Luigi is a simple kid. He always has been. He speaks little. He rarely makes eye contact. He works hard. But he does what he's told, and no more."

"Have you seen him be violent before?" Ali asked.

"No, I have not." Salvatore frowned. "But that doesn't mean he isn't that type of person."

Basso handed over his card. "Please, if you think of anything else."

"Of course."

Ali and Basso climbed into the Citroën and drove away, leaving Salvatore Conti in the rearview mirror.

"What the hell was that all about?" she asked. "People who can handle responsibility. What does that have to do with anything?"

Basso ignored her, checking his phone. "Costa called. Here. Call him back."

She took the phone and dialed. A ring tone came out of the vehicle's speakers.

"*Ciao,*" Costa said. His voice sounded distant and tinny.

Basso turned up the volume. "Basso here. You called?"

"You don't have to go find Luigi."

"Why?"

"Because he just called. He's coming to us."

"I thought we didn't want him coming to us. The press outside, remember?"

"Don't worry about that. We'll sneak him in. Now get your asses back here."

15

"You can slow down now."

"I want to be in that meeting," Basso said.

Ali gripped the edges of her seat as he whipped past another vehicle. "We'll probably beat Costa back to headquarters, what with the psychotic way you're driving."

Basso paid her no mind, revving the engine high. The Citroën's tires rumbled across cobblestone, and the cabin hummed. Up ahead, a group of pedestrians turned their heads toward the approaching siren, then scattered like their lives depended on it.

"Sorry!" Ali called out her open window.

"We're not sorry. We're on official police business."

"Slow down."

Basso took a tight corner much too fast, jerking the wheel, sending them skidding into the parking lot outside headquarters. He slammed the brakes, coming to a halt just past an extremely tight spot.

"You can't fit in there."

"Out."

She jumped from the vehicle, shutting the door. He angled for the parking spot with less-than-expert precision, lurching forward and squealing backward, barely avoiding multiple collisions.

Shaking her head, Ali abandoned the scene.

Gatti was perched by the front entrance, talking on the phone. When he saw her, he hung up. "How was it?"

"Not bad."

"How was the castle?"

"Not quite as pretty as my apartment, but it was nice."

Gatti frowned, staring over her shoulder. She tracked his gaze. The lights of a parked car were flashing, the alarm echoing into the depths of Siena, and Basso was driving out of the lot at speed.

"Is that Basso? *Madonna*." Gatti shook his head. "Let's go inside. Costa is waiting."

They headed for the front entrance, almost colliding with a man walking out.

It was Fabiano.

Gatti froze, then continued past him, colliding hard with his shoulder.

"Watch where you're going, *stronzo*," Fabiano said, descending the steps.

"Excuse me?" Gatti spun around and stomped down to the patrolman.

They squared off, faces almost touching. Fabiano yielded first, glaring at Ali before turning away.

"That's what I thought," Gatti said. "Where you going? Off to see daddy?"

Fabiano lowered his head.

"*Bastardo*," Gatti said under his breath. He brushed by Ali and strode into the building.

She trailed after him, heart racing from the encounter, mind replaying the pain she'd witnessed in Fabiano's eyes. The young patrolman had said some idiotic things over the years, and he had delighted in a viral video of her punching a suspect over the summer, but . . .

"That was a little harsh, don't you think?" she asked.

"Huh?" Gatti looked at her, brow furrowed in confusion. "Harsh? Did you not notice? That was Fabiano."

They reached the stairwell, and Gatti hurried up the steps, pulling away from her. She jogged to keep up.

At the second-floor landing, he turned around. His expression was calm, like the incident had already evaporated from his thoughts. "Luigi's in Interrogation B. He almost seems eager to talk to us."

"Is Costa with him already?"

"No, he's in his office. He'll meet us soon."

They stepped into the squad room.

"Whoa, whoa. Who let you in?" Rossi leaned back from his computer, grinning at Ali and Gatti.

"Focus on your game of solitaire, old man," she said, smiling.

Basso rushed through the door, panting and wiping sweat off his forehead. Being so thin and wiry, the man could sometimes be mistaken for trim and athletic. This was not one of those times.

"Where's Luigi?" he asked.

"Interrogation B," Gatti said. "Costa was waiting for you. He'll be down in a second."

"Good." Basso breathed in through his nose, coughing

out the exhales. "I'm going to get some water. I'll be right there."

"I'm going to hit the bathroom," Gatti said, breaking away, too.

Ali headed straight to the interrogation room. She found Costa standing outside, looking at his phone.

"Oh, you're here," she said. "Everyone thinks you're still upstairs."

"Came in the back." He thumbed over his shoulder. "You got here fast."

"That's Basso's driving for you."

"How were the Contis?"

"Interesting."

Costa's phone rang.

"I must answer this. Excuse me."

Basso came around the corner, face flushed red. Gatti was behind him, sipping an espresso.

"What's going on?" Basso eyed Costa, who was pacing at the far end of the hall, phone pressed to his ear.

Ali shrugged. "He had to take a call."

"Get the car parked, Basso?" Gatti asked with a smirk.

Basso scowled. "*Sì*. It's right outside your mother's house."

Costa returned, pocketing his phone. "Giuseppe's getting discharged now. Ali, you're coming with me to talk to Luigi."

"Me?" She looked at Basso. "But . . . Basso wanted to be in there."

Basso upturned his hands.

Costa ignored him. "He came to you the other night. He spoke with you when we searched his house. I want him relaxed, and he seems to be relaxed around you. He came here and agreed to talk to us. I don't want to screw this up. You're coming with me."

Basso now wore the same expression he donned whenever Inter lost a particularly important game.

"Do you have your notebook?" Costa asked.

She pulled it from her breast pocket, along with a pen.

"Good. Let's go."

"*Signore*, wait."

He stopped. "What?"

"We learned something about Luigi during our trip to Conti Vineyards this afternoon, just before you called us." She shared Salvatore's story about Luigi looking into the window on Martina.

"Okay," Costa said. "That's good to know. Let's go."

Ali followed him into the interrogation room. She had never been in one officially, only during mock exercises at the academy, but seeing the familiar man at the table relaxed her.

Luigi Sala had a mark on his nose and a bruise beneath one eye. He smelled like he hadn't showered in a few days, and his curly brown hair was unkempt and greasy. He wore a sweatshirt with a ripped collar over a T-shirt, both in need of a launder.

"*Signor* Sala," Costa said. "I'm sorry to keep you waiting. Did you want another coffee?"

"No, *grazie*. And please, call me Luigi."

Ali took one of the plastic chairs, placing her notebook and pen on the table. The pen rolled toward Luigi. She lunged for it, missing.

Luigi caught the writing utensil in his lap and set it in front of her.

Her face heated. "*Grazie.*"

"Let's get started," Costa said. "We're going to record this with audio and video, okay?"

Luigi nodded.

"We heard how you met up with Inspector Falco the other night."

"I'm sorry about that. I told her I was sorry."

"That's okay," Ali said. "Sorry about your eye."

Luigi reached up and touched it with a finger. "It's nothing."

"We appreciate you coming in and talking with us, Luigi," Costa said. "It's very helpful for you to do. So, how about we begin with the night of Davide Conti's death? Thursday night."

"Okay."

"Tell me about your evening. What were you doing? Who were you with?"

"I told you the truth before. I was alone at my house all night, watching TV. I did leave once to get a pizza. I brought it home to eat, and I watched more TV. And then I went to bed."

"What time did you go get the pizza?" Costa asked.

"It was around nine."

Ali checked her notes. The time stamp on the pizza receipt had been 9:13 p.m.

"You're sure?"

"*Sì.* I wanted to be home before *Calcio Tonight.* I must have picked it up at nine fifteen, because I was back right when the show started at nine thirty. It takes ten or so minutes to get home from the pizzeria."

Costa folded his arms. "Who were the guests?"

"Excuse me?"

"On *Calcio Tonight*. They had two guests on Thursday. Who were they?"

"Brambilla and Giovanni," Luigi answered immediately.

Ali looked at Costa.

He nodded. "That's right. I watched it, too."

Ali began taking notes, and she was startled to see clumsy scrawls come out of the pen. Her handwriting was all wrong, every line and loop veering in inappropriate directions. She realized her middle finger felt completely dead now, leaving her hand unable to control the pen.

Costa went silent, and she saw he was watching her.

She picked up her notebook and propped it at an angle on her knee so he couldn't observe without causing a scene. Scribbling fast and confident, she made abstract art mixed with words.

Costa returned his attention to Luigi. "And at the end of the show, you know how they always have a special spotlight on a player or a team that's been doing well recently? Where did they go this time?"

"I . . . It was . . ." Luigi frowned, shaking his head slightly. "I don't remember. I must not have seen that part."

"You didn't see that part? It was right around 10:20 p.m. Just before the end."

"No, I didn't."

Utter disappointment crossed Costa's expression. "Well, that's the most important part to me."

Luigi's eyes widened. "Oh, wait. *Sì*, I did see it. Are you talking about the player from England? They went up to some place with the word *little* in it. The small town with the big forward . . . They were talking about something like that. Little . . . I don't know."

"Eaton," Costa said. "'The Big Forward from Little Eaton.'"

Luigi snapped his fingers, pointing at Costa. "That was it! Why? Do you think I was at Conti Vineyards when the neighbors heard the gunshots? That's why you're asking, right?"

Costa studied the young man for a beat, then gestured to Ali. "Inspector Falco, why don't you tell Luigi what you learned from the Contis earlier today?"

"Sure," she said, clearing her throat. "Luigi, we were just at Conti Vineyards."

"I know. Martina told me."

Her eyes narrowed. "Martina did?"

"*Sì.*"

"Okay. Well . . . Salvatore told us—" Ali remembered her interrogation techniques. She had to get him talking. Avoid closed questions. "Why don't you tell us about what happened between you and Davide eight months ago?"

Luigi stared down at his hands, and his face turned red. "When I was looking at Martina?"

"*Sì.* That's what we'd like to know about."

"I was outside, working on some electrical wiring at the back of the house. She was in the bathroom, getting ready for a shower." He shrugged. "And I saw her."

Ali nodded. "Go on."

"Her brother was also outside, and he saw me."

"And?"

"And he came over to talk to me. And I walked away so I could meet him somewhere else. So he wouldn't see what I had seen and think I was looking in on her. But he did, and he got angry."

"And then what happened?"

Luigi's eyes flicked between her and Costa. "He punched me in the nose."

"How would you describe your relationship with Davide?" Costa asked. "Just before his death."

"We were fine. He didn't care that me and Martina have a thing going."

"Wait a minute," Ali said. "You and Martina? You two have a thing going?"

Luigi took his phone from his pocket. He tapped and scrolled, then laid the phone on the table, pushing it over to them. "Here's what I was doing Thursday night."

Costa drew the phone closer. There was a chat open onscreen, displaying half a dozen messages between two participants, L and T. "What am I looking at here, Luigi?"

"Those are the messages between me and Martina on Thursday night. See the time stamps on top of the messages?"

Ali glanced at Luigi. "We've got an L . . . That's you, right? And T? Who's T?"

"That's for *Tesoro*."

"Ah," Costa said. "Martina is your treasure."

"*Sì.*"

Costa scrolled, stopping at one of the messages.

T: *I don't care. She's an idiot. She pretends like she doesn't care, but she does.*

Costa scrolled some more, searching for context, finding the words meant little. Luigi and Martina had been talking about banal subjects.

"You can see I was texting her all night. We do that every night."

Costa swiped up to view the conversation from Thursday, November 15. It had started at 8:36 p.m.

T: Ciao. *Are you there?*

L: Sì, Tesoro. *I'm here. How was your day?*

T: *Nobody wants our wine. Everyone talks about Monaco. The rich get richer. We need a castle, too.*

L: *I'm sorry.*

T: *I miss you. I wish we were together.*

L: *We can be together.*

T: *Lol. Later.*

Martina had gone on to recount the day's events at the Italian Wine Exposition, complaining about the boring lunch she and her father had shared at a restaurant, then about the difficulty of procuring new clients. Apparently, no one had seemed interested in speaking with a small, relatively unknown vineyard.

Luigi had lamented with her, and Ali decided he was an overall good listener. As good of a listener as one could be when texting.

At 8:55 p.m., a message caught her eye.

L: *I'm going to get a pizza.*

After Luigi's declaration, Martina had started a new rant, this time about a girlfriend who'd been posting half-clothed pictures online and declaring herself single. With no more than six minutes between messages, their communication had continued uninterrupted. It was impossible to see when Luigi had left for his pizza, arrived at the pizza place, or gotten back home.

At 9:48 p.m., another series of messages made Ali peer closer.

L: *But I want to be together now.*

T: *Where is your dad?*

L: *At the bar. Where he always is.*

Ali pictured Luigi standing in the field outside the Conti farmhouse, watching Davide and Bianca hook up, then murdering Davide after Bianca left, all during a storm, all while participating in a lively chat with Martina. The scenario seemed unlikely. Then again, it was possible the messages had been staged to make it appear like he'd been home.

"Did you know that Davide was seeing Bianca Monaco?" she asked.

"Bianca Monaco?" Luigi's eyebrows pulled together. His surprise seemed genuine. "No. I didn't know that. Are you sure?"

She nodded. "*Sì*. They were together the night of his death. You haven't heard about them before?"

"No."

"Not even from Martina?"

"No, I swear. I'm telling you. And I don't think Martina knows. Or, if she does, she never said so. But that is something she would have told me. Monaco Vineyards is the bane of Conti Vineyards' existence. We have so few buyers because they can just get cheaper and, well, better-quality bottles from Monaco. Plus, they can sell Monaco's bottles for more money, and sell more, because the name is well known. So, no, I didn't know Davide was seeing Bianca. That would have been big news."

Costa looked back at the phone, beginning to scroll

again. There were a couple of images starting at 10:03 p.m., all blurred due to poor reception. "What's this?"

Luigi reached forward. "That's not—"

Costa tapped the first image. A video player opened, and a circle swirled as the content loaded. Then a disorienting scene materialized, all movement and darkness. Centered in the confusion was a close-up of a face. Luigi's face.

"You don't want to see that." Luigi held out his hand, standing from his chair.

The door yanked open, and Basso stepped inside.

"Sit down," Basso said, pointing at Luigi.

Costa paused the video. "We're okay in here, Inspector Basso. *Grazie.*"

"Are you sure?"

Costa sent him a hot glare, and Basso backed out of the room, shutting the door.

Luigi remained standing, one hand on the table, one reaching out for his phone.

"Luigi," Costa said. "I could give this back to you, but wouldn't you rather we keep looking through it for your alibi? You know just as well as we do that the Contis' neighbors heard gunshots at approximately 10:30 p.m. So far, you've shown us nothing that proves you were home at that time. You could have sent these text messages from anywhere."

"But I told you about *Calcio Tonight.*"

"*Sì,* but you could have learned about that any number of ways. You could have watched the replay on YouTube." Costa set the phone on the table, perhaps sensing the legal boundaries he was close to overstepping. "If you don't show us, we'll have to get a warrant. You see, we'll watch this video one way or another, Luigi. But the cell phone companies work slow, and while we wait, we'll have to keep you close. That means sleeping in a cell."

Luigi dropped onto the chair, putting his hands over his eyes. "You can't tell him about this."

"Tell who?" Ali asked.

He pulled down his cheeks. "Martina's father."

"Tell him what, Luigi?"

"Just watch it. But remember, you asked for it."

Costa grabbed the phone and restarted the video.

The camera shuffled about, but the footage remained dark. It was impossible to make out shapes. Then a light switched on, and Luigi's over-exposed face filled the screen. He puckered his lips and kissed near the lens, whispering gruffly, "Are you ready?"

Ali blushed, realizing what was probably in store for them. Her suspicions were confirmed as Luigi trailed the lens to his waist and grasped his private parts.

"Okay," she said, but before turning her head away, she recognized the Inter Milan sheets from Luigi's bed.

Amusement glinting in his eyes, Costa stopped the video and swiped down to the response, which was another video, this time from Martina. He tapped it, and Martina's face appeared onscreen. Her smile was radiant, so wide it seemed to cut through the scar on her cheek, rendering it powerless against her natural beauty.

Behind her was the tile wall of a shower.

"Are *you* ready, Luigi?" Martina asked in a sultry voice. She waited a few seconds, then flipped the phone around, revealing the rest of a hotel bathroom. When the footage settled, it showed her standing naked in front of a mirror. Her free hand began caressing her breast.

Costa closed the player. Scratching his head, he went to the final video, which had come from Luigi. Ali noticed the time stamp read 10:27 p.m.

"Please," Luigi said. "You really don't want to see that one."

Costa contemplated the warning for a moment, then hit play. Luigi's moans came from the speakers, echoing in the small interrogation room. Quickly, Costa locked the screen, plummeting them into silence. Using a knuckle, he pushed the phone across the table.

Luigi pocketed it, averting his eyes. "Can I go now?"

Costa stared at the wall.

"*Ciao*? Lieutenant Costa?"

"Technically, Luigi, you could have recorded these videos earlier. You could have sent them at pre-determined times to make your alibi seem ironclad."

Luigi's mouth hung open. "Are you kidding me?"

Costa looked at him.

"You don't really believe that, do you?" Luigi asked.

Ali didn't. She had never seen somebody this embarrassed in her life.

Costa sighed. "It doesn't matter what I believe. We'll need the files so we can analyze their metadata. Our experts will verify when and where they were made."

"Fine. Take them, sicko."

Costa relayed his email address, which Luigi used to send over the videos.

"Can I go now?"

"*Sì*. You're free to go." Aiming his voice at the one-way

glass, Costa added, "Gatti, please escort Luigi to his car."

"Of course," Gatti said, entering the interrogation room. He collected Luigi, and they walked out the door.

Ali and Costa joined Basso in the observation room. Costa looked around frantically, then lunged at a bottle of hand sanitizer, squirting far too much onto his palm.

"We're just letting him go?" Basso asked, sounding incredulous. "What did you guys watch? We couldn't tell, but it kind of sounded like—"

"Those were the sheets on his bed," Ali said to Costa. "I recognized them from the visit to his house."

Costa nodded. "I did, too."

"What?" Basso asked. "What does that mean?"

"It means Luigi Sala has an ironclad alibi for the night of the murder," Costa said. "Well, assuming the videos were made around the same times they were sent in the chat."

"We can check the metadata right now," Ali offered.

Costa's eyebrows lifted. "We can?"

"Sì. Just open one of the videos and give me your phone."

He did as instructed. "That's the last video. The one sent at 10:27 p.m. on Thursday night. I would stay away from the play button."

Ali accessed the metadata using a technique she'd learned during her latest training. The date and time displayed onscreen, along with the file size and location. The video had been recorded on November 15 at 10:26 p.m. at Luigi Sala's address.

She gave the phone back to Costa.

"Okay," he said, examining the information. "The alibi is ironclad. Good work, Falco."

"So where does that leave us?" Basso asked.

Costa slipped his phone into a pocket. "Luigi said Martina didn't know about her brother dating Bianca Monaco. He made it sound like the Monacos and the Contis are enemies."

"I definitely got the sense that Salvatore Conti was upset when we told him about Davide dating Bianca," Ali said. "He seemed almost angry."

Basso nodded. "I saw it, too."

Costa checked his watch. "I really don't like the direction this case is taking."

"Have you gotten Davide's cell records yet?" Basso asked.

"No. This delay is ridiculous."

Basso frowned. "It's almost like somebody is stopping them from being released."

"Somebody with a lot of money . . ." Ali mused.

Costa's gaze seared into them. "You'd better not mention something like that outside of this room. Hell, inside of this room, for all we know."

16

Ali walked along Via Fontebranda, lured like a moth to the bright lights blazing from Piazza del Campo. They illuminated a subdued, almost non-existent Monday night crowd.

Flexing her right hand, she thought about the accelerating numbness in her fingers. The little act she had pulled in the interrogation room hadn't fooled Costa. He'd seen her struggle to write. He'd also seen the way she'd failed to grab her rogue pen. The man was too observant to not know what was going on.

The idea was enough to make Ali crave a cigarette. She pulled one from her purse and lit it, savoring the relaxed buzz that traveled through her body with the first drag.

She reached the edge of the square, and the smell of pizza drew her to a restaurant with red awnings. Normally, she despised places like this. They were almost always congested with tourists. But tonight, only a few people were seated on the terrace. Heat towers glowed red above them, billowing out warmth, blocking the chilly air.

"One, please," she said to the man at the host stand.

"Seat outside?"

"*Sì*, please."

The host escorted her to a table. She ordered a Margherita pizza and a glass of red, then sat back to enjoy the peace.

Out in the square, couples strolled by, holding hands, staring into each other's eyes with dreamy expressions. Everything was perfect for them, here in this beautiful place.

Ali thought of Marco and grimaced. Maybe she should just call him back. Get it over with.

The waiter delivered her wine, and she sipped it, finding the taste of the Chianti *riserva* more bitter than she remembered, but still pleasing after a long day at work.

"Falco."

She lifted her gaze to the man in front of her, realizing she had been too lost in thought to notice his arrival at her table. "Gatti. What are you doing here?"

"I came with some friends." He gestured behind him, toward two men being seated at a table across the terrace.

"Oh. *Bello*." She shook her head, feeling dazed. "I didn't even see you come in."

He chuckled. "I thought as much."

She leaned sideways to peer closer at his friends, vaguely recognizing one of them. The man nodded at her and smiled.

Her breath caught as she remembered where she'd seen him before. He was even more handsome now than he had been at Conti Vineyards.

"Who is that with you?" she asked. "The man on the left, I mean. He was visiting the Contis earlier today."

Gatti looked, and in a voice loud enough for the whole square to hear, he said, "That's Nico Villa."

Ali raised a hand to her face. "Okay, wow."

His mouth upturned in amusement.

"Is he . . . ?"

"No. He's not gay, if that's what you're wondering."

"Oh."

Gatti twisted around and snapped his fingers in the air. The man named Nico Villa stood up and strode over.

Ali straightened, face flushing with heat as Nico reached them, stopping beside Gatti. He was dressed in a much different outfit than before, wearing fitted pants and a button-up shirt that showed off his extremely athletic figure.

"*Ciao*," he said, waving shyly. "My name is Nico. I saw you at the Contis' place, right?"

"*Sì*." She held out her hand, letting his warm, dry grip envelope hers. "It's nice to meet you."

Nico smiled. "I can say the same."

Gatti stepped back from the table. "I'll see you tomorrow, Falco."

He walked off, leaving them alone.

"Oh, uh, sorry," Nico said. "I don't mean to bother you, but I am glad I got a chance to say hi and introduce myself. I . . . noticed you earlier today."

She returned his smile. "Nico, you said?"

"That's right. And I didn't catch your name."

"Oh. My name is Ali."

He tilted his head. "Is that short for Alessandra?"

"No, it's . . . My mother was American. It's Ali, with an *i*. Short for Alison."

"Oh. Beautiful."

"*Grazie*," she said, blushing. "So how do you know Gatti?"

He grinned. "We used to play *calcio* together when we were younger. Actually, it's your fault I'm here tonight."

She raised an eyebrow. "Oh? How's that?"

"When I saw you earlier, wearing that badge of yours, you reminded me of my inspector friend, Tommaso Gatti. So I called him to see if he wanted to get a drink." He glanced at their table. "Now here we are, meeting for dinner. I live nearby. Just outside the square." He pointed in the direction of Ali's place.

"It is a small world."

"It is a very small world. Especially here in Tuscany, right?"

Ali laughed. It really wasn't that funny, but she couldn't help herself.

Nico laughed, too.

"What were you doing at the Contis' this afternoon?" she asked.

His face went serious. "My father and I are neighbors. We have a pig farm in Montalcino."

She thought of the prosciutto she'd seen on the patio table. "Quattro Luci Farm?"

"That's right. Have you heard of it?"

She nodded. "I have. I hear your products are fantastic."

"Our crudo was named best in Tuscany two years ago."

"Congratulations."

He shrugged. "*Grazie*."

"If the farm is down in Montalcino, why do you live all the way up here?"

"I have a place there, the family house, and one in Siena. I like to split my time between the country and the city. I often find it more exciting up here."

The waiter placed a Margherita pizza in front of her. "Anything else, *signora*?"

"No, *grazie*."

The waiter moved to another table.

"Anyway, it was great to meet you, Ali." Nico smiled at her, and the warmth of the propane heaters seemed to kick up a notch. "I hope to see you again."

Ali blushed once more, unsure how to respond, but he left before she had to decide. She took a sip of wine to avoid watching him walk away, not wanting to give Gatti any ammunition.

For the next few minutes, she ate her pizza, peeking over at Gatti's table once, seeing Nico looking in her direction. They both pretended not to notice how clearly aware they were of each other.

When she finished her meal, she paid the waiter and rose to put on her jacket, catching a glimpse of Nico telling a story that had Gatti in raucous laughter. The three men were still in the middle of their dinner. She wondered whether she should say goodbye or not.

Again, Nico made the choice for her, approaching and waving his hand. "Have a lovely night, Ali Falco."

She smiled. "You too. See you around, maybe."

He smiled back, then cleared his throat. "Like I said, I have a place up here in the city, so I'm often around. This may be a bit forward, but do you think you'd like to get a coffee with me sometime?"

"Uh," she said, searching her mind for a good way to refuse. "That might be ... I'm very busy at the moment."

"Of course. With the case and everything. That's why I was suggesting coffee only. Nothing that would take too much time out of your busy schedule."

She glanced at the square, considering his offer.

"You don't have to decide right now." He pulled a business card from his pocket and held it out. "If you're bored one day and you'd like to have some nice conversation—but not too much conversation, nothing overbearing, of course—you can text or call."

She took the card. "I'll think about it."

He grinned, stepping back. "That's all I ask. That you think about me."

Seeing Gatti and his other friend were watching from their table, she kept her face impassive as Nico walked away. But when she turned and left the restaurant, she was thinking about him.

17

The next morning was bitingly cold, the coolest of the year yet. Ali's puffs of breath glowed in the early light as she made her way to work, keeping her eyes on the cobblestone, thinking of Nico Villa and his smile.

After returning home the night before, she had done a bit of internet sleuthing. Nico's Instagram account was private, so no luck there, but his LinkedIn profile was up to date and polished, listing him as the public face of Quattro Luci Farm. He was only twenty-six years old, five years her junior, but that didn't put him out of consideration.

Her phone chimed in her pocket, and she took it out, stomach dropping as she saw the name Marco Vinci.

Hi, Ali. I'm going to be in Siena today for work, and I was hoping you might be available to meet up? I'll be free from 2 p.m. onward. I hope to hear from you. And I hope you're doing well.

Ali stared at the message. When she eventually blinked, she realized she had been standing still in the middle of the street. Pocketing her phone, she resumed walking.

Today? Today he was in town? And what? She was supposed to just drop everything and meet him? After he'd spent months ignoring her calls? Now he was ready to talk, and so she should be, too?

Cursing under her breath, she strode up to the headquarters building. Before she went in, she grabbed her phone and typed a response.

I'm sorry, Marco. I can't. I'm very busy today.

There. It was done.

Ali headed through the entrance and up the stairs, depositing her backpack under her desk and hanging her jacket on her chair. The door to Ferrari's office was open, and she spotted Basso, Gatti, Costa, and Longo inside. They were all holding packets of paper, studying the documents intently.

She checked her watch, making sure she was on time. She was. Everyone else had just arrived early. That made her feel late.

"Come, Falco," Ferrari called. He sat behind his desk, looking at his computer screen. "And shut the door, please."

Ali complied.

"Falco." Costa held out a packet for her, keeping his eyes on his own.

"What's this?"

"Vodafone finally sent over Davide Conti's cell records."

She took the packet and went to stand along the rear wall, next to Gatti.

"We are all here now." Ferrari took off his glasses and rubbed the bridge of his nose. "This case is going to give me an ulcer."

"I thought you already had an ulcer," Basso said.

Ferrari grunted. "Another ulcer. Now, before we dig into this information here, everyone should know that Giuseppe Sala was released yesterday evening. And Luigi Sala, so I hear, has an alibi."

"Correct," Costa said.

Ferrari picked up the packet lying in front of him. "What are we looking at here?"

Basso began pacing. "We have many text messages between Bianca and Davide, some from the day of the murder. The first one was sent in the morning to ask about their dinner plans."

Ali flipped through the pages of her packet, searching for the relevant messages.

Gatti presented his to her, pointing at the bottom of the third page.

She nodded.

"The next few messages, as you can see, were the same," Basso continued. "Reiterating that they were going to have dinner at Davide's house. Davide responded with banter, telling Bianca he had something special planned. She was intrigued. Blah blah blah."

He went back a page. "Davide also had a phone call that lasted a few minutes with his father. A text message from Martina, where she reminded him to send an email about a purchase order . . . Blah blah. Going back to older activity, we see he spoke to Bianca numerous times throughout the days leading up to his murder. Sometimes with texts, sometimes with phone calls."

For a full minute, the inspectors studied the packets in their hands. Nothing jumped out as extraordinary to Ali, or out of place.

"Let's move to the GPS locations," Basso said.

Ali found the map and saw there was a single blue dot on it.

"As you can see, Davide Conti did not go anywhere the entire day of his murder. He stayed right at home."

"Or his cell phone did," Ali said.

Basso nodded. "Right."

"Then his phone was rendered completely untraceable at 10:28 p.m.," Costa said. "Somebody either shut it off, took the battery out, or removed the SIM card immediately after Davide sent the cryptic break-up message to Bianca."

"The woman he had just proposed to," Gatti said. "If we can believe what Bianca told you, that is."

Costa shot him a look.

Gatti threw up his hands. "What? It's not hard to fake an engagement ring. Especially with Monaco amounts of money."

"Moving on." Ferrari dropped the packet onto his desk with theatric finality. "What else? Because right now, we can't be thinking we have to look closer at the Monacos."

Nobody spoke.

Ferrari looked at Longo. "What else?"

Longo raised a finger. "I do have one thing we've figured out."

"Ah, the great forensic expert has come up with the clue that will solve the case for us." Ferrari smiled. "Go, Dr. Longo. Shine the light to lead us out of this black hole."

"Right," Longo said, pulling a folder from under his arm. He plucked out a piece of paper and set it on Ferrari's desk. It was a printed screenshot of a pair of boots for sale online.

"Brunello Cucinelli boots. They have a detailed tread pattern that is unique to only them."

He put another paper on the desk. The left side had a screenshot of the famous Brunello Cucinelli boot tread, and the right had a close-up photo of the boot prints Ali and Gatti had discovered in the trees below Conti Vineyards. "You can see they match perfectly."

Ferrari stood and faced his window. "Those boots are exceptionally expensive, are they not?"

"*Sì*," Longo confirmed. "Well over a thousand euro for any of the models."

Gatti's eyebrows shot up. "That limits the pool of suspects substantially, does it not?"

"It does," Ali said, an idea forming in her mind. It was far-fetched, but . . . She cleared her throat, drawing everyone's attention.

"What?" Costa asked.

"I just had a thought."

"Speak your thought then," Ferrari said, voice rising.

"When Gatti and I were interrogating the owner of Mickey's Bar, Pino Acquaviva, he made a comment that I've been wondering about since."

Ferrari and Costa assaulted her with impatient looks.

"He believes the Monacos are involved with the Mafia. He mentioned that we should look into a possible connection."

Basso snorted. "Mafia? Really?"

Ali shook her head. "I'm not saying it's true. I'm just saying it's an angle we need to consider. The Monacos don't seem like killers, but if they are connected to the Mafia, then they wouldn't need to be. The Mafia could do their dirty work for them. All it would take is one call from Enzo."

The room fell silent, growing considerably more tense.

At last, Ferrari said, "It's something I've wondered myself." He looked at Costa. "You have a friend in the DIA, don't you? He had a German name?"

The Direzione Investigativa Antimafia. She eyed Costa.

"*Sì, signore*," he said. "Becker is his name. I can talk to him today."

Ferrari nodded, and his expression turned resolute. "*Grazie*. But be discreet. I don't want word to spread that we are asking such questions."

"Of course."

"What *else*?" Ferrari slapped his desk, the noise booming like a cannon, and dropped into his chair. "There has to be something else. To open an investigation into Enzo Monaco . . . To even hint at such an incendiary idea outside the walls of this office . . . It is career suicide. For all of us. I want to know anything you're thinking that could draw us in any other direction."

Again, nobody spoke.

Ferrari glared at them one by one, Costa first, and then Basso, and then Gatti, and then Longo. When his hooded blue eyes finally landed on Ali, she raised a finger.

"*Sì*?" he prompted.

She frowned, trying to form her muddled thoughts into words. All last night, she had been thinking of one man. One man who had randomly come into her life yesterday afternoon, and then again that same evening. Who had been popping up in her imagination ever since, always in sexual imagery. Just a minute prior, she had been thinking about calling him to get coffee. And now . . .

"What?" Ferrari barked. "What?"

"It's just that . . ." She turned to Gatti. "Who is this Nico Villa?"

"Nico Villa?" Ferrari asked. "Who is Nico Villa?"

Gatti straightened his posture. "Well, he's a friend of mine. We used to play *calcio* together growing up. Why?"

"Because he was at Conti Vineyards yesterday afternoon," Ali said.

"One of the men in the Range Rover?" Basso asked.

Ferrari scowled. "What are you three talking about?"

"Well, *signore*, we went to speak to the Contis yesterday afternoon—"

"I know," Ferrari snapped, cutting Basso off. "And?"

"And two men were there when we showed up."

"Nico Villa and his father," Ali said. "They were speaking to the Contis. They gifted some prosciutto from Quattro Luci Farm, which they own."

"They own the farm?" Basso's eyes bugged out. "Those two men?"

"*Sì*," Gatti said. "They own the farm."

"That's very high-end prosciutto. I wish I would have known it was them. I would have introduced—"

"Who is this Nico person?" Ferrari demanded, nearly shouting now. "Why does he matter?"

"He's young and good-looking," Ali said. She glanced at Gatti. "And he's now poking his nose into your life, isn't he?"

Gatti shrugged. "I mean, I guess you could say that. But what does 'young and good-looking' have to do with anything?"

She blushed. "I'm just saying . . . I don't know, he's young and good-looking, and rich, too, given his family owns Quattro Luci Farm, so he could know Bianca Monaco. Maybe he was jealous of her relationship with Davide, so he killed Davide and shot him in the crotch."

Basso chewed his lip in thought. "Gatti, when was the last time you saw this Nico Villa before last night?"

"A year or so ago."

"And now he's suddenly having dinner with you?" Ali asked.

"Well, it's not so much of a random occurrence that he was out with me last night."

"Oh?"

"No." Gatti chuckled. "He noticed you were an inspector. He saw the badge. He was interested in you, so he called me out of the blue. Of course, I didn't know any of this until after we left dinner. That's when he confessed the entire reason why he was there with me. He wanted to get inside information on you."

Ali felt her face bloom with heat as the men stared at her. "That could have been a fake story. He knows I'm working the case. Maybe he wants to get close to me to see what we've learned."

"How old is he?" Ferrari asked.

"My age," Gatti said. "Twenty-seven, I think. Could be twenty-eight."

"Twenty-six," Ali said.

Costa folded his arms. "What if Falco's right? We need to consider the possibility."

"Whoa," Gatti said. "The man is a good person. I've known him all my life. He's never hurt a fly."

"You know him that well?" Basso asked. "You haven't seen him for a year, but you know him that well?"

"I know him well enough. He's smitten with Falco. That's all that's going on. He's always been like that."

Basso laughed. "Like what? Smitten with women? So smitten he'd be willing to kill over it?"

Gatti put his hands up, eyeing Ali as if to say, *What have you done?*

She looked down, shame spiking into her suspicion. Suddenly, she felt like the lead torch carrier in a witch hunt. Nico had expressed interest in her, and she'd responded by labeling him a murderer, setting the provincial police on him. Meanwhile, she was ducking text messages from another man, equally eligible and good-looking, while sitting in her apartment during her off-hours, drinking and smoking alone.

"Just look into him," Ferrari said.

Basso turned to Gatti. "What's Nico's phone number?"

Heaving a great sigh of frustration, Gatti pulled out his phone.

Ali blushed yet again, remembering Nico's card was still in her pocket, readily accessible. She handed it to Basso before Gatti could find his friend's contact information.

Basso took the card, memorized the number, and then studied Davide's cell phone records, sliding a finger down each page. "No calls or messages to or from this number."

"Just look into him," Ferrari repeated. "And make sure we're using the same discretion as—"

Three knocks on the door cut off the chief's train of thought.

Clarissa poked her head inside without waiting for an invitation. Her eyes were wide. "You have a call on line four."

"I'm in a meeting, Clarissa."

"It's an emergency, *signore*."

Ferrari huffed, then picked up the phone and poked a button. "Ferrari . . . *Sì*. We'll be right down."

He hung up and closed his eyes.

"What is it?" Costa asked.

"Salvatore Conti is dead."

18

"*Cazzo*, it's a frenzy," Basso said.

Chaos had descended upon Mickey's Bar. *Polizia* vehicles were parked and flashing along the road, which was now closed in both directions, and the dirt lot outside the building was barricaded. Nobody stood near the single vehicle parked there: a Volvo wagon Ali recognized as Salvatore Conti's.

Beyond the vehicle, at the edge of the lot, a blue tarp was spread across part of a shallow drainage ditch, weighted at the corners by rocks. Longo, Fontana, and another crime scene investigator were close by, stepping into their forensic suits.

Sergeant Rustica, the local officer who had assisted with Giuseppe Sala's arrest, noticed their arrival and headed over to them.

"Rustica," Costa said. "How are things?"

Rustica gazed at the tarp. "Could be better."

"Is that him?"

"*Sì*. We covered the area to keep his body safe from the

elements, and also to keep him out of sight from the press." Rustica lifted his chin toward the road, where a small crowd had gathered at the barricade. A television camera aimed in their direction as a reporter talked into a microphone, gesturing wildly.

"What happened?" Costa asked. "Tell me everything you know."

Rustica nodded. "At approximately 8:30 a.m., the owner of the bar called in. The place is closed on Tuesdays, but he said he was swinging by to get a jacket he forgot the night before. He noticed the vehicle in the parking lot, and then he noticed some birds congregating, making a ruckus. He went to investigate and discovered the body."

Ali glanced at the ditch and saw Longo's team had begun erecting a white tent around the area, blocking it from prying eyes and cameras.

"Did you check the plates on the vehicle?" Costa asked.

"*Sì*," Rustica said. "It's Salvatore Conti's."

Costa snapped on his gloves, then handed out pairs to Ali, Basso, and Gatti. "Where is the owner of the bar?"

"He's up by my cruiser."

"Good. We'll talk to him in a few minutes, okay?"

"I'll see you soon." Rustica strolled back to the road.

"Let's check out the vehicle first," Costa said. "Be careful where you step."

Ali looked at the ground and saw little detail to be gleaned from the dirt. It had been raining for hours, washing away most evidence. Tiny droplets pulsed on puddles with increasing frequency, telling her the storm's intensity was ramping up again.

They approached Salvatore's Volvo from behind, and

Costa strode directly to the driver's side. Ali tried the opposite tactic, circling the vehicle before choosing where to start. At the front bumper, she saw a pair of vague lines leading straight toward the ditch. From this angle, she could hardly make out the tarp.

"Do you see these marks?" She pointed down. "Looks like the body was dragged from here."

"I see them," Costa confirmed.

Ali walked to the front passenger door and peered inside. The rain-streaked window reflected her image until she got very close, almost pressing her face on the glass. She saw a newspaper sitting on the seat closest to her. Otherwise, everything was immaculate.

She moved to the rear passenger window. The back seats had been put down, making room for a pile of wire and wood. There were also some metal tools and a plastic toolbox. It seemed like Salvatore had been gathering materials to protect plants from rodents.

Costa opened the driver's door, so Ali tried the front passenger door. The cold metal button popped under her latex-covered thumb, and the door opened with a tiny squeal.

The newspaper she had spotted was a copy of yesterday's *Corriere della Sera*. It was folded neatly, prominently displaying the headline: *Murder at the Vineyard*. Ali had already read the sensational account of Davide Conti's vicious killing. The national story had upset her, so she could only imagine the angst and anger it must have stirred in Salvatore.

She checked under the newspaper, finding nothing, and then the glove compartment, finding registration paperwork, a parking permit, and some insurance cards. The only place left to look was under the seats and floor mats. She came up empty.

Kneeling to the ground, wetness seeping through her pants, she peeked under the car. The shiny screen of a phone captured her attention.

"Phone," she said. "On the ground near the inside of the front tire. Your side, Costa."

Costa got on all fours and retrieved it. "Battery seems dead. Could have been damaged by the rain."

Basso strode to him with an evidence bag held open. Costa dropped the phone inside.

Ali joined the men by the hatch as Gatti popped it open. The four of them conducted a thorough search of the back, yielding no obvious clues. With nothing else to check, they closed the doors and traveled the short distance to the ditch.

Salvatore Conti's body now lay uncovered beneath the white tent.

"*Madonna*," Basso murmured.

Yesterday, the man's skin had appeared deeply tanned from hours spent among the vines. Today, it was pale gray. Numerous tiny holes and lacerations covered his face. One eye stared up, the other looked like it had exploded out of its socket.

"Birds?" Costa asked.

Longo nodded.

The stench of death caught in her nostrils. Combined with the crisp scent of fresh rain, it reminded her of the Falco family boathouse after her father had cleaned fish. Only much worse.

Ali thought of her father's misshapen face. A high-pitched tone rang in her ears. She turned away from the body, feeling then that she had been holding her breath for some time.

"We found a phone," Costa told Longo. "Could be water damaged."

"We'll dry it out and see what we can do. Fontana! Take this phone."

Fontana rushed over, collecting the evidence bag from Costa.

Longo kneeled beside Salvatore's body and indicated his neck. Among the damage caused by the birds, there was an angry red mark and a bloodless cut. "Signs of strangulation."

"Looks like he was dragged from the car to this spot," Costa said. "Time of death?"

"Rigor mortis is strong, so within twelve to twenty-four hours, I'd say. We're not going to get a precise window since he's been out here all night. We'll see what the autopsy can give us."

Ali studied the ditch. It was a meter or so deep, and a steady stream of water ran through it, passing underneath and around Salvatore's body.

"What are you thinking, Falco?" Basso asked.

She glanced back at the bar. "It was difficult to see the body from the parking lot, but it was pretty easy when we got closer to the ditch. Why didn't the killer completely hide it? Or take it somewhere else?"

"He weighs a good two hundred pounds," Longo said. "Maybe it was all the killer could do, or would do, to get him here."

"True," she said.

"Longo, we'll leave you to it." Costa looked at Ali, Basso, and Gatti. "Let's go talk to the owner of this place."

The barista from Mickey's Bar was leaning against one of the police cruisers, smoking a cigarette. He watched them approach.

"My name is Lieutenant Costa. I hear you are one of the owners of this establishment."

"*Sì*. Vincenzo."

"Nice to meet you, Vincenzo."

They shook hands.

Costa tipped his head toward each of his three inspectors. "Basso. Gatti. Falco."

Vincenzo took a drag. "I've met Inspector Falco and Inspector Gatti."

Ali and Gatti nodded in acknowledgment.

"Good," Costa said. "Now, can you tell us in your own words what happened?"

Vincenzo pointed with his cigarette. "I came to get some things from inside. I locked back up. I went to my car. I noticed the Volvo, but I didn't think much of it. It was the same one that was here when I closed the bar last night."

"You saw it last night?"

"*Sì*. It was the only one left in the lot besides mine. It happens. People have too much to drink. They catch a ride with one another."

"That's when you were closing up?"

"*Sì*."

Ali's brow pinched in confusion. "I thought your brother-in-law, Pino Acquaviva, always closed."

Vincenzo shrugged. "We had to switch shifts. It is a rare thing, but it happens."

"What time did you kick everyone out?" Costa asked.

"Right around eleven. Normal closing time for a Monday. Maybe a few minutes earlier. It was slow last night."

"And was somebody sitting in the vehicle?"

"Not that I saw." Vincenzo shook his head emphatically. "I would have noticed that."

"And then this morning?"

Vincenzo took another long drag. "It was those crows that had me wondering. They were really making noise. One of them had a piece of something in its mouth. I really got scared, I tell you. It's like I knew what I was going to see before I saw it. And then, well, I walked up to the ditch and found his body. Then I called the police."

"*Grazie*," Costa said. "I know that must have been difficult to discover."

"*Sì*. I'll never forget what those crows were doing."

Costa let a moment pass before asking, "Did you know him well?"

"Salvatore?" Vincenzo shrugged again. "I knew who he was. More so now, what with his son's murder investigation."

"Did Salvatore come in last night?"

"*Sì*, he did. It was actually strange. He was waiting for somebody. But the person never came."

"How do you know he was waiting for somebody?" Basso asked. "Did he mention this?"

"No, it just seemed that way. I never spoke to him. Well, other than to take his order. Nobody did. I think we were all afraid. Didn't know what to say, you know? What with his son being murdered."

"I guess I don't blame you," Costa said.

For a few seconds, they stood in somber silence.

Basso broke it first. "What time did he come in? Do you remember?"

"I think it was around eight, eight thirty, but I couldn't tell you exactly."

"And you say nobody spoke with him?" Gatti asked.

"That's right. He arrived alone. He drank alone. He left alone."

"When was that?" Costa asked. "What time did he leave?"

"I don't remember the exact time, but I do remember he paid with a credit card, so I could tell you. I would need access to the register to find the receipt, though."

Costa nodded. "Getting that receipt would be very helpful. Falco, you can escort him. Rustica!"

"*Sì?*" Rustica asked, coming over.

"We need to give Vincenzo here access to his bar."

"Of course."

Rustica led them to the building, then unlocked the front door and handed the keys to Vincenzo. He waited on the porch as they went inside.

Vincenzo used his keys to open the register. After some searching, he handed Ali a receipt. "Here it is."

"*Grazie,*" she said, eyeing the paper in her hand. The signature read, *Salvatore Conti*, and the time stamp told her he had paid at 9:32 p.m. "He left immediately after paying? Or did he stick around?"

"He left right after paying."

She nodded. "Can I have this?"

"*Sì.* I have a copy."

"Great. *Grazie.*"

She pocketed the receipt and allowed Vincenzo to usher her outside. He locked the front door behind them, handing Rustica the keys as they made their way back to the group.

When they were close, Costa broke free from a conversation and met them halfway. "Did you get what we need?"

"*Sì, signore*," Ali said. "I have Salvatore Conti's receipt right here." She handed it to him.

"That's very helpful. *Grazie*, Vincenzo."

"*Prego*."

Costa looked at Rustica. "Could you escort Vincenzo to his vehicle, please?"

"Of course," Rustica said.

"You're free to go now, Vincenzo." Costa handed him a card. "Please call if you think of anything that can help us. We'll be in touch soon in case we need to talk some more, okay?"

"Okay." Vincenzo took the card. "I am happy to help however I can."

"*Grazie*."

Rustica and Vincenzo walked away, and Costa steered Ali back to Basso and Gatti.

When they were all together, Costa examined the receipt. "There's his name, and there's yesterday's date and time."

"He paid at 9:32 p.m. and left right after," Ali said. "He didn't stick around, according to Vincenzo."

"We found something in his pants pocket."

The inspectors turned at the unexpected voice. Longo stood behind them, holding a plastic evidence bag. Inside, there was a square piece of paper.

Costa took the bag from Longo's hands and put his face to the plastic. Once he'd seen enough, he passed it around.

The bag reached Ali, and she saw a single word written in blue pen. The ink was seeping off the waterlogged paper, collecting in beads at the bottom of the bag. She handed it to Basso.

"Monaco," he read aloud.

19

Ali walked by a man enjoying a cigarette outside headquarters and savored the scent of the second-hand smoke. After such a long, eventful morning, she had wanted a large lunch. Now, after satisfying her craving at the Egyptian kebab place down the road, she wanted an after-meal fix.

"*Ciao*," the man said, smiling, mistaking the ogling of his Marlboro for something else.

Ali gave no reply as she hurried into the building. Upstairs, she found Gatti's chair was empty. So was Basso's. Costa's door was closed.

She stopped at Clarissa's desk. "*Ciao*."

"The Conti girl is here," Clarissa said. "They're in Costa's office."

"Martina?"

"*Sì.*"

"What's happening?"

"I don't know. They've been talking to her for twenty minutes."

"Why didn't somebody call me?" Ali checked her phone and saw two missed calls: one from Basso, one from Gatti. "*Cacchio.*"

Flipping the switch to take her phone off silent mode, she rushed to Costa's office. The door opened before she could knock.

Martina Conti appeared on the other side. Fresh tears streamed from her red-rimmed eyes, down her face. Basso put a hand on her shoulder and escorted her out with quiet words.

Ali lowered her gaze, moving to let them pass. They walked by Clarissa's desk and disappeared into the stairwell.

"Get in here, Falco," Costa called.

She stepped inside. "I'm sorry I'm late."

Costa waved a dismissive hand. "Shut the door."

She did.

Sitting across from Costa, Ferrari nodded at her. She nodded back.

"Where have you been?" Costa asked.

"I'm sorry, s*ignore*. No excuse." After a brief silence, she asked, "What was Martina doing here?"

"Take a seat." Costa grabbed his mouse and began clicking.

Ali looked at Gatti, who stood against the back wall. He ignored her.

She took the chair next to Ferrari. The wood was still warm, and the air still smelled faintly of perfume.

"Martina came in when you left for lunch," Costa said as he typed. "After hearing about her father this morning, she discovered she had an important voicemail from last night."

The computer speakers hissed, and Costa tapped a key, turning up the volume as high as it could go.

Ali braced herself for loud dialogue to fill the room, but none came. Instead, there was a sudden blast of chaotic noises: a male grunt, more male grunts, sounds of struggling, sounds of scuffling, and then a loud crack.

The noises shifted to a lower register, like the fight had moved away from the phone. More violence came out of the speakers, including repeated groaning that sounded like a man being killed. Slowly, the groans became less angry and more desperate, like the man was giving up. Then they stopped.

"*Sì . . . Sì, sì . . .*" a man whispered. He said something else, but it was impossible to hear clearly.

A loud grunt, a long scraping sound, shuffling footsteps —all of it coming to a crescendo before dissipating into silence.

Ali said nothing, listening, waiting.

Costa grabbed his mouse and scrubbed the audio forward, skipping ahead several minutes. A few seconds ticked by, and then a car engine revved to life, sounding distant. It drove away, tires crackling as they passed the phone, fading into the static of the recording.

Costa closed the audio file and sat back.

"When did she get that voicemail?" Ali asked.

"Nine thirty-five last night. We checked the time stamp on her phone. She sent us this recording for further analysis."

She frowned. "Only three minutes after he paid."

Basso came into the room and looked around. "Did you just listen to it again?"

They nodded.

"Where were you?" he asked Ali.

"Eating. I'm sorry."

Basso went to the window and peered down at the parking lot. "Damn fine way for Martina to wake up this morning. Learning about her father's death, then discovering she has the act recorded on her phone? *Madonna*."

"She didn't hear this voicemail last night?" Ali asked.

"She did, but only the first few seconds," Costa said. "She didn't think anything of it. Apparently, her father often pocket-dialed her and left long messages of nothing. Only when she heard the news this morning did she realize what she had. That's why she came to us."

Ali nodded. "Did Salvatore tell her anything relevant before he died?"

"No. Their only other communication last night was a short text exchange. She told him that she was over at a friend's house. A woman named Gina. Said she was going to stay the night there and to not wait up."

"Who's Gina?" Ali asked.

"Gina Capriati. Martina's lifelong friend, so she told us. We'll look into her."

"And what did he say in return?"

Costa eyed a handwritten note on his desk. "Quote, 'Have a good time, Marti. I'm headed home right now. Love you.' And then he called a couple minutes later, at 9:35 p.m., and that's when he left this voicemail."

"What about his phone?" she asked. "Anything yet?"

"Longo is working on it," Basso said. "It's still waterlogged."

"What about the note in Salvatore's pocket? Did you ask her about that?"

Costa and Ferrari exchanged a look.

Basso shook his head. "She didn't know what that meant."

"Costa and I need to talk," Ferrari said. "Alone."

Ali, Basso, and Gatti left the office, shutting the door softly behind them.

"Answer your phone next time, Falco," Basso said, striding to his desk. He veered off toward the espresso machine before he got there.

Ali grimaced, then threw Gatti a glance. The man was smiling at her.

"What?" she asked.

"That voicemail was left at 9:35 p.m. last night."

"Yeah. So?"

"Don't you get it? That's right about the time Nico was chatting you up at the *ristorante*."

"So?"

"So, Nico couldn't have been killing Salvatore Conti while he was up here with you and me." Gatti raised an eyebrow. "I told you, he's a good guy. Now give yourself permission to accept his advances. If you need some help, I can call and let him know you're interested."

"How about I feed you your own *coglioni*?"

Gatti laughed.

"You two!" Basso barked, lowering an espresso from his lips. "Get away from that door and get back to work!"

20

Ali took the long way home from headquarters, craving movement after a day spent sitting in the car and then at her desk. She kept clear of Piazza del Campo, stopping for a few groceries at a small market before continuing to her apartment.

With another reason to dig into Enzo Monaco, his business, and the two women in his life, the mood in the office this afternoon had been one of preparing for a particularly intense battle. While Ali and Gatti had spent the last few hours combing every piece of information at their disposal, Ferrari and Costa had kept themselves locked in Costa's office to talk on the phone with the brass down in Rome.

Ali's gut told her that tomorrow was going to be big. She needed to make sure she was sharp and ready. So tonight, she planned to eat in, lay off her vices, sleep well—and forget about Marco Vinci.

All day, her mind had been drifting to his earlier text message. It was different, knowing he was in town. She kept asking herself the same things: Why had he come? Was he here for work? Or was he visiting just to see her?

Unfortunately, her questions would continue to go unanswered, because Marco had not responded after she'd denied his request. It seemed she might have given him the final brush-off. She felt hollow inside for it, and she wondered if he would answer if she called. Not that she should even try.

Her thoughts shifted to Nico Villa. *Back* to Nico Villa. Ever since Gatti's annoying yet accurate comment, Nico's charming smile had resumed looping in her mind. So often that she hadn't been able to resist looking into him a bit more during a short break this afternoon. Her favorite discovery had been an obscure fluff piece spotlighting Quattro Luci Farm.

According to the old *Corriere della Sera* article, Nico's mother had moved to America shortly after his fifteenth birthday, leaving him and his father alone to run the business. It was a small tidbit of information in a larger story about the farm's operations, but Ali had latched onto it, feeling warmth in her heart for the young, extremely handsome, available, and interested man. They had something in common. They both knew the pain of not having a mother.

In her pocket, the weight of the business card seemed to grow heavier.

She reached her apartment building, stopping at the gate and digging into her work backpack for the key.

"Ali."

She spun around, dumbstruck to be staring into the blue-green eyes that had haunted her dreams for months. "Marco."

"*Ciao.*"

She blinked, then turned back to the gate, putting her key into the slot and twisting. She pushed it open and paused before heading through.

Marco stepped into the light beaming down from the gate's arch, and she saw his face had a day's worth of stubble on it. His jawline was sharper than she remembered, almost gaunt.

"You look beautiful," he said.

She blew air from her nose. "What do you want, Marco?"

"Can I come up?"

"I don't think it's a good idea."

"I think it is. I think we need to talk."

Ali closed her eyes. "Fine."

Holding the gate open wide, she motioned Marco through. As he walked by, the scent of him registered in her brain, and the hurt inside her began to ache. Then the anger sparked.

She let the gate fall shut and marched ahead of him, up the stairs, past closed apartment doors swelling with the sounds of televisions and the scents of cooking food. She hurried as if she were alone, with no regard for the person following her, but Marco stayed close on her tail, catching the doors she threw open.

"Nice building," he said.

She ignored him. Reaching her unit, she slid her key into the lock and pushed inside.

"*Ciao*, Ali!" Isabella called from the hall.

"*Ciao*, Isabella."

"*Ciao, signore!*"

"*Buona sera*," Marco said, flashing an earnest smile.

The man looked good, Ali had to admit.

Suddenly, his expression dropped, and he lunged into the hall.

Ali rushed from her apartment, seeing Isabella sitting on the ground, as if she had fallen.

Marco kneeled beside her, cradling her back and shoulders. "Are you okay?"

"Oh. I think so. *Sì*."

Ali watched, frowning, noting the pitiful way Isabella grunted as she tried to rise to her feet. When had the spry older woman transformed into a helpless waif?

Marco took Isabella's hands and lifted her fast.

"Whoa," Isabella said, laughing. "Now I'm up!"

"Are you okay?"

Isabella patted and swiped her rear, exploring Marco's body with her eyes. "*Sì*. I'm just fine."

"Good. Are you okay to go back inside by yourself?" Marco asked, concentrating hard on the older woman's every move, searching for any sign of injury.

"That's not an invitation, Isabella," Ali said. "Don't worry, Marco. She's not hurt."

He turned to Ali, expression incredulous. Once his back was to Isabella, the older woman winked, kissing her fingertips and tossing them into the air. Her joyful disposition disappeared when Marco faced her again.

After helping Isabella into her living room, he returned to the hall. "That was close."

"Real close." Ali let him come inside her apartment, shutting the door behind him. "Take a seat if you want."

"*Grazie*."

She removed her coat and hung it on a hook.

Marco eyed the pictures she had on display, stepping

close to the one with her mother, father, and her standing on the beach in Liguria. "I remember this picture."

"Why are you here?" she asked.

"Right." He pulled a chair from her kitchen table, and when she made no move to sit, he pushed it back in. "It's really good to see you, Ali."

She said nothing.

"Listen, I'm sorry about avoiding your calls. I can see how it would be upsetting that I would do that, especially when you left such nice messages for me."

"Okay."

"No. It's not okay. I would be pissed off if I were you. I was just . . ." He looked down at the table between them. "It's just that I was trying to take it one day at a time, you know?"

Trying to take it one day at a time? She almost vomited, but again, she said nothing.

"I was in a bad place. A place, mentally and physically, that I couldn't get out of. I had complications with my injury. With the gunshot."

"Me too. With the gunshot to my shoulder. I'm still having them."

"Oh?" His eyebrows lifted. "I'm sorry to hear that. What's going on?"

She waved away his question. "It's nothing."

He nodded. "Well, my complications weren't nothing. They were awful. They involved my intestines. I had trouble being out in public for long stretches of time. Or, if I was out, I needed to know where bathrooms were." He blushed, looking down again.

The tension in her chest relaxed a bit, and she exhaled,

feeling a stab of sympathy for him. "I didn't know about that."

Marco shook his head. "Of course you didn't. I never told you."

"That's right. You never did. We never spoke."

"I didn't want to tell you about it. It was embarrassing."

"And now? How are you?"

"Much better. *Grazie.*"

"Good." She put her hands on her hips.

Marco sighed. "I was in the middle of those complications when you were calling. I listened to your messages, and I was so happy to hear your voice. I was so happy to hear the excitement for your new job. But I guess I was also just feeling sorry for myself with my career situation."

"What do you mean?"

"You know I wanted to be transferred down to Rome. Well, with Colombo and Dante gone, we had a whole shake-up of our division, and any prospect I had of being transferred disappeared. And that just made our chances . . . yours and mine . . . even more hopeless in my mind."

"Pointless, you mean?" Ali clarified, a hint of poison entering her voice.

"Hopeless."

"But you got out of your bad place," she said. "That's why you're down here?"

"I did."

"And your fiancée, what was her name again?"

"Valentina."

"She helped you through everything?"

Marco shook his head.

"Please don't spare my feelings. I saw the picture online

with you two. I know you are back together. Which is weird, since when I saw you in the hospital, she hadn't even come to visit." It was her turn to blush now. She had just admitted to stalking him online—and to being jealous.

He opened his mouth to respond, but she cut him off, asking, "What's this all about, Marco? I have a big case going on. It's my first big case, in fact. I've had a long day today, and I have another long day tomorrow."

"I read about it," Marco said. "It seems exciting."

Ali stared expectantly.

"Fine. I came to tell you I'm moving down to Rome, after all."

"With Valentina?"

"What? No. She and I were just . . ." He grimaced. "No, I'm moving alone."

She shrugged. "Oh."

Marco rubbed his jaw in frustration. "That picture you saw online was when we met for lunch one day. Nothing more."

"It looked like a good lunch."

"No, it wasn't a good lunch, Ali. Listen to me. She was upset about me breaking off the engagement. More than upset, actually. She was livid. She considered it a great embarrassment. A hit to her pride. So she told nobody. She pretended to her friends and family that everything was fine, that we were still together, and she was helping me heal. Then, when I was released from the hospital, she invited me to lunch. That picture was orchestrated to make it look like we were still happily together."

"Why?"

"Because she wanted to show the world we were in a good place just before *she* broke it off with *me*."

"That makes sense," Ali said, voice dripping with sarcasm.

"If you knew Valentina, you would think it makes perfect sense. She had to be the one to break it off, not me. So she found a way. She offered me a deal. In exchange for me going along with her plan, she pulled some strings with her father and got my transfer down to Rome."

"Okay."

"Ali, I'm trying to tell you I'm close. I'm trying to tell you I . . ."

"What? What are you trying to tell me?"

"I'm trying to tell you that I'd like to see you again."

"Oh. Okay. Well, you have my phone number. Maybe we'll chat. Take it one day at a time, you know?" Ali took delight in slinging his earlier words back at him. She walked to the door and opened it.

Marco stared at her long, then nodded. "I get it."

"Have a good night, Marco."

He strode past her. "Bye, Ali."

Ali shut the door behind him, securing the lock, and stood motionless. Marco did the same on the other side, his feet casting twin shadows under the door.

She glanced at the picture of her family. A tear fell from her eye, sliding down her cheek. When it hit the floor, Marco's shadows were gone.

21

"I'm telling you, go to Monte Vida. Say I sent you, and you'll get the best *fiorentina* you've ever had in your life."

"I've been there," Gatti said. "It was decent. But I prefer Pianone."

"Pianone." Basso scoffed. "The chef stirs the risotto with his cazzo."

Lowering the music, Basso eyed Ali in the rearview mirror. She eyed him back.

"What's your problem?" he asked.

"Excuse me?"

"You've been quiet the whole ride. What's wrong?"

"Nothing."

"It's not nothing. I know you. Something's wrong."

She looked at the castle looming above them. "Maybe it's the constant, pointless arguments about *calcio*, or about restaurant food, or about other *merda* nobody wants to listen to."

"That's not it. Tell me."

She shook her head, almost smiling despite her foul mood. "Nothing."

"Fine."

"Maybe she's sick of this drive," Gatti said. "How many days in a row are we going to come down here?"

Basso snorted. "It's impossible to get sick of this drive. It's too beautiful. And there are no clouds for once. It doesn't get any better than this in mid-November."

They crested the flat-topped hill, and Castello Monaco came into full view. It was teeming with activity today. People milled about on the vast lawn, enjoying the break in the weather, and streamed through the castle's southern entrance, coming and going from tours and the gift shop.

"We're supposed to park in the tourist lot and walk to the back of the property from the eastern side—the opposite of where we went last time," Basso said. "Let me do all the talking."

"As opposed to . . . ?" Gatti asked.

"As opposed to you opening your smart mouth and causing trouble. This is a delicate situation."

Gatti held up his hands.

Basso eyed Ali in the mirror again, then slowed the Citroën and turned into the large dirt parking lot designated for tourists. Vehicles choked the space, and it took them a moment to find a spot. As soon as the engine cut off, they got out.

Ali sucked in a deep breath. The air was crisp and cool, but without wind, the overhead sun made her sweat beneath her various layers.

"This way," Basso said.

They rounded the southeast corner of the castle,

following a gravel path, and came face to face with a man standing outside a small guardhouse. He wore a blank stare and a three-piece suit.

The inspectors flashed their badges, and Basso made a quip about being there for a special tour. The guard raised a radio, said something into it, then waved them past.

"*Madonna*," Basso said, gesturing to the east.

Ali put a hand up against the sun, looking toward the slope. Rows of grapevines furled out in all directions, terminating where the mountaintop cut downward. The land beyond overlapped itself in a sea of hills.

"I'm going to see if they have any extra rooms to rent," Basso said.

Gatti snorted. "I'm sure your family would love that."

They continued along the path, feet crunching on gravel, sounds of frenzied tourists vanishing into the background. Soon, the rear of the property opened up before them, revealing an enormous patio, half the size of a *calcio* field, threaded with sculpted marble and foliage. The entire area had been invisible from the approaching road.

"There they are," Basso said under his breath.

Up ahead, Enzo Monaco strolled toward them. His lawyer, Torrero, and muscular manservant, Girardo, trailed a dutiful step behind.

"Welcome back," Enzo said.

"*Grazie, signore.*" Basso offered a hand.

Gatti stepped up next, and then Enzo turned to greet Ali.

"*Buongiorno, signore,*" she said.

The man's eyes bore into her as they clutched hands. He squeezed a bit too hard, and her gaze flicked down in time to see him run a finger across the numb edge of her palm.

She pulled away, but Enzo let go at the same time, ensuring the entire interaction went unnoticed by Basso and Gatti. He flashed her an amused smile.

"Quite the property you have here, *signore*," Basso said.

"*Grazie*." Enzo inspected the view, interlacing his fingers behind his back.

Girardo hovered a few paces away, but Torrero remained close, watching them with the intensity of a father supervising his young daughter's first date.

"Where's Lieutenant Costa?" Enzo asked.

"He had another press conference and a number of meetings to attend."

"Ah, *sì*. I've seen the news."

"It's hard to miss. *Grazie* for agreeing to host us at this great property again."

"Cut to the chase," Torrero said.

"Nonsense." Enzo scowled at his lawyer, then looked back at Basso. "*Prego*. I would give you a personal tour of the oak rooms, but the public is here en masse today, and they'll be doing tours until this afternoon."

"Oh, I've seen the barrels," Basso said, laughing. "Many years ago, with my wife. We sampled a number of wines as well. That was before children, of course."

Enzo nodded, acknowledging the mirth without partaking. "What can I do to aid in your ever-complicating case, Inspector?"

Basso folded his arms. "I'm afraid we have to ask you some difficult questions, *signore*."

"Difficult?"

"*Sì*."

"Of course." Enzo pursed his lips. "I take it the papers are correct, then. You have no suspects, and you're grasping at straws. So, you would like to know what I was doing the night of Davide Conti's murder, and also the night of Salvatore Conti's."

Basso's expression turned sheepish. "That's exactly what we are hoping you can tell us."

Torrero stepped forward and whispered in Enzo's ear, blocking his mouth with his hand, leaking no sound. After a moment, he backed away.

Enzo's gaze slid to Ali, resting on her for a heartbeat before tracking back to Basso. He smiled curtly. "My lawyer says I do not have to tell you anything, but of course I have nothing to hide, so I'll tell you the simple truth of it: Davide Conti died last Thursday. I was home all night. As for Monday, when Salvatore was killed, I was here all night as well. I can have Torrero send over security footage of the interior of our home as proof. I'm sure there are plenty of clips of me grabbing one too many snacks from the refrigerator."

"Okay. That might be very helpful. *Grazie.*" Basso nodded at Enzo, then Torrero.

"What about the guardhouses?" Ali asked.

Basso stared at her, frowning deeply. She ignored him.

"What about them, Inspector . . . Falco, was it?" Enzo asked.

"Are the guardhouses constantly manned?" she asked. "Like the one we just walked past?"

"*Sì.* Twenty-four hours."

"And does every entrance to the castle have a guardhouse?"

"*Sì.*"

"Perfect. Corroborating witnesses—the guards—would be very helpful. Much better than just footage from the house, since that kind of thing can easily be doctored to show any time and date one might want to show. We'll have them verify the whereabouts of your family and close personal staff during each murder."

Basso's eyes widened in shock. Gatti cleared his throat.

Enzo smiled. "That's ambitious."

Ali looked at his feet. He wore a pair of brown leather dress shoes that matched a watch band on his wrist.

Enzo lifted one foot. "I heard you found a set of boot prints. Expensive brand."

"I don't think we told the newspapers about that."

"You didn't."

"Oh. You mean, you learned it from somebody on the inside."

Enzo kept his gaze locked on hers.

"In that case," she said, "you probably heard Salvatore had a note with your family's name written on it in his pocket."

"I have heard about that, sì."

"Well, maybe you could let us take a look at your shoe collection, then."

"Falco!" Basso snapped. He sent Enzo an apologetic smile. "I'm terribly sorry, signore."

"No," Enzo said. "That's okay. Inspector Falco is direct. I like that."

"I'm not sure I do," Torrero said. "I want—"

Enzo held up a hand, which served as an electric prod to his lawyer's vocal cords. "And what if I just so happen to have a pair of boots that just so happen to match the killer's?

What if we just so happen to wear the same size? I wouldn't want you thinking I had anything to do with the killings because of a coincidence."

Her eyes narrowed. "I've changed my mind, so you don't have to worry about that. Since you knew about all this beforehand, you've had ample time to get rid of the boots. A search of your closet would be pointless."

"Precisely," Enzo said.

Basso glanced between them. "Well, *signore*, I . . . look forward to receiving the security footage we were talking about."

Enzo shook his head. "Like Inspector Falco, I have changed my mind. Torrero will not be sending over any footage without a warrant. Good luck getting one."

"I see." Basso exhaled, glaring daggers at Ali.

"You may leave the way you came in. Girardo will show you out so you do not get lost."

Enzo walked away, Torrero on his heels.

22

Basso's driving was unnervingly subdued on the ride back, and he spoke sparingly, only to Gatti, always in a soft monotone. There was no eye contact in the rearview mirror.

Ali wondered what it would be like to return to desk duty. If she had a problem with it, perhaps she would get into teaching, or some artsy profession. She had once taken a pottery class and enjoyed it.

When Basso shut off the Citroën's engine in the head-quarters parking lot, he finally raised his voice loud enough for her to hear from the back seat. "Falco, stay here. Gatti, we'll see you inside."

Gatti nodded and got out, shutting the door behind him with little noise.

Basso released a weighty sigh, unclipped his seat belt, and turned to face her. "What in the hell was that back there?"

"I . . . I don't know, *signore.*"

"No, what you don't know is how much damage you've just done to your career."

She shrugged. "I was being direct. He told you himself that he didn't mind it."

"Shut up!" Spittle flew from his lips and hit the headrest in front of her.

Ali held her breath, bracing herself. She had seen Basso explode on others, but never her.

"I want to know what happened back there, Falco."

"He rubbed my hand."

Basso frowned. "Excuse me?"

"He rubbed my bad hand. And he looked at me with an amused glint in his eyes, just like Fabiano's father did when he came out of that meeting in Ferrari's office. You think I'm blind? That I don't see the writing on the wall? My days have always been numbered, Basso. From the moment I became an inspector, they have been looking for an excuse to get rid of me. Well, now they have it."

"That's not what's going on."

"At least now I know it's coming. I don't have to hold my breath. I don't have to sit on desk duty for a couple of months, watch my nerve damage fail to heal, and get dismissed when the doctors give up trying or when the Fabianos get their way. It's better like this."

Basso arched his eyebrows. "Do you really mean that, Ali?"

She closed her eyes and laid her head against the seat. She saw her mother and father looking at her with disappointment. "Are we done?"

Basso hesitated. "*Sì.*"

She opened the door and stepped out.

They walked to headquarters in silence. Basso outpaced her, not looking back, as if he didn't care whether she came or not. But she followed, anyway. She was a Falco, and Falcos never quit. Ferrari would have to fire her before she handed over her badge.

The third-floor squad room was empty. Ali didn't have time to wonder where everyone had gone, however, because Gatti leaned out of Ferrari's office and motioned them inside. She and Basso hurried to join the meeting, taking up position along the rear wall beside Gatti.

A man wearing a Carabinieri uniform sat with Costa in front of the desk. He had the insignia of a captain on his shoulder and looked to be in his fifties. His blond hair was combed close to his scalp, held firm by glossy product. She didn't recognize him from any of her previous encounters with the local Carabinieri station.

"Everyone," Ferrari said, "this is Captain Becker. He's with the Direzione Investigativa Antimafia of Florence."

The man with the German name nodded to each of them, revealing he had bright-blue eyes. Ali returned the gesture, curious to hear what he would tell them today.

"Nice to meet you all," Becker said in fluent Italian, no hint of an accent. It was a rare occasion when somebody with a non-native name spoke the language so well.

Ferrari pinned Ali with his stare. "Costa and I heard about your meeting with Enzo Monaco this morning."

Of course they had. Ali lifted her chin, feeling the pit in her stomach grow deeper.

"We'll discuss the specifics of that later. Right now, we

need to know what kind of Mafia activity we're dealing with in the area. At least, activity the DIA is aware of. That's what Captain Becker is here to tell us about this morning. Captain?"

Becker rose to his feet and turned around. His body was a hulking mass of muscle, standing two meters tall. He gave the inspectors a thin smile. "*Grazie*, Chief. I'll keep this as brief as possible for you. I know you have your hands full here with this investigation. I don't envy you."

He produced a presentation remote from a pocket, tiny in his big hands, and clicked a button. A flatscreen television, which had been brought in on a wheeled cart and pushed against the side wall, sparked to life. A photograph came onscreen, cast from the laptop that sat on the desk.

The image was gruesome, much like the ones Ali had seen in dramatic movies and during her training at the academy. There was a man lying in a field, shot dozens of times. An old Fiat 500 was parked haphazardly nearby. The driver's door was open, as if the man had stopped the vehicle during a high-speed chase and tried to run, only getting so far before being gunned down.

Becker clicked the remote again, revealing the body of a different man, who had also been shot multiple times. He lay in a ditch, face down. "These two killings happened here in Tuscany in the last five years. You may remember them. The first was near Lucca, the second just west of Siena."

Costa grunted.

Becker clicked to a third photograph. This one had been taken in a city. A scooter leaned up against a car, both doused in smeared streaks of red. A river of blood flowed out from under a sheet, which covered a body lying on the ground. A mass of civilians looked on from an overhead bridge as a crime scene team investigated.

"This killing was carried out by the Prima, which, as you probably know, is becoming one of the most influential, powerful, and brutal Mafia organizations operating in Italy, right behind the 'Ndrangheta. They are based in the south, but this killing took place up in Milan.

"The point being, the territory for Mafia violence has no tight borders. And the organizations are becoming more brazen, more brash. This Milan killing took place in broad daylight, perpetrated by a man who hit two innocent bystanders with his bullets."

Ali suddenly felt sick to her stomach. She had just gotten done standing toe to toe with Enzo Monaco, one of the richest men in Italy. If he was tied up in an organization like this, then she'd kicked the hornet's nest.

Ferrari cleared his throat. "What about Montalcino? What investigations are leading you there?"

Becker shrugged. "I can't tell you that information. It's classified."

"Do any of them involve Enzo Monaco, the financier and winemaker?" Costa asked. "Monaco Vineyards?"

Becker shook his head. "Nothing is leading in that direction, no. And I can tell you we have looked at him in the past due to his connections in the financial world. However, Mafia money laundering is largely done in the UK and other global markets, not local. There's always the possibility of corruption with global men like Enzo Monaco, though. We just didn't see it. And we have bigger, more obvious leads to chase."

"And the other name we sent you?" Ferrari asked. "Salvatore Conti? Does that name, or his business, Conti Vineyards, ring any alarms?"

Again, Becker shook his head. "I've never heard of him before."

"What about the Villa family?" Basso asked. "They own a farm. Quattro Luci."

Becker squinted in thought. "No. Anybody else?"

Silence descended on the room.

He shut his laptop and powered down the television. "I showed you these grisly images of the Mafia's latest activity to make a point very clear: the killings you are facing here don't fit the modus operandi for any of the organizations we're investigating. I read your reports. The Conti young man—his phone was taken, and the killer's boot prints were wiped away, correct?"

Ferrari nodded.

"And his father, killed two days ago—he was strangled, and his body was dragged away from his vehicle and deposited in a ditch. Why? To hide it from plain sight?" Becker folded his arms. "The Mafia don't care about stealing phones or mopping boot prints. They don't care about hiding bodies. They are confident and proud. It seems to me you're dealing with somebody who cares if they get caught. They seem to be protecting their identity, whereas the Mafia don't worry about that part of the game."

"*Grazie*, Captain," Ferrari said, standing.

"Good luck to you." Becker tucked his laptop into his bag and slung the straps over his shoulder. "Please don't hesitate to contact us for any further help."

"Of course." Ferrari escorted him to the door, saw him out, and returned a few minutes later. He moved slowly, sitting behind his desk with a grunt, as if the tense atmosphere in the room held crushing weight.

Gatti dared to speak first. "What progress have we made on Salvatore Conti?"

Costa retrieved a piece of paper from the desk. "We were able to dry out his phone, get the passcode from Martina, and see his recent activity. Salvatore made no calls that night, other than the one to his daughter at 9:35 p.m., when he was being killed."

"No other calls all day?" Ali asked.

"No."

"Text messages?"

"Just the one from Martina at 9:29 p.m. telling him she was at Gina's house and wouldn't be coming home that night. He texted her back at exactly 9:33 p.m., saying, 'Have a good time, Marti. I'm headed home right now. Love you.' It's not clear why he called her only two minutes later."

"So nothing new," Basso said, picking at the fabric of his pants.

"*Cazzo!*" Ferrari went to the window. "I want everyone out there investigating, not sitting here talking. And I want to know who our next suspect is by the end of the day."

"What about Enzo Monaco?" Ali asked. "Isn't he our next suspect?"

Ferrari chuckled softly. Dangerously.

"I don't see what's so funny," she said. "He had motive. His daughter was engaged to Davide. And he was playing cat and mouse with us today."

Basso and Gatti looked away, refusing to back her up.

"He knew about everything," she said. "Things that the newspapers don't know. He knew about the expensive boots that left the prints. He knew about the note we found in Salvatore's pocket with his name on it."

Ferrari turned around. "That's not saying anything about his involvement in these murders."

"It's not?"

"No, Falco, it's not. Let me explain to you how things work in this province. You're a little new, so I can understand it might not be clear yet. I get the information from you— from my inspectors—and I pass it up the chain to my superiors. My superiors give Enzo Monaco any and all information he wants to know."

"Well, that's not good," Ali said.

"But that's the way it is." Ferrari indicated the door. "Everyone out. Except for you, Falco."

Her insides felt like they were in freefall as Gatti, Basso, and Costa left the room.

"Sit."

She lowered onto a chair.

"Sometimes I talk to the higher-ups, and they talk to Enzo Monaco." Ferrari's voice was a low rumble. "Sometimes my inspectors talk to Enzo Monaco, and he talks to the higher-ups, and then they talk to me. You see how it is? He is a link in this chain. Just as much of a link as you or I. Do you understand?"

She nodded.

"And Giulio Fabiano? He's a link. And the mayor? There's another link."

"And Dimitri Fabiano?" she asked.

"*Sì.*" Ferrari wiped the top of his desk. "He's a link now, too, because he'll be taking your place in this investigation."

Ali had been expecting as much, but the news still soured her stomach.

"You're to come into work and sit at your desk for the time being, backing us up from headquarters as needed. There's still a lot to be done."

"Desk duty."

"That's right."

"And no firearm proficiency test?"

"No firearm proficiency test."

"Because of how I spoke to Enzo Monaco?"

"You're injured, Falco. And *sì*, because of how you spoke to Enzo Monaco."

"I don't understand. There's training. Fabiano just gets to waltz in off foot patrol and become an inspector without it?"

"Fabiano has been undergoing training in his off-time."

Ferrari might as well have reached across the desk and stabbed her in the chest.

"So he's been preparing to take my place. And now the time has come."

He said nothing, but the defeated look in his eyes told her everything.

She shook her head. "I can't believe this. You said you purged this building of the Fabianos. You said that."

Ferrari stared at her. "I know what I said. But I learned you can't purge somebody from a place they already own."

"Am I fired?"

"No."

"Am I going to be fired?"

"Go home, Falco. Come back tomorrow."

"Because if I'm going to be fired, I'd rather you just tell me now. If I'm—"

Ferrari slapped his desk, and the ferocity of the outburst shocked her upright.

"Please." He closed his eyes. "Go home for the rest of the day. When you come back tomorrow, you are on desk duty until you are healthy enough to return."

"*Sì, signore.*"

23

Ali climbed the final flight of stairs with a bottle of wine and a bag of groceries tucked under her left arm.

Isabella was outside her apartment door, sweeping the hallway. "Oh, *ciao*, Ali."

"Hi, Isabella."

"Who was the man last night?"

"I don't want to talk about it."

Ali fumbled with the keys in her pocket. When she managed to pull them out, her numb hand struggled to select the one to her apartment. She tried and failed until she lost her grip and dropped them.

"*Porca vacca,*" she said, bending over. The groceries shifted, and she barely kept hold of the bag.

"I've got it. I've got it." Isabella picked up the keys. "Which one?"

Ali pointed. "Where was that spryness last night?"

Isabella unlocked the door and handed back the keys. "I wanted to get a closer look at him."

"You're a dirty old woman."

"He's one of the good ones. I could tell. Strong. Smelled nice, too." Isabella followed her inside.

Ali put the groceries on the table. "*Grazie*, Isabella."

Isabella eyed the apartment, bending at the hip to see her bed around the corner. "Is he here?"

"What? No."

"Well, I hope we see him again soon."

"Bye, Isabella." She ushered the older woman out into the hall. "Have a good night."

"You too."

Ali shut the door with a sigh. Standing in a cloud of antique floral perfume, she unloaded the groceries, stocking half a shelf of her refrigerator with food she no longer wanted for dinner.

She shut the fridge and stared at the bottle of wine. After popping the cork and pouring a couple of fingers' worth into a glass, she donned her house clothes, grabbed a cigarette from her pack, and went out on the balcony to light it.

The sun had already dipped below the horizon, and the city hummed with the sounds of late rush hour. Purple shadows painted the valleys between the hills, whose tops glowed pink with the final rays of daylight.

Her phone vibrated in her pocket. She pulled it out and saw Clarissa's name lighting up the screen. Ali needed to talk to somebody, but not her. Not now.

She silenced the call, picturing Marco's expression when she had summarily kicked him out. The man had been pouring his heart out to her, and what had she done? Pushed him through the door, ignoring the pain in his eyes.

For the tenth time since, she thought about his story,

about the lengths he had gone to for a transfer down to Rome.

Taking a deep drag of her cigarette, she scrolled to his contact information and hovered her finger over his number.

A few seconds passed, and then she pressed the screen, bringing the phone to her ear.

She took another drag, steeling herself for the call. It rang four times, then five, and just when she was about to hang up, he answered.

"*Ciao.*"

"*Ciao,*" she said. "Um. It's me. Ali."

"*Sì.* I know."

"Listen, I'm glad you picked up. I just wanted to let you know that I'm sorry for the way I acted last night. I was . . . I was hurt from earlier. I mean, I guess I'm still hurt. So I probably wasn't listening to what you were saying with a clear head."

"Okay."

"And I just want you to know that I'm very happy you're moving to Rome. That's so exciting. It's your dream, and it's coming true."

"Okay."

"And . . ." She hesitated, registering his distracted tone. "Well . . . listen, if you're busy, we could talk later, maybe."

"Mar-co!" a woman called in the background.

"One moment . . . *Sì?* . . . No!" He cleared his throat. "Sorry, Ali. What were you saying?"

"Oh, nothing. I was . . . I was just saying you seem busy. We can talk later."

The woman spoke in the background again. Her voice was familiar, chiding.

"Ali . . . here . . . in Como."

"I can't hear you," Ali said. "You're breaking up."

He didn't respond.

"Talk to you later." She hung up, sucked in one last drag, then flicked the cigarette off the balcony and into the growing darkness. To herself, she said, "Bye, Ali."

Her phone chimed.

I'm sorry. I'm terribly busy. Moving some final things. I'll call you later, okay?

No problem, she responded, wondering about the woman in the background.

Not that she particularly cared. It was just that she had been hoping Marco was sitting in a lonely apartment, yearning for human connection. Like she was.

Ali pulled up Clarissa's name and typed a message.

Are you doing anything tonight?

Staring at the screen, she decided the response didn't matter either way. She needed to go out. There was no sense in moping when she had a choice.

She changed into a pair of jeans and a sweatshirt, put on her shoes, and left.

Wednesday evenings in Siena usually bustled with activity, the middle of the week bringing out the restless crowd, and tonight was no exception.

Ali paused in the courtyard, watching people stream past as she decided where she should go. She had a choice of three directions. All roads led to Piazza del Campo eventually, but she wasn't quite sure she was in the mood for that level of excitement right now.

As she exited the gate, emerging onto the cobblestone road, her phone chimed with a message from Clarissa.

I heard about today. I'm sorry. Sì, *we're headed out now. Do you want to get a drink with us?*

Where? Ali asked.

We're going to Il Rose. Want to come?

Ali knew the place. It was near the square, but not in it. *I'll be there.*

Okay. See you in twenty minutes.

Perfect.

And it was perfect. For once, she wanted to hear the raucous carousing of other people. It was better than listening to the depressing lamentations of her own mind.

Joining the flow of people, she decided she would take a little tour of the city until it was time to meet Clarissa. Before she got far, however, a man caught her eye. He stopped suddenly, and she realized she knew him well.

"Ali?"

"*Ciao.*"

"It's Nico. Remember me?"

She smiled. "*Sì*, of course."

The young man had proven impossible to forget over the last few days.

He was holding his phone in front of him, as if he'd been in the midst of messaging somebody. He shoved it in his pocket. "It's great to see you. What are you doing here?"

"I live here." She nodded toward her building.

"You're kidding."

"No."

"Here?"

"*Sì*. It's true."

"I live just up the road. Right off Via Domenico. This is amazing."

"Wow," she said, eyebrows lifting. "It is amazing."

"Well, what are you up to?"

She shrugged. "I was just on my way out."

"For a drink? I myself was just going out for a drink. Would you care to join me?"

Ali smiled at his directness and recalled the way he had left her last, telling her to think of him. If only he knew how much she'd been thinking about him—as a potential lover, as a potential murderer, and again as a potential lover—he might have run.

"Unless, of course, you already have plans."

"I'm actually hungry," she said, surprising herself. She couldn't believe she was accepting this man's invitation. "If we're going to have a drink, there has to be some food there."

His answering grin was brighter than the moon. "I'm ravenous, too. I know a great place that is somewhat nearby. My uncle owns it. It's called Vaporo. Have you heard of it?"

"No."

"It's small. Off the beaten path. But it's very good."

She nodded. "Okay."

"Okay."

Side by side, they began walking. Ali noticed he smelled nice.

"I can't believe I haven't seen you here before." His dark hair hung over an inquisitive eyebrow. "How long have you lived in that apartment?"

"Three years."

"Wow. Three years?" He chuckled. "I only bought my

apartment one year ago. But still. Maybe our schedules are just so that we miss each other."

"Maybe."

"Oh, if you'll excuse me, I have to send a quick message." He pulled out his phone.

"Canceling your other plans?" she teased.

"Something like that." He smiled sheepishly, pocketing his phone. "I was going to meet a friend. I just told him I have something else to do."

She blushed. "You didn't have to do that."

"I wanted to." He gave her a charming smile.

"So, Gatti tells me the investigation is slow and challenging."

She said nothing.

"You can't talk about it, though," he said. "Of course. I understand. This way."

They took a right onto a street with a row of brightly lit posts. She snuck a peek at Nico, catching him sneaking a peek at her, too.

"You look very nice," he said. "Were you already on your way out to meet some people? Or . . . ?"

She shrugged. "There's always the possibility you might see somebody you know in such a small town."

"Right."

They cut through a large group of people walking toward Piazza del Campo and continued north, heading into the heart of the city.

"You seem preoccupied," he said.

"I do?"

He nodded. "It must be hard to turn off your brain after work."

"You're right. It's not easy."

"It's easy for me. I feed pigs. I watch them roll in mud."
He laughed. "Then I do it again."

"Ah, *sì*, the pig farm. I've heard a little about you and
Quattro Luci since our last meeting."

He grimaced. "I know. I spoke to Gatti. I heard you've
been talking about me as a potential suspect."

Ali closed her eyes, tamping down her embarrassment.
"Glad to know Gatti is keeping his mouth shut."

"But I'm not a suspect now, right?"

She looked up at Nico. His facade had completely fallen
away, leaving behind a scared man instead of a confident
hunk. His eyebrows were arched with concern, and when he
visibly swallowed, she worried he might be sick to his
stomach.

"I told you, I feed pigs. That's what I do. I can't even
stand the thought of sending some of them off to die. They
have personalities, you know. When we send them to get
slaughtered . . . it's difficult. And to hurt a man?" He shuddered. "*Oddio*, I can't picture it."

They went quiet, turning their attention to navigating
the swarms of revelers filling the narrow side street.

"No need to worry," she said after a while, hoping to
comfort him. "You're in the clear. You have quite an alibi for
the other night, I must admit."

"When?"

"When you were chatting me up instead of sitting at the
table with your friends." She flashed him a smile.

"You mean, an alibi for Salvatore Conti's death?"

She sobered. "I think we should change the subject."

"Right. I'm sorry." He held up his hands. "Gatti told me I

was nosy, too. It's just that nothing this interesting has happened in this area in years. And you're right there in the thick of it, investigating. What a fun job it must be."

"It was."

"Was?"

"I've been put on desk duty for the time being."

"Oh no. What happened?"

She shook her head. "Long story."

"The life of an inspector. I imagine there are politics."

"There are, *sì*."

They fell into an easy silence, glancing at one another every so often, smiling. His hands were in his pockets, his pace leisurely. He gave off an air of comfort, of certainty.

"Do you know Bianca Monaco?" she asked suddenly.

He took the question in stride. "Of course. Everyone knows the Monacos. Why?"

She, too, wished to know why she had asked the question. Perhaps it was like he'd said, and the case was never far from her thoughts. Even if she'd been demoted.

"Is she somehow involved in the case?" he asked.

"Never mind. We really should change the subject now."

"Because she was dating Davide Conti? Is that why you're asking?"

Ali froze. "Who said she was dating Davide Conti?"

He stopped beside her. "Well . . . everyone knew that."

"Nobody knew that." She folded her arms. "They were dating in secret."

He shook his head. "I beg to differ. They were out with each other all the time."

They resumed walking, slower now.

"Who all knew?" she asked. "This is very important."

Shadows hid Nico's expression, but she could see him tilt his head in thought. "Every one of my friends in Montalcino. Davide's friends. I don't know. People."

"What about his little sister?"

"Martina? I think so. She'd have to be blind to have missed that."

A single lamp hung off the wall ahead. Ali stared at the cone of light shining down from it, questioning what the hell was going on. Had Luigi lied to their faces about him and Martina not knowing Davide and Bianca had been together? If so, why? Were they scared to admit they knew? Again, why?

"What about Enzo Monaco?" she asked.

"What about him?"

"Do you know him?"

"Everyone knows Enzo Monaco."

"What do you think about him?"

Their feet scratched on the cobblestone as Nico considered his answer.

"Enzo Monaco," he said, chuckling softly. "That man is . . . well . . . a *pezzo di merda*."

She laughed, cutting herself short as she realized he was dead serious. "And why do you say that?"

When Nico didn't respond, she looked up at him again. His face was still shrouded in shadows, but there was just enough light from the lamp to illuminate his eyes. The deep hatred she saw burning in them made her stumble.

His gaze slid to her, and she was alarmed by the way the hatred remained.

Ali lowered her head. A few steps later, she noticed he

was wearing a pair of shiny leather work boots. *Expensive* shiny leather work boots.

She checked over her shoulder, heart pounding, and saw they were well into a long straightaway. The alley had no windows, no service entrances to the businesses on either side. Another alley, located several meters ahead on the left, was her only chance at escape. Otherwise, she was trapped.

"What's the matter?" Nico asked.

"Nothing," she said, though something was definitely the matter.

She couldn't figure out why or how, but in that very instant, she knew she was walking next to a killer.

"You were looking at my boots," he said.

She kept her eyes down, barely hearing him over the blood rushing in her ears.

"I had to get new ones," he said. "The others had mud all over them."

On her next footfall, Ali twisted away and ran. But he was too quick, pulling her to the ground in a single fluid motion. One second she was upright, and the next she was on her back, the brightness of the alley lamp filling her vision.

"No!" she screamed, and then his hand was over her mouth and nose.

"Shhh," he said, pushing his weight into her torso. He wrapped his legs around hers and pinned her arms to the ground with his elbows, like he was an Olympic wrestler, and she was a child.

Rage flared inside her, and she jerked her legs up, kneeing him in the crotch.

He grunted, then seemed to double in density, sinking onto her even harder, forcing the breath from her chest. She gasped, panicking as his hand pressed tighter against her face, preventing fresh air from reaching her lungs.

Something sharp stung her neck.

Ali jerked again and again and again, but she was in a straitjacket.

Nico's eyes were shimmering pools of oil, wide with intensity, as he watched her fight. "Shhh. Shhh. Shhh."

A warm sensation radiated out from her neck, relaxing her limbs. It was as if peace itself had been injected into her bloodstream, filling her body and mind with tranquility.

A figure loomed large over Nico's shoulder.

With detached interest, she observed a pair of impossibly long legs, stilts that reached up into the stratosphere, attached to a being that looked down from the heavens.

There was a tearing sound. Nico removed his hand, and another hand slapped something over her mouth.

The being was a wizard, she decided. He had sealed her lips shut with a magic spell. She couldn't even slip her tongue past them. But there was no fear. There had been pain for a moment—she remembered hitting her head on the ground—but it was a distant memory, fading away without leaving a trace.

A moan slipped from her throat, muffled by the silent spell.

The wizard pulled her to her feet, and she felt dizzy, as if she were falling over. His hands wrapped around her like vines, keeping her stable and upright. Something snapped her hands together behind her back, and then she felt the same snap around her ankles.

Floating now, she peered up at the smattering of stars visible through a crease in the stone canyon above. She knew she had been made from those stars, crafted by them with intention, and so had these two men. They were under a spell of their own, one that filled them with palpable fear and made them handle her like an animal.

The stars disappeared, and then she was inside a dim box, being molded into position like a piece of clay. She felt only ecstasy.

"She needs another."

"I know. It's in the back seat."

Nico looked down at her, then glanced behind him. Eyes wide, he slammed the box shut.

The darkness was complete now, save a vague orange light streaming in through the crystalline wall above her.

She moved her lips, feeling a flat piece of tape across her mouth. That's what it was—tape. Not a magic spell, after all. Panic surged inside her, disappearing just as quickly.

The box jolted and swayed, and then a hand grabbed her arm. Something stung her neck again, spreading more warmth through her veins.

A song rose up, the rapturous notes of angels.

And then there was nothing.

24

"And I'd prefer you kept your opinions on the hush for at least the next couple weeks," Basso said. "Right now, you're here to observe. Got that?"

Inspector Fabiano nodded, though his attention seemed split.

Basso's eyes bounced between Fabiano and Gatti, who sat at their respective desks. They were both pointedly ignoring each other. Clearly, there was some kind of bad blood between them. That would have to change if they were going to be on the same squad together.

"Anyway, get comfortable at your new desk, Fabiano. And since you two are right next to each other, you might as well kiss and make up." Basso frowned. "Hey, where's Falco?"

No one responded.

"Gatti, I'm talking to you."

Gatti looked at him, upturning a hand.

"Use your words. Do you know where Falco is?"

"She hasn't been in yet, *signore*."

He checked his watch: 8:24 a.m. It wasn't like her to be late. It was more like her to be early. Then again, it wasn't like her to ignore calls, either, and yet she had missed two at lunch on Tuesday. Maybe something was wrong with her phone. He only hoped she hadn't gone out the night before and self-medicated on alcohol after being relegated to desk duty.

Sipping his espresso, Basso pointed at Gatti, and then at Fabiano. "I don't know what's going on between you two, but you're on the same team now. Got that?"

They remained silent.

"I said, got that?"

"*Sì, signore.*" Fabiano nodded.

"*Sì, signore,*" Gatti said.

Blowing air through his lips, Basso looked around. His gaze latched onto Clarissa, who was seated at her desk, typing on her computer. He could tell she had gone out the night before by her puffy eyes. He'd been young once, without kids, drinking in the bars and English pubs. Most women he knew could hold themselves to one or two drinks and call it, but Falco and Clarissa had the same gene he did, so one or two for them often became four or five.

He went to her desk. "Where's Falco?"

"I don't know."

"Is something wrong with her phone?"

"I don't know. I don't think so."

"Did you see her last night?"

Clarissa sat back, sighing. "She was supposed to meet us. She never showed up."

Basso walked away, pulling out his phone. He scrolled to Falco's number and dialed. It went to voicemail without ringing. He hung up, then shot her a text message asking her to call him, warning that she'd better not still be asleep.

Longo emerged from the stairwell and entered the squad room.

"What's happening?" Basso asked, gesturing at the folder under the forensic specialist's arm.

"I may have something interesting. I was going to tell Costa."

"You *may* have something interesting? Or you *do* have something interesting? I wouldn't knock unless you're dead sure about what you have in that little folder of yours."

Longo stared at him, then knocked on Costa's door.

"Come!" Costa called.

Basso followed Longo inside.

"I may have found something interesting," Longo said.

"What is it?" Costa looked exhausted, like he had spent the night sleeping upright in his desk chair.

Basso whistled, getting Gatti's and Fabiano's attention, then waved them inside.

"I have discovered an interesting anomaly in the mud we found at the crime scene." Longo opened the folder and splayed a pair of papers in front of Costa. Each was covered in jagged line graphs. "These are spectral signature plots. One for the mud from the bottom of our killer's boots, and one for the mud surrounding the Conti farm."

"And?" Costa picked up a paper and studied it.

Basso took the other, utterly confused by the numbers and accompanying jargon.

"As you may remember from that first morning at the Conti house, there were rather large boot prints found on the front porch. Well, more like mud smears."

"*Sì*," Costa said.

"Vineyards typically fertilize in the fall, generally after harvest, using commercially processed compost containing a variety of plant matter and animal manure. Many of these vineyards have a custom blend they use, making the soil on their land unique."

"And?" Costa twirled a hand.

"And the mud found on the front porch, in the smears left by the killer, doesn't exactly match the soil found on the Conti property."

"How is that even possible?" Basso asked. "He walked through the vineyard to get to the house."

"I said it doesn't *exactly* match. It mostly matches, but not identically." Longo folded his arms. "You see, when the killer stepped onto the porch, he shed the mud he had accumulated from the walk through the vineyard. But he also shed mud that he had accumulated from somewhere else. Somewhere he'd been before coming to Conti Vineyards."

"I see," Basso said.

Longo pointed at the different peaks in the graphs. "You can see the unknown mud has a higher ratio of manure to plant matter than the mud covering Conti Vineyards. The type of manure is completely different at that, having more sus, less bovine."

"Sus?" Basso asked.

"Pig," Longo said. "The unknown mud is heavily concentrated with pig manure. In fact, the bovine element seems to be missing."

"So it could be pure pig," Costa said.

Basso's eyes widened. "Remember that stench when we

were at the Sala house? It was coming from a pig farm. Rustica said as much."

Costa leaned back, bridging his fingers. "Whose farm?"

"I'm checking." Gatti approached the desk, staring at his phone, pinching and swiping the screen.

Basso scowled as a single name came to his mind. "Gatti, if you tell me that's the pig farm of your friend . . ."

Gatti lowered his phone. He looked stricken. "Quattro Luci Farm neighbors the Sala property to the west."

"Any other pig farms nearby?" Costa asked.

Gatti consulted his phone once more. "No. The second closest one is over ten kilometers away."

"Too far to smell, even with perfect wind," Longo said.

"Then the unknown mud most likely came from Quattro Luci Farm." Costa rubbed his jaw. "That makes Nico Villa's sudden interest in reconnecting with Gatti quite suspicious."

Gatti swallowed.

"I want you to think very carefully, Gatti," Costa said. "Was he talking to you about the case?"

Gatti shook his head. "No way he's the killer. He was there with us the night Salvatore Conti was killed. He couldn't have done it."

"Answer the question, Gatti."

Gatti frowned.

"Speak!"

"Okay, fine. He was asking about the case. But I told him I couldn't talk about it."

Basso stood up, prodded by a half-formed thought.

"What?" Costa asked.

Basso walked out of the office, striding quickly toward Falco's desk. He willed her bag to be sitting on the floor in its usual spot, but there was nothing there. He pulled out his phone and dialed. Again, the call went straight to voicemail.

What did that mean? Was her phone completely shut off?

He hurried to Clarissa's desk. She was speaking on the handset in a bored tone.

"Clarissa." He pressed the hook switch, ending her call.

"Hey—"

"I need to know what Falco told you last night. What did you speak about? What was the exact conversation?"

Clarissa looked like she wanted to protest, but she must have seen something in his expression that made her return the handset to its base.

"Let me check." She grabbed her phone, swiped, and held it out.

He read the messages.

Ali: *Are you doing anything tonight?*

Clarissa: *I heard about today. I'm sorry. Sì, we're headed out now. Do you want to get a drink with us?*

Ali: *Where?*

Clarissa: *We're going to Il Rose. Want to come?*

Ali: *I'll be there.*

Clarissa: *Okay. See you in twenty minutes.*

Ali: *Perfect.*

Clarissa: *You coming?*

Clarissa: *You're not coming, I guess.*

Clarissa had sent the final messages at 9:04 p.m., a little over an hour after Falco had last responded. They were still unanswered.

"She really never showed up," Basso said.

"That's what I told you earlier. She was supposed to come out with us."

"But she was the one who texted you first. She asked if you were going out."

"*Sì.*"

"I thought you meant she just never committed to meeting you. Why didn't you say she was missing?"

"Missing?"

"She didn't show up where you were going to meet last night, and she didn't come in this morning. Now she's not answering her phone."

Clarissa's mouth dropped open. "I . . . We were out with a man she kind of stood up on a blind date once. I figured she saw he was there and decided not to come inside the place."

"What man?"

"Francesco. A kid's dentist. Why?"

He waved a hand. "Did she ever mention a man named Nico to you?"

"Nico?"

"*Sì*, Nico!"

"No. Why?"

Basso turned to leave.

"What's going on?" Clarissa asked, sounding worried. "I'm calling her."

He stopped, waiting with bated breath as Clarissa put her phone to her ear. Immediately, she pulled it away.

"Straight to voicemail?"

"*Sì.*"

Basso strode back into Costa's office. Inside, a heated discussion was taking place between Costa and Longo.

"Something's off," he said.

They ignored him.

"Hey!" His shout silenced the room. "Something's off.

Falco's not answering her phone. More than that, it's going straight to voicemail. She was supposed to meet Clarissa last night out on the town, and she never showed up. Now she's not showing up to work."

Costa looked past him.

Clarissa was in the doorway, nodding.

"I don't like it," Basso said. He pointed at Gatti. "You said Nico Villa was hitting on her the other night."

Gatti shook his head.

Basso stepped up to him, gripping his shirt. "Look into my eyes and tell me you can vouch one hundred percent for this man."

Gatti shook his head again. "I cannot."

Basso let go. "We need to leave right now."

25

Ali opened her eyes.

For several seconds, she blinked, trying to focus the brilliant, amorphous colors that made up her vision.

Her mouth was sticky and dry, her tongue crackling as she moved it.

"She's up!"

The man's voice made her flinch. Footsteps led away, and then she was in silence.

A cloud of leather cradled her body, hot and sticky against her skin. Slowly, she attempted to sit up, falling to one side when her hands remained pinned behind her back. She tried again, using her core muscles this time, and managed to swing herself upright.

Vision swimming, she wobbled precariously. Her head and torso were heavy, and it took all her strength just to stay seated. After a minute, she gave in to her exhaustion and slumped into the leather cloud.

At the snap of a hypnotist's fingers, she was ripped from

her trance. Ali realized with a start that the leather cloud was a couch, and her hands were tied at her rear. Struggling to remember where she was and how she had gotten here, she scanned her surroundings.

The living room was large and eerily quiet. Matching end tables sat on either side of the couch, and a rug decorated the ceramic tile floor. A flat-screen television was mounted on the stucco wall amid hanging iron implements, paintings, and ceramic plates. The space was a mix of old Italy and new, furnished with taste and money.

Daylight streamed in through windows to her left. Beyond the glass, she saw the hilltop city of Montalcino in the far distance, recognizable by the clock tower poking up over an undulating landscape of plowed hills.

A strange noise came from outside. It sounded like the intermittent squealing of animals. She peered closer at the windows and caught sight of movement in her peripheral. Turning her head, she found more windows behind her. Several mud-covered animals ambled in and out of view behind the glass.

Pigs.

All the memories flooded back, latching into place, completing the puzzle in her mind. *Quattro Luci Farm.*

Heavy, thudding feet approached from a hallway to her right.

Ali uncoiled and sat straight, feeling for the first time that her pants were wet. Had she peed herself?

Her eyes landed on a pitcher of water and an empty glass. They were placed on an antique wood table in the dining room, which was connected to the living room via an open floor plan.

She ran her tongue across the dry inside of her mouth again. She was so thirsty.

Nico Villa came into the room, followed by an older man. They looked similar, and she recognized the older man from the other morning at the Contis': Nico's father.

"Rise and shine, beautiful," Nico said. The charm was gone from his voice. His smile appeared foreign, almost painful, like somebody had just told him his favorite pet had died and then said they were joking.

His father's face was blank. Clinical. When he looked at her, his eye contact made her shiver. "Ali Falco, are you there?"

She didn't respond.

"My name is Armando. I'm Nico's father." He turned to Nico. "Get her a glass of water and then give her 0.25 milliliters. Be exact. We don't want her passing out."

Nico sprang into action, pouring a glass of water and bringing it to her.

She wanted to turn away, to refuse anything from this crazy man, but her instincts forced her to open her mouth. The glass hit her teeth as she tilted her head. Water gushed down her throat. She controlled three gulps, then couldn't keep up and coughed, spraying liquid outward.

Nico jerked back. "Watch it, *troia*!"

He splashed the remaining water on her face.

Ali sank into the cushions, icy liquid running down her chest, across her thighs.

Nico's lips curled into a snarl, and he stepped forward, acting like he was going to hit her with the glass in his hand.

"Stop!" Armando yelled.

Nico froze, holding the glass high overhead. The predatory glaze in his eyes vanished as he lowered it and stepped away.

"Now give her the dose."

"Dose of what?" she asked. Her voice was deep, scratchy from disuse.

"Ketamine." Armando went to the windows and looked out. He had a handgun tucked into the back of his pants.

Nico unzipped a leather case on the dining table, taking out a syringe and a vial.

"That's too much," Armando said, watching his son fill the syringe. "Push some out."

"I know how to do it."

"We need her talking. Not dying."

"I know, old man."

They spat the words at each other like they were mortal enemies.

Nico flicked the syringe and walked to her. She recoiled, but there was no stopping him. His movements were too fast, hers too slow. Hooking his fingers into the neck of her sweater, he pulled it down to expose her shoulder and jabbed the needle close to her surgical scars.

Ali winced at the pain, but only for a moment. The drug took immediate effect. Warm, familiar ecstasy flooded every cell of her body.

"There you go, sweetheart," Nico said, smiling again.

In this new state, Ali saw the disease inside his mind, knew the soul trapped within him was kicking to get out of such a toxic shell.

She collapsed into the soft cushions, examining Armando. The older man had the same affliction. She could see it in his eyes. Both father and son were under the control of an alien parasite, one that she needed to be respectful of if she wanted to get out alive.

Ali understood she was in mortal danger. These men were murderers, and they wouldn't hesitate to kill her, to destroy the evidence of her existence in the digestive tracts of the animals outside. But the cold logic didn't bother her in the least. The drug had made her a spectator.

Armando moved in front of her, snapping his fingers.

She looked at him.

"What do the *polizia* know?" he asked. "Who are your suspects?"

She said nothing.

"You'll have to tell us, or we'll simply kill you. If you tell us, we'll let you live. It's as simple as that."

"I don't believe you," she said. Her voice sounded kilometers away, but also everywhere at once.

"She's out of it." Armando glared at his son. "How much did you give her?"

"Only 0.25, like you said!"

"Okay. Okay." Armando held up a hand, then dragged a wood chair from the dining table and sat down in front of the couch. "You were looking into Enzo Monaco, right?"

Ali nodded. She knew she was supposed to fear dying, but she wasn't afraid. She decided to respect her feeling of calm, understanding that cooperation would give her the best odds of survival.

But why should she bother? Who cared if she lived or died?

The thought came as a small shock. And then Marco flashed in her mind, pleading to her, his hand outstretched.

Marco. There was a goal. She had to get back to Marco. He

cared about her. He had come over. He had apologized for what he had done.

Armando snapped his fingers. His hand was centimeters from her face. "*Ciao*?"

"*Sì*," she said.

"What do the *polizia* know? Speak to me, or we'll have to kill you, Ali." His voice was matter of fact. A boss talking to an underperforming employee.

"We're looking into the Monacos, but we're afraid to get too close. He's too powerful."

"Do they know about Nico and Bianca?"

"Nico?" she asked. "He was dating her? When?"

Nico's gaze turned distant, and his mouth moved silently, like he was saying a curse under his breath.

"They weren't dating." Armando glanced at his son. "She wouldn't accept his advances."

Ali shrugged. "Once we get her cell records, we'll see as much."

"I doubt it. Their last messages were six months ago."

She wanted to argue, but he was right. They would never dig back six months into Bianca Monaco's cell phone records.

"Nico killed Davide because he was jealous," she said.

Armando chuckled. "Jealous is a soft word for the emotion my son was feeling about their relationship. I'm sure Bianca will turn up dead soon." Lowering his voice to a volume meant just for her, he added, "If I don't do something about it."

He stood up and walked away.

Ali blinked. "What are you going to do about it?"

"I'll show you both what I'm going to do," he said. "Nico

did a good job of bringing you in, but now there's more that needs to be done. Nico, you have to do exactly as I say."

Nico scowled at his father. "Do what? We already brought her here. She doesn't know anything. Let's just kill her and feed her to the pigs before the *polizia* come sniffing around."

"That's not good enough." Armando studied his son. "Do you remember when we used to play chess?"

Nico nodded, expression curdling like he wasn't very fond of the memories.

"I am thinking many moves ahead here. I told you how to pick her up by her apartment. I told you the perfect place we could park the car. I told you exactly how we would get her out here without making a scene. So, do you trust me?"

"*Sì*," Nico said.

Armando's gaze came to rest somewhere behind her. "Cut the zip tie on her wrists."

"What if she tries something?"

"Then you'll stop her."

Nico shook his head. "Fine, grand master."

He removed a foldout knife from his pocket, rounded the couch to stand behind Ali, and pushed her forward. "Don't try anything, *troia*."

She felt his large, strong hand wrench up her arms and knew that without the drug, the pain in her shoulder would be unbearable. When the pressure released, her hands fell apart. She brought them around to her lap, enjoying the smooth, silken quality of her skin as she rubbed her palms against one another.

The numbness of her right hand was almost complete. She used her left to straighten the curled fingers, then let go and watched as they pulled back into a shape that reminded her of a sloth's claw.

She eyed Armando. "They'll be looking for me. I was supposed to be at work first thing in the morning."

"That's good," he said. "Nico, go get some rope to tie her wrists in front of her."

"She's right," Nico said. "They'll be looking for her. And I just cut the zip tie. What do you need rope for?"

"Get it, please, son." Armando's voice was pure menace. The parasite was angry.

Nico left the room.

"Stay where you are, or I'll shoot you." Armando turned again to the windows, folding his arms in front of him.

A minute later, Nico returned with a length of rope. "Is this good?"

"Perfect. Tie her hands in front of her."

He came over. "Put your hands up and your wrists together. Like this."

Ali stared at him, thinking about her self-defense classes, evaluating what moves she would need to subdue him and Armando, who now stood a good ten paces away. Then she remembered her ankles were still bound. There was no getting out of this with force.

Putting her wrists together, she watched Nico wrap them. When he finished, she tried to ball her hands into fists. She could only make one. Her right hand was not moving correctly.

"What are you doing?" he asked.

"I have nerve damage. I can't move my right hand."

He tugged the rope tighter, clearly not concerned by her affliction.

A tiny voice told her to keep her wrists spaced ever so slightly apart.

"Ah," she hissed, baring her teeth in mock pain.

"*Cazzata*," Nico said. "You can't feel anything."

"Make sure it's tight," Armando ordered.

Nico cinched Ali's wrists completely, squashing the miniscule space she'd fought for to nothing.

26

"Where are they?" Basso yelled into his radio.

"They're on their way," Costa said, voice scratching out of the radio speaker. "They'll meet us at the farm. You need to slow down."

"With all due respect, *signore*, you need to speed up."

In the rearview, Costa's vehicle trailed at least a half kilometer behind on the two-lane road.

Basso swerved around another car, not waiting for it to pull over. Fabiano gripped the edges of his seat, eyes locked on the windshield. His face was pale.

"Armando Villa has created a renowned brand of international products," Costa said. "Many of which can be found in the pantries of dignitaries across the world."

"So what?"

"Must I remind you again that we have no proof that the Villas are involved in this at all? We are not driving in there at a hundred kilometers per hour with guns blazing."

He shook his head. "That's not what I want, either. We need to plan this out and act carefully."

"Agreed."

He thought for a moment. "Has Gatti been to the farm before?"

"Negative," Costa said.

"I have."

Basso looked at Fabiano in surprise.

"Watch out!" Fabiano pointed.

Dropping the radio, Basso swerved to meet the upcoming turn. They were going too fast for the curve, so he let off the gas and pumped the brakes, sending them into a skid. Quickly, he corrected, and they fishtailed back into the center of the lane. A vehicle going the opposite direction passed by, flashing their headlights.

"Can we slow down?" Fabiano asked.

"No, we can't slow down. If you ask me that again, I'll throw you out of the vehicle. You say you've been there?"

Fabiano nodded, swallowing, still preoccupied with the road ahead.

"And? What is it like?"

"I don't know. It's been a while. Things might have changed."

"Well, what's the road into the property like?"

"There's a driveway. It's very long, a couple of kilometers. A hill blocks your view of the farm most of the time because it sits down in a valley. There's a river that runs behind it."

"What else?"

"There are trees that line the river."

"Enough to provide cover if we want to get a good look at the property?"

"I think so. I don't know . . . It's been years." Fabiano scratched his head. "But . . . I'm pretty sure."

"*Cazzo*," Basso said, reaching for the fallen radio.

"Slow. Slow!"

Basso rolled his eyes but slowed down anyway, rounding the next turn easily, keeping between the lines as he lifted the radio to his mouth. "Okay. Fabiano has been to the farm. He remembers a river passing behind the—"

"Can I please talk and you drive?" Fabiano interrupted, holding out his palm.

Basso handed over the radio, and Fabiano relayed the information to Costa.

"Okay," Costa said. "We'll follow your lead. Rustica and Umberto are close now."

"Copy."

"How many more minutes?" Basso asked Fabiano.

The kid had his eyes closed, his hands still clutching the seat on either side of him.

"Fabiano!"

"Sorry." He read the dashboard touch screen. "Five minutes before we turn."

"Keep your eyes open, then."

Fabiano nodded.

"I'm counting on you," Basso said. "Don't you dare let us down."

Fabiano ignored him, his lips moving silently, his hand crossing his chest.

27

The old man was staring outside, watching a smattering of leaves tumble past the window, blowing on the wind. His eyes were telegraphing terrible messages about the things he had in store for them, and the fear twisting Nico's face was palpable. Still, Ali felt only peace.

Armando swiveled, pointing behind her. "Take that plate off the wall and shatter it on the floor."

"What?"

"Just do it, son."

Nico mumbled to himself as he once again walked behind Ali's couch.

She turned to see him pull a plate from the wall. He looked at it front and back, then slammed it into the ground. A cacophony shattered the air—a crash followed by a dozen ceramic pieces ringing at different notes as they tumbled across the floor.

"Good." Armando came over and examined the splayed shards. He ducked down, out of sight, and then straightened, holding one carefully in his hand. "This is perfect."

Ali and Nico watched Armando round the couch. The old man's demeanor had changed. She could see he was about to act, and she predicted that whatever happened next would be a surprise to both her and his son.

Terror reached her brain for the first time since the shot of ketamine. A whooshing sound snuffed out all other noise as her heart pounded in her chest.

"What are you doing?" she asked.

Nico hovered close by to observe. His father stopped in front of her.

Ali eyed the jagged edges of the ceramic shard in Armando's hand, and her self-preservation instincts began to kick in. If she could get the shard, she could cut him across the carotid. Then, if she could reach the gun tucked in his pants, she'd really have a fighting chance.

Her muscles began coiling, preparing for action.

Armando smiled at her. "It's wearing off. Grab her from behind. Keep her still."

Nico hurried to comply, clamping his hands on her shoulders, pulling her into the cushions.

Armando bent forward, grabbing the rope around her wrists with his powerful grip. She kicked up her legs in protest, and he put an end to her leverage by sitting on her lap, sagging his full weight down.

"*Vaffanculo!*" she screamed, thrashing at the sudden horror of imminent death.

But Armando just stood up and released her hands.

"What did you do?" Nico asked.

"Let her go and come around here," Armando said.

Out of breath, Ali looked at the rope and saw a section had been cut. She wrestled her hands back and forth and found the binding remained tight. However, with some more movement, she estimated she could pull free, eventually.

"What the hell are you doing?" Nico asked his father, staring down at Ali. "She'll get free."

Armando waved a hand toward her. "I made it look like she's been cutting through the rope. Now give me your gun. I have to make it look like she was shooting at us with it."

Nico frowned.

"Son." Armando held out his hand. "Give me the gun."

Nico pulled a pistol from his pants and passed it to his father.

Armando dropped it into the pocket of his jacket. "Okay. Go on. Take a look. Make sure it seems like she was cutting through."

Nico seized her wrists and glared at the rope, eyes filled with disgust. "So what? Why?"

Armando put the piece of ceramic to his son's neck and swiped sideways. There was a swish of fabric, a soft nicking sound, and then Nico was holding his throat, eyes bulging wide as blood sprayed onto Ali's lap.

"Gah!" He turned around to face his father, making sickening gurgling sounds.

Armando flung the shard to the floor and pulled his gun, taking aim as he backed away.

Nico stumbled forward, one hand clutched against his wound, the other reaching out. His eyes were wild with confusion, fear, and betrayal.

Armando put the table between himself and his dying son, gun held at the ready.

Nico lunged to one side, trying to catch his father as wet coughs racked his frame, but Armando shuffled just out of reach, and Nico collided with a chair. He fell, slamming into the wall before landing on the floor.

Ali watched in horrified fascination as he convulsed, blood pulsing out from under his pressed fingers. He rolled onto his back and let out a wailing moan. Then his hand flopped to the ground, and she saw the light leave his eyes at the exact moment of his death.

Time stood still as she and Armando looked down at Nico's freshly dead body.

"Don't worry," Armando said, breaking the silence. "It will be easier for you."

Ali realized she'd been holding her breath. She sucked in through her nose, smelling the metallic stench of blood. A lake of crimson had spread out from under Nico, enveloping the chair's feet, and her lap was warm with the glistening gore that had sprayed across her.

"What the hell are you doing?" she asked.

"I'm removing the problem."

28

Basso pressed the binoculars to his face, and the property bobbed into view. He identified the main farmhouse nestled at the bottom of the valley. Behind it sat a large barn surrounded by pig enclosures. The animals moved inside a maze of fencing, eating and frolicking.

"You see anything?" Costa asked. He was kneeling next to Basso, pressing his own set of binoculars to his eyes.

Basso dialed up the magnification to the maximum level, focusing on the farmhouse's windows. All he could see were bright reflections of the outside world.

"Not yet," he said, shifting to examine the two vehicles parked out front. He recognized one of them as the Range Rover they'd seen outside the Contis' place. The other was a wagon-type hatchback.

Basso scanned the farmhouse again. This time, he caught movement in the window—a man standing, looking out, barely visible behind the reflections.

"Wait. In the front windows. Do you see it?"

"What? No. Where?"

The man turned, and metal glinted in his hand. He disappeared inside.

Basso frowned. "I think I saw a gun."

"I don't see anything."

"He moved away from the window."

They stared through their lenses, but there was no more movement.

Costa grunted, lowering his binoculars and getting to his feet.

"Careful," Basso said. "Stay down."

Costa scoffed, waving a hand as he strode downhill toward their parked vehicles.

Basso scurried after him, keeping low until they were out of sight of the farmhouse.

"*Cacchio*," Costa cursed, stumbling on a huge chunk of tan earth that had been tilled from the field they were traveling through.

"What's the plan?" Basso asked.

"We drive in. We knock on the door. And we have a conversation with them. That's our plan."

"He had a gun. I swear I saw it."

Costa stopped and looked at him. "I didn't see it. And I was watching the same windows."

"Maybe you need to have your eyes checked."

Costa's expression cooled. He continued walking.

Basso followed in silence. Maybe he had been seeing things. Maybe the man had been holding something else in his hand. A television remote, perhaps.

But he had called Falco a thousand times on the way down, and each and every time, her phone had gone straight to voicemail. That had never happened once in their six-year history together. Something was off, and Costa wasn't respecting that enough.

Basso spat on the ground. Normally, he didn't mind the smell of agricultural activity. It was simply part of life in the country. Today, however, the pungent odor of pig manure coming over the hill disgusted him.

They arrived at their vehicles, and Basso scowled at the *polizia* cruiser that had joined them at the property. If they descended into the valley with that thing, the blue-and-white paint job would be like a neon sign announcing their presence.

"Anything?" Gatti asked. He and Fabiano stood next to Rustica and Umberto.

"Nothing," Costa said. "So we're going in. Slowly, like nothing is out of the ordinary. Because nothing is out of the ordinary. We go knock on the door, and we talk to them."

Basso shook his head. "I don't like it."

The rumble of an engine pulled their attention up the road. A vehicle was approaching, kicking up a plume of dust in its wake.

"Wait," Basso said. "Who is this?"

The old Toyota pickup truck slowed as it drew closer. There was a sticker, or a magnetic sign, stuck to the side of it. The logo read, *Quattro Luci Farm*.

Basso stepped into the driveway, putting his hand out.

The truck stopped.

One hand on his Beretta, he went to the driver's lowered window. "*Polizia*. Who are you?"

The man had both hands on the wheel, and his face was twisted in confusion. "My name is Ricco."

"Ricco, you work here?"

"Sì."

"Is there a woman inside that house?"

"What house?"

"Don't play stupid with me. The house! The Villas' house down there."

The man's eyes widened. "I don't know. I haven't been there yet today. I'm just going in to speak to *Signor* Villa— Armando Villa. He's the owner."

"We know that. What are you talking to him about?"

"About work. About my hours next week."

Basso read Ricco's face and decided the man was telling the truth. "Ricco, I need you to give me your cell phone."

"Basso," Costa warned. He was standing nearby, watching.

"Why?" Ricco asked.

"Do it!"

The man reached over to the front passenger seat, picked up his phone, and handed it to Basso. "What's happening?"

Basso pocketed the phone, then opened the door. "Get out."

29

"I don't understand how you're fixing anything," Ali said. "By killing your own son?"

Talking seemed like her way out now. She had to distract him. She had to delay the inevitable.

Armando edged toward Nico's body. "It's simple. I put the gun in his hand, I aim, and I shoot you. He was the one who kidnapped you last night. He was the one who drugged you and brought you here." He shrugged. "We have another living quarters up above the barn. That's where I often spend my time. I had no idea any of this was happening until it was too late. He walked in on you cutting yourself free with the piece of ceramic plate. You sliced his neck. He shot you with his gun before he died."

Her adrenaline spiked, burning off even more of the pleasant feelings the ketamine had given her, unveiling the heavy dread she harbored underneath. And then she realized something.

"No. Wait," she said. "You're not thinking this through."

Armando scoffed. "I've been living with this problem for

years. Cleaning up all his messes. Believe me, Inspector. I've thought this through."

"But you killed Salvatore Conti."

He paid no mind to the accusation, sidestepping the pool of blood under his son, assessing how to best stage her death.

Ali had a point to make, but thoughts failed to form in her sluggish brain. She slid forward on the couch and saw the ceramic shard lying in three pieces by her feet. "It was you, right? You killed him. It had to be you."

He pulled the gun from his jacket pocket. Nico's gun. "*Sì*, it was me. He came by here the other night asking too many questions."

"What kind of questions?"

He shook his head, eyeing her.

"Please. I want to know."

"Okay, inspector Falco." Armando smiled pitifully. "You must solve the case before you die? Fine. Salvatore was distraught about a memory and came over to discuss it. Apparently, months ago, Davide had told him in passing that my Nico had been infatuated with Bianca Monaco—that it was the big news around town that the pig farmer was going after the princess in the castle and was getting nowhere fast. At the time it had meant nothing to Salvatore, but this recollection about my son was apparently jarred loose when you detectives went over the other day and told him Davide and Bianca had been together when Davide was killed. Salvatore was doing the math—That Nico was still infatuated, and still jealous, and that he may have killed Davide."

"Salvatore came to talk to you here?" she asked. "I don't get it. Why did you kill him at Mickey's Bar? Why not here?"

He shook his head impatiently. "I would have killed him right here, but I had too many employees around. So I drove after him, and followed him to Mickey's Bar. I waited while he was inside, and then when he came out into the parking lot, I took action. With the people walking in and out of the place, it was too risky to load him into my car. So I pulled him to the ditch and left him out of sight." Armando blinked out of his memory. "Before I left, I put a note in his pocket that read 'Monaco' for misdirection. I had heard suspicions were raised about the Monacos."

"And Davide? Was that you who killed him? Or Nico?"

"Nico."

She kept talking. "He stole the gun from Giuseppe Sala's workshop, returning it after the kill, leaving one of the spent shells with Giuseppe's fingerprints on it to throw us off. He wiped his boot prints. The evidence pointed to Giuseppe, and no one else."

"I wish." Armando scoffed. "Nico came home upset that night. I knew he'd done something, and I made him tell me everything. And then I made him return to his mess and clean it up. By dumb luck he'd left the spent shell inside that kitchen. But he'd left his boot prints everywhere. He still had the gun in his car! I told him to go back and wipe the boot prints. I told him to return the weapon back to Sala's workshop. My son isn't...*wasn't* clever enough to think of all those details. He couldn't see past the anger. If it weren't for me, he'd already be rotting in a jail cell."

"And then there's me," she said. "Why am I here? Why not just leave me alone? Why the hell did you take me?"

Armando's head tilted towards his dead son, but he kept his eyes on her. "I killed Salvatore because I thought there was a chance to resolve everything. But you and I know, sooner or later, somebody was going to get smart, and things were going to point to Nico."

Armando looked at his son's body. "He had been talking about you, you know—Ali Falco, the pretty inspector on the case. Believe me, it wasn't going to end well for you either way. I simply took the pieces left on the board and came up with a way to protect my legacy." He shrugged. "So here you are."

"Your legacy is lying there with a slit neck."

"He's not my legacy." Armando knelt over his son, measuring angles.

"So . . . you . . ." She searched for words. "The farm is? But now you have nobody to pass it down to."

"Nico was never going to get the empire," he said absently. "I always knew his activities would catch up to him at some point."

"Are you saying he's killed before?"

"When Nico loved a woman, he proved, twice now, that he would do anything to keep the competition at bay."

"Who's the second man he killed?"

He raised Nico's gun and aimed at her head.

"Tell me," Ali begged, voice strained with desperation. She would take every opportunity to prevent the inevitable from marching forward. "Please. Tell me."

The gun lowered. Slowly.

Armando's eyes glazed over. "He killed a man, an employee of mine, who was screwing my wife. He killed him with an axe. Davide got off easy, compared to what this man got."

"*Madonna,*" she whispered, goosebumps rising on her arms.

"*Sì.*"

"That's why Nico's mother, your wife, moved to America?"

Armando laughed, and then his expression went dead serious. "That's why I took that same axe, chopped her into pieces, and fed her to the pigs. So she and her lover could be together forever."

He raised the gun and aimed at her again—right as the point she'd been trying to make finally came into focus.

"But you screwed up." Ali stared past the barrel of the gun, meeting his gaze. "Nico was out in Siena at the exact time you killed Salvatore Conti."

Armando's eyes flashed. The aim wavered.

"Salvatore was calling his daughter when you attacked him. You left the phone. We found it kicked under the car. It was all caught on voicemail. And the time stamp was 9:35 p.m., which happens to be the same time I was up in Siena, talking to your son. My fellow inspector was there, too. He's friends with Nico. Every inspector on the case knows Nico couldn't have killed Salvatore."

Crushing astonishment filled Armando's eyes. Then anger.

In a rush, she continued, "So if you kill me and stage all this to look like your son did everything, the *polizia* are going to know that somebody else was involved. That there's still another suspect out there. That there's still *you*. They'll know you planted everything."

His face was frozen, eyes unblinking as he calculated.

"They're coming for you," she said, hoping to drive her

point home. "You're going to have to come up with a better plan."

Armando straightened and stepped away from his son. Putting a hand over his mouth, he looked at the floor, deep in thought.

She eyed the gun in his hand again.

A rumble drew their attention to the windows.

Ali squinted, making out the form of a pickup truck in the distance. It was coming closer, driving down the dirt road leading to the house.

Armando tucked the gun in his jacket pocket and faced her.

"That's an employee of mine," he said in a low, quivering voice. "He has two children at home. A wife. If you make a sound in here while I'm out talking to him, I'll have to kill him. You don't want that, do you?"

She shook her head, enthralled by the prospect of him leaving her alone.

The truck rocked to a stop outside, sending a cloud of dust rolling past the windows.

Armando hurried out of the room. She heard the front door open and shut, and then a key twisted in the lock.

Slumping to the floor, she picked up one of the shards of ceramic. With it gripped tight in her good hand, she began sawing back and forth on the rope.

30

"Who's that?" Basso wrenched up the parking brake and shut off the engine.

"That's Armando Villa," Costa said from the front passenger seat.

"Why's he locking the door behind him?"

"Because he's a security-conscious man? Okay, listen, you wouldn't shut up, so I let you talk us into this idea. Now you keep quiet and let *me* do the talking. Got it?"

"*Certo.*"

The stink of the pig farm hit Basso like a punch in the nose as he got out. He heard the twin thumps of Gatti and Fabiano jumping down from the truck bed, then the squeak of Costa's door opening.

On the porch, Armando pocketed his keys and turned around. He gave them a double take, stopping in his tracks. "What is this?"

"*Signor* Villa, how are you?" Costa asked.

Armando took a step back.

Basso's eyes narrowed, flicking between the front

windows of the farmhouse and Armando. The man was hiding something.

"We just want to talk with you." Costa shut his door and joined Basso by the bumper.

"What is the meaning of this?" Armando asked. "Who are you?"

"*Polizia*," Basso said. "Do you have Ali Falco in there?"

"*Signor* Villa," Costa said, putting up a hand to Basso. "We're sorry to bother you, but we're trying to find the whereabouts of—"

"You're sorry to bother me? You are driving one of my employee's trucks. What the hell is going on? Hey, where are you going?" Armando pointed at Basso.

"Basso!" Costa shouted.

Basso disregarded them, pulling his gun and running fast toward the front windows.

"Hey!" Armando cried. "What are you doing? Get away from there!"

He felt a flood of certainty at hearing Armando's tone. It was too appalled. The man definitely had something to hide.

Stepping up to the house, Basso put his back against the stucco siding and leaned over to peek inside. The windows were dirty, hard to see through, so he pushed his face right into the glass.

The first thing he saw was bright-red blood. And a body.

His insides spasmed as he realized they were too late. Then he noticed it was not Falco lying on the ground, but somebody else. Involuntarily, he let out a cry of relief. It took him another second to recognize who the body belonged to. "What the hell?"

"Gun! Gun!"

Basso pivoted toward Armando, who was aiming a handgun in his direction. He raised his Beretta to fire, but Armando's muzzle flashed first. The window next to him shattered into a million pieces.

Lightning quick, Armando spun and shot at Costa. Costa jerked, falling to the ground like a sack of rice, colliding hard with the earth.

Gunshots erupted from Gatti and Fabiano. One of them screamed.

Leveling his Beretta again, Basso shot once at the front door. But there was no target to hit.

Gatti sprinted away, rounding the far side of the house, firing his gun three times. A moment later, he reappeared, pointing. "He's around the back!"

"Is he hit?" Basso asked.

"Costa?"

"Armando!"

"No," Gatti said. "I don't think so."

"*Cazzo*." Basso ran to Costa.

The lieutenant was unmoving.

"*Signore!*"

Costa grunted in response.

Basso dropped to the ground, rolling Costa to his side to assess the damage. The lieutenant's hands were covered in blood, clutching his stomach.

"You're going to be okay," Basso said, but it looked bad. Very bad. He had never seen a gunshot wound in real life. He pulled out his phone, finding it already vibrating. Rustica's name lit up the screen. "*Sì!*"

"What's going on? I heard shots!"

"Call an ambulance! Costa's hit!" Basso hung up and pocketed his phone. "Fabiano. Get over here."

Fabiano, face ashen and hands gripping his gun, rushed to them.

"Where's Nico?" Gatti asked. He stood nearby, swiveling his aim between the sides of the house.

"He's dead," Basso said.

"What?"

"He's dead. I saw his body inside."

"*Cazzo*. What about Falco? Did you see her?"

Basso rose to his feet, gun at the ready. "No. I'll go this way. Gatti, you take the other side of the house."

"And me?" Fabiano asked, kneeling beside Costa.

Basso glanced at Rustica's cruiser, which was screaming down the road, closing in on the property. "Stay with Costa until they get here."

31

Ali had given up on trying to cut the rope from her wrists. It was no use. The angle wasn't there, and none of the ceramic shards were big enough to breach the braided twine.

Now she was on the ground, sawing at the thin plastic zip tie holding her ankles together, hoping she could get it off before more shots came inside. She had screamed Basso's name after the window had shattered, but he hadn't heard. Probably because her voice had been snuffed out by gunfire.

The first piece of ceramic she tried on the zip tie wasn't sharp enough, but the second one seemed promising. Unfortunately, it was also stained with Nico's blood.

She kept her eyes off his dead body, concentrating on cutting the plastic.

With a snap, the zip tie split open. Her legs fell apart, fresh agony blooming in her ankles as blood rushed into muscles that had been starved of oxygen for the last however many hours.

With a flash of insight, she decided to put the ceramic

between her pressed together heels, and then rubbed the rope against the sharp edge, sawing up and down. The rope finally broke free, and she pulled her arms apart.

For a moment she sat motionless, acquainting herself with the sensation of freedom, then she pulled herself up using the couch and stood on shaky legs. After a moment, she attempted a step. Her feet were concrete slabs of aching pain. A wave of dizziness washed over her, and the room spun. She found herself on the couch, watching as darkness crept into the corners of her vision.

Breathing slow and deep, she waited for the vertigo to pass. When it finally did, she sat up from the couch and looked out the window. Gatti was removing his face from a pane, running away.

Had he seen her? Most likely not. She had been blocked by the back of the couch.

"*Cacchio*," she whispered, rising again.

Somehow, she managed to stumble over to where she had seen him. Nine panes made up the large square window. The upper left slab of glass had been shot out, letting in a cool, fluttering breeze that washed over her skin.

Shivering from a combination of the frigid air and her adrenaline, Ali peeked outside to evaluate the scene. She needed to gain her bearings before joining the fray, especially since she was weaponless.

In front of the pickup truck she'd watched drive in, Costa lay on the ground, clearly shot, two *polizia* officers bent over him. Somebody else was jogging across the driveway. Squinting, she saw it was Fabiano, body slunk low, both hands cradling his Beretta.

Ali was lifting her hand, preparing to bang on the glass, when she heard a scuffling noise.

"What are you doing?"

She spun around.

Armando stood next to the dining table, pointing his gun at her. His free arm dangled at his side, covered in crimson blood that oozed from a tear in the fabric at his shoulder. "Come here. I need a hostage."

Ali listened to Fabiano's footsteps as he passed the window, but she didn't dare call for help. He would put his face to the glass and Armando would shoot.

The living room had an exit to her left, leading to the front door, and there was a hallway behind Armando, which presumably led to a rear exit.

Armando took a step closer. "Don't you dare move."

Ali turned and lurched into a sprint, bare feet slapping painfully on the tile as she ducked low, expecting gunshots to ring out at any moment. None came.

Boots thumped fast after her, accompanied by Armando's frustrated cursing.

She skidded to a stop at the front door, hurrying to release the deadbolt.

"Come here!"

A wet hand grabbed her by the neck. Armando's fingers slipped, then grasped her sweater. Fabric ripped. Her hand whiffed the doorknob, but as she fell in a twisting heap, the door flew open, swinging inward.

Armando's grip let up, and she collapsed to the tile.

Light poured into the entryway. Fabiano stood on the threshold, looking down at Ali. His eyes were wide, unsure. Naively, he held out a hand and stepped forward.

"Watch out!" she yelled.

Armando rose up behind the heavy wood door and slammed it closed, smashing Fabiano's bicep against the jamb. Fabiano cried out in pain, but then he pushed back with surprising ferocity. The door hit Armando square in the face, driving him into the wall.

Fabiano barreled inside.

The men collided, and Armando's gun dropped to the ground. It skittered across the tile, kicked by Fabiano's flailing foot, into the living room.

Ali surged to her feet and ran for the gun. Reaching down with her right hand, she was shocked to see she had sustained some major damage from the fall. Her pinkie finger was jutting backward at a ninety-degree angle, and her ring finger had shifted sideways.

She picked up Armando's gun with her left hand and turned back to the brawl, wondering why Fabiano hadn't fired his weapon yet. Her breath caught as she saw the reason.

His hands were at his throat, trying desperately to pry Armando's blood-soaked forearms from their death grip on his neck. The men were sitting upright, leaning against a display cabinet, Fabiano in front of Armando.

Face beet-red, eyes wild with panic, Fabiano changed strategies, punching behind him. Armando only locked his arms and squeezed tighter, wrapping his legs around the rookie's midsection for leverage.

"Let him go!" Ali screamed, raising the gun.

Fabiano's gaze whipped to her. He looked at her mangled hand, then at her face.

Armando ignored her demand, removing one arm from

his choke hold to reach for the Beretta, which Fabiano had dropped just beyond his grasp.

"Stop!"

Armando touched the weapon, spinning it. And then he clutched it.

Ali fired.

The shot grazed Armando's upper arm. A chunk of flesh on his bicep erupted in blood, and the Beretta fell from his hand. He grunted, reaching for it again, somehow maintaining his powerful grip around Fabiano's neck.

"Stop! Drop the weapon!" she yelled. "Let it go!"

Once again, Armando ignored her.

Ali closed one eye as she aimed, finding the sight lined up wrong in her off-hand. She corrected, then hesitated. The opening she had was too close to Fabiano's exposed chest. There could be no missing. Moving forward would guarantee the bullet's trajectory, but she was out of time. Armando had the gun now, and he was readying to shoot.

She squeezed the trigger. The gun kicked, flashing.

Through a purple blotch in her vision, she saw Armando's body slump. Blood pulsed from his upper right chest, flowing out of his flannel shirt and onto the tile.

Fabiano wrestled free from the pig farmer's hold and got to his feet, coughing.

Ali stepped past both men and kicked the Beretta away. Her vision was worsening, darkness creeping in around the edges. The entryway tilted sideways, back and forth, leaning and righting.

Fabiano said something in a muffled voice.

She sagged to the ground.

He kneeled, wrapping her in his arms.

Slowly, her vision expanded, brightened, and sound began penetrating her ears.

"You okay?" Fabiano asked.

Ali nodded.

Movement caught her eye, and as she looked, she already knew she was too late. Armando had pulled Nico's gun from the pocket of his jacket. The gun she had long since forgotten about. It was in his hand, pointed at Fabiano's back.

"No!"

He fired.

A flurry of shots came from the open front door.

Armando's body shuddered and went still.

"Are you okay? Are you—" Basso rushed into view. His gaze landed on Fabiano.

Still kneeling beside her, the young man's eyes were wide, his chest bowed out, his back arched. Spittle flew from his mouth.

And then he fell.

32

F ive days later...

The top floors of the Università di Siena hospital were engulfed in a dense fog, rendering them invisible from the sidewalk below.

Ali stopped and set the bouquet on a bench so she could adjust her sling. Covered in a hard cast, her right hand was on fire. She'd felt it burning, tingling, aching, and itching over the last couple of days. Dr. Stefani had told her those were all good signs that the shoulder surgery had worked, that her nerves, along with her dislocated ring finger and twice-fractured pinkie, were healing.

But she wasn't getting her hopes up. Not yet.

The automatic doors to the main hospital building opened as Ali walked inside. People streamed past in all directions, their feet squeaking on the floor, their hushed conversations echoing off the vaulted ceilings.

She spotted Basso across the reception area and strode over. He was in the middle of an argument with a coffee vending machine, pounding the side of it, cursing under his breath.

"After you select, you have to press Enter."

"Where?"

She pointed.

"*Pezzo di merda*. Finally."

She waited patiently for the foamy espresso to flow out into the tiny cup.

"You want one?" Basso asked, offering it to her.

"No, *grazie*."

He sipped, staring at her arm. "You're late."

"I had to get some flowers."

"Good call."

"He's up?"

Basso headed toward the elevators. "That's what they told me an hour ago. He could be asleep now."

"Either way, I'd like to see him before they transfer him," she said.

He called the elevator. When it arrived, they climbed inside and rode up to the seventh-floor step-down unit.

"Costa?" she asked.

"He's better." Basso sipped his drink. "I saw him yesterday. He's going home tomorrow. Have you visited him yet?"

"*Sì*. After my surgery, I went in and saw him."

"And you?"

"Good."

"And the surgery?"

"I can feel my hand."

Basso nodded. "That's good. That's very good."

"It hurts like hell."

"Better than numb."

"So they tell me."

The doors parted, and they stepped out into another reception area. Basso checked them in with the woman behind the desk. After examining their badges, she waved them through, pushing a button. A set of doors clicked as they unlocked.

"Seven-twenty-one," Basso said.

Passing a bank of windows overlooking the gray Siena sky, Ali watched water streak down the exterior of the glass.

They found the door to Room 721 propped open. Inside, machines beeped and whirred.

Basso stopped at the threshold and knocked softly. Nobody answered, so he gestured for Ali to lead the way.

She walked in. "*Ciao*?"

Fabiano came into view as she rounded the corner. His eyes were open, staring at a muted television on the wall. He turned to her, offering a weak smile. She reciprocated the gesture.

"Hey. How are you doing?" She held up the flowers, then went to the windowsill and set them down next to three other bouquets.

"*Sì*, how are you feeling, Fabi?" Basso asked.

"I've been better." Fabiano's voice was hoarse, like he'd been screaming for the last five days instead of lying in a medically induced coma and undergoing three surgeries on his spine. He eyed his palm, opening and closing his fingers. "I can move my hands. They're telling me that's good."

"*Bene, bene,*" Basso said. "We hear you're transferring out of here."

Fabiano nodded. "That's right. My father's got some idea that I can get better treatment in Lucerne."

"I'd believe it. Those Swiss—the food is *merda*, but they know what they're doing with everything else."

"I would kill for a raclette right now," Fabiano said, chuckling. He looked at Ali, and his joviality vanished. "*Grazie.* I've been waiting to tell you that."

She stepped to the foot of his bed. "For what?"

"For taking that shot. For saving my life."

She shrugged, wincing as pain lanced through her shoulder.

"Are you okay?" Fabiano asked.

She studied him, floored by the compassion in his eyes. They must have put him on some good drugs.

"I'm fine," she said. "I had a couple of broken fingers. I wasn't shot in the spine."

"And Costa? My father told me his surgery went well. That the bullet missed all vitals."

Ali and Basso nodded.

"Good." Fabiano looked at her again. "I'm serious. I've been thinking about that a lot."

"About what?"

"The shot. It was left-handed. It was amazing under the circumstances. And after all the trouble I've given you in the past . . . I've been such a *stronzo*." He sighed. "You could have just shot me, and I would have deserved it."

She raised an eyebrow. "I was aiming at you."

He laughed, then frowned. "Ouch."

"Oh no," she said. "What hurts?"

"My . . . I don't know . . . Something deep in my chest. That's new. That's gotta be good."

Ali wiggled her aching fingers under her cast, understanding what he meant. She glanced down at his legs. One foot was splayed sideways, the other straight up, toes to the ceiling.

"I can't feel them yet," he said.

A tear slipped from her eye. "I'm sorry."

"For what? Because of you, I'm not dead."

She shook her head, more tears falling.

"Hey," Basso said. "He's gonna be fine. Right, Fabiano?"

"I have to tell you something," she said.

Fabiano tilted his head. "Tell me what?"

"I knew Armando had another gun in his pocket. I mean . . . I forgot. It was stupid. I should have known. I watched him put Nico's gun in his pocket earlier, before he killed him. I knew he had two. So when I got that gun away from him, I should have expected the other one to come out. But I forgot."

"Falco . . ." Basso said, but he left the sentence unfinished.

"I'm sorry. It's my fault that you are in here. I should have warned you. I should have remembered."

Fabiano's forehead creased with a smile. "Falco, the last thing I remember is looking at you. Your fingers were pointing different directions, and your eyes were rolling into the back of your head. You did your best. This wasn't your fault."

"What wasn't her fault?"

They turned and saw Giulio Fabiano standing behind them. He had entered without making a sound.

"*Ciao, signore,*" Basso said.

Ali only nodded.

Giulio's eyes burned into hers. "What wasn't your fault? What are you talking about?"

"Nothing, *Papà*," Fabiano said.

"That will be for me to judge."

Ali wiped the tears from her cheeks, lifting her chin. "That day, I knew Armando Villa had a second gun in his possession. But I forgot. And because I forgot, Armando was able to shoot your son in the back."

"Falco, that's not how we see it," Basso said.

Giulio glared at Basso. "Your sons are fine and healthy at your home, Inspector. Mine is paralyzed in a hospital bed. So, forgive me, but I do not care how you see it."

"*Silenzio,*" Fabiano hissed.

Giulio's eyes widened.

"Nobody asked what you think! What you think doesn't —" Fabiano coughed. And then he kept coughing, unable to stop.

"*Cazzo,*" Basso said. "Call a nurse or something."

Drool streamed from Fabiano's mouth between painful hacks, and one of the machines started beeping. A nurse rushed into the room, another one following close.

"Everyone out!" they ordered.

Ali watched, dumbfounded, as the nurses went to work trying to calm Fabiano down.

"Now!"

Basso pulled her toward the door, and when they stepped into the hallway, Giulio was already gone.

33

Three Months Later . . .

Ali's breath barely accelerated as she climbed the stairs, emerging into the third-floor squad room. It had been six weeks since she'd had a cigarette. Six weeks since she'd committed to running every other night and completing her shoulder exercises daily.

Perhaps the effort was paying off, after all.

She stopped at Clarissa's desk. "Hey."

Clarissa looked up from her computer screen, smiling. "*Ciao, bella.*" She tilted her chin toward Ferrari's office. "They're in there."

"Who?"

The door opened, answering her question before Clarissa could. She saw Costa in his wheelchair, Ferrari and Tiraboschi gathered around him, and Giulio Fabiano off to one side, talking to somebody else.

It had been months since her encounter with Fabiano's father in the hospital. Her lungs constricted at the prospect of having to interact with him again—and then her heart began pounding when she realized whom he was talking to.

Dressed in a suit that made Giulio's attire seem like a peasant's, Enzo Monaco stood a half head above the others, gazing down on them.

"See you later," Ali said.

Taking a seat at her desk, she dropped her shoulder bag and snuck another glance at Ferrari's office. Giulio and Enzo were now staring at her, calm expressions on their faces. She ignored them, picking up a pen and concentrating on the paperwork in front of her.

She had been using handwriting as a meditation tactic. It relaxed her breath, and she savored the way the ink stroked across the page with the smallest amount of effort, the way her penmanship improved each time. In her estimation, it was better than ever before.

The edge of her palm slid across the paper, and she smiled inside at the ticklish feeling.

Enzo broke off from the group and approached her desk. She pretended not to notice.

"Inspector Falco."

"Oh. *Buongiorno*." She set down the pen and stood up.

"It's been a while since I've seen you."

"*Sì*. It has." She peeked around him. Ferrari and Costa were still speaking in the office, but Tiraboschi and Giulio were walking out. "Listen, *signore,* I'm sorry for the way I spoke to you last time we saw one another."

His eyes never left hers. "Are you?"

"*Sì.*"

He put his hands in his pockets, somehow making the simple gesture look regal. "I have a very strong-willed daughter, Inspector Falco. I am used to being spoken to in a direct manner."

Ali said nothing.

"I hear you went through quite the ordeal to catch the real killer. Or killers, as it were."

She nodded.

"And I hear you did a good job when it came down to crunch time. In fact, I'm to relay thanks from my daughter."

"Oh. Um, tell her *prego.*" Was this what they had been talking about in Ferrari's office? If so, with Giulio in the meeting, she doubted they'd been singing her praises.

"Anyway." Enzo checked his watch. "I'm glad everyone involved ended up being okay. I'm harboring no ill feelings."

"*Grazie, signore.*"

He left without saying goodbye, a trace of pleasant cologne lingering in his wake.

She sat back down and picked up her pen.

"My office in five minutes," Costa called to her, wheeling out of Ferrari's office and into his own. She got the sense that her superiors had been watching the interaction.

Gatti exited the stairwell, eyeing Enzo as they passed one another.

"You too, Gatti," Costa added, leaving his door open. Before the gunshot, his door had been shut at all times. After returning from medical leave, however, he'd adopted the opposite practice.

"What am I supposed to do?" Gatti asked, pausing beside her desk.

"Costa's office in five minutes."

"What's happening? Tiraboschi, Giulio Fabiano, and Enzo Monaco?"

"I guess we'll find out," she said, sifting through her memories, trying to find a clue. The only peculiarity she could come up with was Costa's recent shift in demeanor.

Lately, he'd been acting nice to everyone, making statements of gratitude at regular intervals. Last week, for example, he had called her into his office to commend her quick action during the conflict with Armando. He had already told her the same in November.

It was almost as if he were a dying man. But he wasn't, as far as she knew. Costa often reminded them that his ailments were temporary. Just another couple of weeks and he would be back on his feet. Of course, he'd been saying that for over a month.

Unable to sit with her thoughts any longer, she went to Costa's office.

His wheelchair was parked backward at his desk, facing the window, but instead of enjoying the view, he was looking at his phone. Again, Ali saw a picture of a baby onscreen.

She knocked. "*Signore?*"

"Falco. Come." He made no move to hide his activity this time, swiping to see another photo of the smiling child. After a moment, he twirled in his chair and put his phone on the desk. The swift movement made him grimace. "I spoke to Dr. Stefani yesterday. He says your last checkup was good."

"*Sì, signore.* Almost one hundred percent." More like eighty percent, but she wasn't about to say so.

"That's excellent."

"And your intestines?" she asked.

He smiled. "Progressing nicely, *grazie.*"

Gatti came in, standing beside Ali along the rear wall. Basso trailed after him, talking animatedly.

"—wasn't fit for prison food. How do you screw up a carbonara?" He nodded at Ali and took a seat in front of Costa's desk.

"You have to get the *penne strascicate,*" Gatti said.

"Why? So I can take it home and feed it to my dog?"

"You don't have a dog."

Basso flipped a hand.

Longo joined them next, hanging back with Ali and Gatti. Costa eyed the door.

"Should I close it?" Longo asked.

"No," Costa said. "We have another guest, but I'm not sure exactly when he'll be here. Let's get started without him."

"Who?" Basso asked quietly, as if trying to break into a private conversation with the lieutenant.

Costa ignored him. "Longo, give us your news."

"It's been twelve weeks," Longo said. "We've found three of Genevra Villa's teeth a meter beneath that foul pig muck, but nothing else. No trace of the Quattro Luci Farm employee who allegedly cheated with her, Bruno Tarantino. We've decided to end the search. His remains might be out there, but I'm not willing to put any more manpower into it. Ferrari agrees with me."

Costa raised an eyebrow at Ali, Basso, and Gatti, seeking their approval.

"I agree as well," Basso said. "No sense continuing any longer. The man disappeared eleven years ago, on exactly the same day Genevra allegedly left for America, quitting without a word to any of the other employees. And with what Armando told Ali, I think the case is closed. Clearly, the man's bones were ground into a fine paste inside those pigs, deposited as *merda* long ago."

"Thank you, Basso," Costa said.

Basso looked at Longo. "Eleven years ago, they were killed."

Longo nodded. "*Sì.*"

"Eleven."

"That's right. What's your point?"

"Normal aging time for prosciutto is fourteen to thirty-six months. That means none of the stuff they have down there is tainted."

Costa folded his arms. "Basso, I am sorry to tell you this, but the farm will remain shut down indefinitely. There will be no more meat for sale at any point in the future."

"*Ma-donna.*" Basso slapped the desk. "I'm running out of my supply."

"You still eat Quattro Luci Farm prosciutto?" Gatti asked, horrified.

"Have you tasted it?"

There was a knock on the door.

"Ah, there's our guest," Costa said. "How are you doing, Fabiano?"

"Fabiano!" Basso jumped up from his chair. "You're back."

Fabiano went around the room, shaking hands and sharing smiles with everyone but Gatti, who held himself conspicuously apart.

Ali was last in line, and she gave Fabiano a perfunctory hug. He felt thin, but his face was pink with color and his arms were strong as they briefly wrapped around her. When he smiled, he looked healthy.

"Sit," Costa said. "I'm glad you are here."

"*Grazie.*"

"How are you feeling?"

"Great. Almost back to normal."

"How was Switzerland?" Basso asked.

Fabiano laughed. "I've had enough raclette for a while."

"Okay, everyone." Costa raised his hands. "Quiet down. I have a couple of important announcements to make."

"I think I'll take my leave now," Longo said.

"Thank you, doctor," Costa said. "Have a good rest of your morning."

Longo left the room and Basso moved to Costa's side, putting his hands behind his back.

"First off, I want to welcome our newest member of the team." Costa gestured to Fabiano. "Dimitri Fabiano, assuming you pass all your final checks—and I'm sure you will—I want to welcome you as a full-time inspector."

"Congratulations, Fabiano," Basso said.

"Oh, congratulations," Ali said. But her insides flipped. She pictured Giulio's calm stare from earlier and realized now it had been a knowing glare.

Fabiano beamed. "*Grazie,* everyone."

Gatti said nothing, and his face remained blank.

Costa's gaze landed on Ali. "Falco, I'm sorry . . ."

She swallowed, steeling herself for the news she sensed coming.

". . . but we no longer need your services on desk duty. Assuming you can shoot with that hand of yours, we need you back on full duty as an inspector."

Basso grinned and began clapping. Gatti joined in.

"I'm sorry," Costa said with a laugh, shaking his head. "That was Basso's idea."

"I told you," Basso said. "You should have seen your face, Falco. This isn't a funeral."

Ali nodded. "Ah. Good one."

"Okay, quiet down again, everyone." Costa's humor faded. "This is not a goodbye for Falco, but it *is* a goodbye for me. At the end of April, I will be transferring from this department to Rome headquarters."

"Why?" Gatti asked, eyes wide with shock.

Costa looked at Ali. "Care to tell them?"

Her brow furrowed in confusion, and she racked her brain for why she would know the reason. Then it clicked. "You are leaving to be with your daughter and grand . . . son, is it?"

He nodded. "*Sì.* I've come to understand my life is too short to be wasting any of it, to be that far from my family. I put in for a transfer to Rome, and with the help of some friends, I've been moved expeditiously. So . . ." He lifted his hands, shrugging.

"Who's our boss, then?" Gatti asked. "Ferrari?"

"Ferrari?" Basso scoffed. "No."

"Basso will be taking over my role," Costa said.

Gatti laughed out loud, then stopped when Basso narrowed his eyes. "You're telling the truth?"

"*Sì*, he's telling the truth," Basso said. "What's so hard to believe about that, Inspector?"

Gatti's mouth hung open.

Ali cleared her throat. "I think what Gatti meant to say is that you're so young, *signore*. It is unbelievable that somebody would move up so quickly."

"*Sì*," Gatti said. "Especially somebody so good-looking."

She shook her head. "Okay, well, you ruined it."

They laughed, and Basso joined in despite himself.

Costa raised his hands once more. The room quieted.

"We'll talk about this in depth later. I still have two months left. Until then, I'll be working closely with Basso to ensure he is prepared for the transition." Costa looked at them each in turn. "But one thing I'm certain of? Siena is in good hands."

"*Grazie, signore*," Basso said.

Ali, Gatti, and Fabiano repeated the sentiment.

"Now get out," Costa said, shooing them. "Basso, with me."

Ali returned to her desk and noticed that Fabiano had followed her.

"Hey," she said, sitting down. "Congratulations."

"*Grazie.*"

Wiggling her computer mouse, she woke the screen. "How was Switzerland?"

"It's nice up there," he said. "Good medical facility, for sure. But I missed it here. I'm glad to be back."

"I bet."

His focus drifted from her. She tracked his eyes and saw Gatti leaving the squad room, descending the stairs.

"What's up?" she asked.

"I just . . . It was a little intense the last time we talked. I've had a lot of time to think about what you told me, and I want you to know I still stand by what I said back then. You did the best you could, and I'm not holding any grudges."

"*Grazie*," she said quietly. "If only your father agreed."

Fabiano's gaze went distant. After a moment, he blinked into the present. "I don't care about what he thinks, and I hope you don't either. What he thinks doesn't count."

She picked up her pen.

"And I hope you're not holding any grudges against me," he continued. "But after the way I've been treating you since I got here, I wouldn't blame you."

"No. We're okay."

"*Bene.*" He remained in front of her desk, ruminating. "It's not easy being his son, you know. But I guess I can't complain. I'm not dumb or ignorant. I'm aware of my privilege. I wouldn't be on this team if it weren't for him."

"I don't know about that."

He stared at her. "My father helped make Costa's transfer happen in exchange for me becoming a permanent part of the team."

"Oh," she said. Now Giulio's earlier presence made sense to her.

"I thought I might as well make that known officially. It'll probably be the rumor going around, anyway."

She shrugged. "Not from me."

"It doesn't matter. I just want you to know I will be working hard to get up to speed."

"Well, I'm not that up to speed, either," she said. "We can help each other."

Fabiano offered his hand. "That sounds like a good idea."

She reached out to shake it, but before their palms met, he pulled away.

And then, with a deadly serious expression, he presented his left hand instead. "*Grazie*, Inspector Falco. For saving my life."

Grinning, Ali swapped hands, too. "*Prego*, Inspector Fabiano. Now let's pray you never have the chance to return the favor."

————

Thank you so much for reading Tuscan Blood, Ali Falco's second adventure in this brand new series I've begun writing. I hope you enjoyed the story. My wife and children are dual citizens of the United States and Italy, and we often travel to the areas featured in this novel. In fact, I'm writing this while sitting at a table in a rented apartment in northern Italy, where my family and I are spending the next 5 months.

People often ask me if I've given up on the David Wolf Series, and the answer is no! I would't know what to do with myself without writing about those characters and that setting, both of which I love so much. But I've found that now I enjoy writing about the Falco Series characters and setting as well. Which is something I wasn't sure would happen.

I embarked on the Falco series to prove to myself I could do something new. That I could get out of my comfortable place with the Wolf series I'd tucked myself into. And now that I've proven I could, I'm grateful the two Falco books exist and excited for the future of the ever-complicating characters populating her world.

If you enjoyed the story, I hope you'll consider leaving a review on Amazon, as it helps so much with other people discovering the book, sales, helping my family buy more pizza while we're here in Merate, Italy.

—>You can Leave a Review for Tuscan Blood by Clicking Here.

And I also hope you'll consider sharing this book with friends, loved ones, strangers with obvious hankerings for international mysteries, and anyone else you think might like the novel.

You can contact me at jeff@jeffcarson.co (no "m"), and you can sign up for the New Release Newsletter by clicking this link— https://jeffcarson.co/newsletter/ (Sign up to receive a free story sent to your inbox.)

ALSO BY JEFF CARSON

THE DAVID WOLF SERIES

Gut Decision (A David Wolf Short Story)– Sign up for the new release newsletter at http://www.jeffcarson.co/p/newsletter.html and receive a complimentary copy of the David Wolf story.

**NEW! Echoes Fade (David Wolf Book 17)

THE ALI FALCO SERIES

The Como Falcon (Ali Falco Book 1)

Tuscan Blood (Ali Falco Book 2)

Made in United States
Orlando, FL
02 September 2024

51046382R00176